Dee Williams was born and brought up in Rotherhithe in East London, where her father worked as a stevedore in Surrey Docks. Dee left school at fourteen, met her husband at sixteen and was married at twenty. After living abroad for some years, Dee moved to Hampshire to be close to her family. She has written twenty previous novels including *A Moment to Remember*, *This Time for Keeps*, *All That Jazz* and *After the Dance*.

To find out more about Dee, go to her website at www.deewilliams.co.uk

D1514018

Dee
WILLIAMS

Lights Out Till Dawn

headline

First published in 2011 by
HEADLINE PUBLISHING GROUP

First published in paperback in 2011 by
HEADLINE PUBLISHING GROUP

1

Cataloguing in Publication Data is available from the British Library

ISBN 978 0 7553 5891 5

Typeset in Palatino by Avon DataSet Ltd,
Bidford-on-Avon, Warwickshire

Printed and bound in Great Britain by CPI Group (UK) Ltd, Croydon, CR0 4YY

Headline's policy is to use papers that are natural, renewable and
recyclable products and made from wood grown in sustainable forests.
The logging and manufacturing processes are expected to conform
to the environmental regulations of the country of origin.

HEADLINE PUBLISHING GROUP
An Hachette UK Company
338 Euston Road
London NW1 3BH

www.headline.co.uk
www.hachette.co.uk

This is for all the children who were evacuated during the Second World War. For some it was an adventure, but for others it was misery.

I would like to dedicate this book to the memory
of my good friend Gilda O'Neill
who sadly passed away Friday 24 September 2010.
I will never forget you.

Chapter 1

BLITZ KIDS

August 1939

'WHAT SHOULD WE do, Mum?' Rene Morgan was sitting at her mother's kitchen table, tears running down her cheeks. She was holding the letter that had arrived that morning after she had left for work. 'We knew it might happen, but we thought it would be just a trial run, you know, so that they can get all the kids together and in the right place, but this . . .' She threw the letter on to the table. 'It sounds as if it's going to be the real thing.'

'I don't know what to say, love.' Maud looked at her sympathetically. 'Perhaps it is just a rehearsal, as you said, you know, to get the kids to school and show them what they have to do if the worst happens.'

'It says here that they have to be at the school at seven o'clock on Saturday, September the second. They

1

have to take a change of clothes, all with their name in, a toothbrush, a comb, a handkerchief and a bag of food to last them all day. Drinks will be provided. What shall I do, Mum?' she asked again. 'Do I let 'em go?'

'I can't tell you what ter do with your kids, and we know what John thinks about all this.'

Rene knew what her husband John thought. They had discussed it for weeks and he wanted them to be safe. Air-raid shelters were being set up all over London. Gas masks and identity cards were being distributed. Leaflets were being delivered nearly every day telling them about the precautions they had to take: how to make blackout curtains and put strips of sticky paper over their windows.

'I ain't putting no sticky paper all over my windows,' Maud had said when that leaflet arrived. 'I'll never get 'em clean again.'

'It's to stop the glass splintering and flying about in an air raid, Ma,' said John.

It was all very frightening for everyone.

'John was only saying last night that he reckons Rotherhithe could be a target, with having the railway lines at the bottom of the road and the docks just over the bridge. If Hitler does start bombing, it'll be the docks he'll be after.' Rene sniffed back a tear.

Maud Stevens gently patted her daughter's hand. 'Don't say that, love.' She picked up the letter and reread its contents. 'Poor little buggers, being sent off ter God only knows where. And to God knows . . .' She stopped. She didn't want to say any more. She didn't want to voice her fears that her precious grandchildren could be harmed.

'P'raps there won't be a war,' said Rene, dabbing at her eyes. 'After all, the wireless said that Mr Chamberlain has given Germany an ultimatum.'

'Hmm. The Germans.' Maud pulled her floral wrap-around overall tighter round her slim body. 'Yer father always reckoned they were a right bunch of trouble-makers.'

Rene knew her father's opinion about any foreigners. He had been a merchant seaman since he was fifteen, and Rene and her sisters Betty and Maggie had loved it when he came home with wonderful presents, telling them tales about the far-off lands he'd been to. For a few years Rene's two children Hazel and Peter had also enjoyed his presents and stories. Everybody was very sad when he'd died last year from pneumonia, but his memory and sayings still filled their lives.

'What do the kids have ter say about it?'

'The teachers have made it sound like a big adventure, but what if they get ill or, heaven forbid, badly treated?'

'John'll be wherever they're sent like a shot.'

'Mum, John reckons he'll be called up. Being a car mechanic ain't a reserved occupation.' Once again Rene burst into tears.

Maud stood up and went round the table and held her daughter close. She patted Rene's dark wavy hair. If there was a war, what was going to happen to them all?

Rene was still sitting at her mother's table when Hazel and Peter came racing in, Hazel stomping in her roller skates. It was August and the children were on school holiday, and like all their friends they had been playing in the street on their skates and scooters.

'How many times do I have to tell you to take those off before you come in?'

'Sorry, Mum,' said Hazel, looking a bit sheepish as she sat down to unbuckle her skates.

Years ago the tarry blocks that were the road in Glebe Street had been taken up and a nice new concrete surface had been laid. The kids loved it as it was so smooth and they could skate, scooter and push their home-made carts up and down. Rene remembered when the blocks were ripped out; nobody went cold that winter, as they were quickly picked up and stacked in every back yard.

'What we got for dinner, Gran?' asked Hazel.

Rene and John and the two children lived upstairs at 38 Glebe Street, while Maud and her unmarried daughter Betty lived downstairs. It was a very amicable arrangement. Rene worked at the local shirt factory; Betty, who was also a machinist, worked for a London fashion house. Maud loved looking after the children, and cooked dinner for the whole family every evening.

'As it's Monday, we've got cold meat, potatoes and pickles, and fer afters a lovely rice pud. How does that sound?'

'Good,' said Hazel. She was ten years old and had short straight dark hair cut in a fringe that framed her brown eyes. Her face was rosy, as almost every day since they'd broken up for the school holidays, she had been playing in the street with her friends. Now she saw the letter on the table. She knew exactly what it contained. She and her friends talked about the evacuation all the time, and a few weeks ago they'd had to go back to school to be given gas masks and lists of what to take with them when the time came. She pointed to the letter. 'Connie's mum said she could go.'

'Billy's mum said he could go as well,' said Peter. At seven, he was a complete contrast to his sister. He was small for his age and had a shock of dirty blond hair and blue eyes. 'Billy said we'll have labels tied on us like a parcel. And we have ter take our identity cards and gas masks.'

'I don't like them gas masks,' said Hazel. 'They make me feel all sweaty and I can't breathe.'

'I know what you feel like, love,' said Maud. 'I told that there warden who came to fit them I ain't wearing one.'

'You have to, Gran,' said Peter in alarm. 'If the Germans drop tear gas on us, we don't want you to die.' He rushed to be cuddled by his gran.

The children loved Maud. She was always there for them, telling them stories and giving them little treats, and sometimes she took them to the pictures. It was a very happy family, and nobody wanted things to change.

The discussion that evening as they sat round the table in Maud's kitchen was about the children being evacuated.

'Well I don't want them to go,' said Rene softly, looking at her children sitting on the floor playing a rowdy game of snap.

'We can understand that,' said John, leaning forward and also speaking softly. 'But think of it this way. If we do have a war, remember what Hitler did in Spain when he helped Franco and bombed the people of Guernica. I reckon it'll be twice as bad for us. He ain't got no time for us Brits; he ain't got over the last war when we pasted him.'

'Oh yes,' said his mother-in-law. 'The war to end all wars.'

'Look, why don't you two go on up and get ready for bed, then I'll come up and we can play snakes and ladders,' said Betty, who could see that the children were beginning to look a bit worried.

'All right,' said Hazel, glad to get away from all this talk about war.

Upstairs, the two children went into their bedroom and got undressed ready for bed. Their flat consisted of a very small scullery, a kitchen cum living and dining room and two bedrooms. The front bedroom was also their front room, with a brown Rexine three-piece and their father's pride and joy, a piano. Every Sunday afternoon he would sit and 'tickle the ivories', as he called it. The children loved it and would sing along with him. He always told them that he was disappointed that neither of them wanted to learn to play; they were more interested in being out in the street with their friends.

Hazel loved her home, but she also liked her gran's downstairs. Gran and Auntie Betty shared the bedroom, and their front room wasn't used very often, not like upstairs. Gran's front room had lace curtains at the window and a large table in the bay with a great big pot on it. The pot had pictures of old-fashioned ladies and gents walking in a park, and in it was a large aspidistra. Gran would wash its leaves with milk to make them shine. It was always cold in that room, and Gran's three-piece was very hard, but they only went in there at Christmas and when Grandad had died. Hazel suddenly felt very sad. She loved her home and family and she didn't want to go away and leave them.

'Thanks, Bet,' said Rene after the children had gone upstairs. The sisters had a very good relationship.

'I could see they were trying to make all this out. Don't worry, I'll soon have 'em laughing,' Betty said as she left the room.

'We could send them to Maggie's,' Rene said to her mother and husband. 'That way they would be out of London.' Maud thought about her other daughter. Blackheath wasn't that far away. But would Maggie and Tom want the worry of Rene's kids? They didn't have any of their own. Maggie, who was the eldest and the brainy one of the three girls, had a lovely home and a very good job in the City.

'Blackheath's not really out of London,' said John. 'No, I reckon we should leave it up to the government. They know what they're doing.'

An hour or so later, Betty came back down to the kitchen. 'They've settled down,' she said as she walked in.

'Cuppa, Bet?' asked Rene.

'Please. Those two were asking so many questions.'

'It must be really hard for the poor little mites to take this all in,' said Maud.

'It's hard for all of us to take it in,' said Betty as she sat at the table and waited for the tea her sister was bringing in from the scullery.

They sat in silence, each with their own thoughts.

Lights Out Till Dawn

Was Saturday, September the second going to be the day the children were leaving for real? Or was it just a rehearsal?

Chapter 2

THE FOLLOWING MORNING, Maud went next door to her neighbour and friend Hilda Ford. The Fords had moved into number 36 soon after they were married. Hilda was older than Maud, and she and her husband Ron had lived here a long time. They had been a great source of comfort when Bill was away at sea and Maud had the three girls to look after. The Fords had two children; both their son and their daughter had married many years ago and moved far away. Penny, who had two girls, lived in the West Country, while Adam and his three boys had moved to Scotland. Hilda and Ron were upset when their children went away and missed them constantly.

Like most houses in the road, the key to the front door of number 36 hung behind the letter box on a piece of string. Maud pulled it through, opened the door and walked in. 'It's only me,' she called out as she made her way down the passage. The two friends always let themselves into each other's houses; they had nothing to hide.

The kitchen door opened and Hilda appeared, smiling. 'Come on in. You all right, gel?'

'Yes. I just need to talk to someone.'

'Why? What's wrong? I've made a pot of tea, d'you want one?'

'Yes please.'

'Sit yerself down and I'll pour you a cuppa.'

'Where's Ron?'

'Just gorn across the road to get his paper. Don't know why he bothers; he only sits and carries on about the news.'

Maud sat at the kitchen table in a room that was as familiar as her own, and Hilda pushed a cup of tea in front of her.

'Now come on, what's wrong?'

'It's the kids. Rene thinks they're gonna be evacuated on Saturday.'

'What? But we ain't at war.'

'Not yet we ain't, but . . .' She shrugged.

'Just a bloody lot of scaremongering if you ask me.'

'But surely the government wouldn't spend all this money on air-raid shelters, gas masks and identity cards if they didn't think it might happen?'

11

'I ask yer, identity cards. What d'we want them for? I know who I am.'

'I know.'

'Now come on, what's bothering you?'

And Maud drank her tea and told her friend all that had been said yesterday.

Every evening they listened intently to the news on the wireless, and as the week progressed, everybody knew that on Saturday the children going to the school weren't going for a rehearsal; they were really being evacuated

On Friday evening the tin bath was brought in from off the hook in the yard, and after it had been filled with water, Peter went in, then Hazel. This was the usual ritual, with more water added for the grown-ups, but tonight the bath was emptied after Hazel stepped out. Her father wrapped her in a towel and carried her upstairs to their flat. Peter was already dry and was sitting eating a bar of chocolate.

'Cor, where did you get that?' Hazel asked her brother.

'Dad gave it to me,' he said with a big grin on his face.

John smiled lovingly at his daughter. 'Don't worry, there's one for you too.'

Hazel looked surprised. 'A whole bar?'

He nodded. 'Now come here and let me dry your hair.'

Hazel sat on the floor in front of her father while he carefully rubbed her hair dry. She loved this time after a bath. Her dad was so gentle and she felt very safe and close to him. She knew that tonight was extra special, as she had never had a whole bar of chocolate to herself before, but she was frightened too. She didn't want to go away. Why couldn't they stay here? Hazel wanted to cry, but she knew that would upset her mother.

John slowly rubbed his daughter's hair. He was very worried about what was going to happen. He loved his children so very much. He didn't want anyone to hurt them. Would they be well looked after? Why did there have to be a war? He wanted to cry, but grown men didn't do that sort of thing.

When they had their nightclothes on, Hazel and Peter went downstairs to say good night to Gran and Auntie Betty.

Betty hugged Hazel very hard. 'I'm sorry I won't be able to come to the school with you tomorrow, but I have to go to work.'

'I know that, Auntie, but don't worry, I'll write to you and Gran. Dad's given me some paper and envelopes and stamps, so I can let you know where we are.'

Betty wiped her eyes and hugged her niece again. 'You're a good girl, Hazel.'

Maud was sitting watching them, as she often did. Betty and Hazel had a special relationship and did

13

many things together. In the winter they would paint, and sit and string beads to make necklaces. On summer evenings Betty would take a chair out in the front for Maud to have a chat with the neighbours, and after the man had been round selling cherries she would watch Betty and Hazel sitting on the coping that ran round the bay window with cherries dangling from their ears like earrings. The two of them were always laughing together. It was Betty who had bought Hazel her red tap shoes. That was one thing she would never forgive her daughter for, she thought fondly, as Hazel was always tap-tap-tapping upstairs till Rene confiscated the shoes.

Peter was sitting on his gran's lap. 'D'you know, Daddy gave us a whole bar of chocolate each.'

'Well you are lucky children,' said Maud, trying hard to keep back the tears.

'I think he's worried we might not come back home again if the people we stay with are nice to us,' said Peter.

'Course we will, silly. Sometimes you talk such a lot of rubbish,' said Hazel.

Rene came into the kitchen. 'Right, come on, you two, up to bed. You've got to be up early tomorrow and you've got a long day in front of you.'

Hazel hugged her gran and gave her a big loud kiss. 'You won't forget us, will you?' she asked with a worried look on her face.

'Of course not. As if I would. Besides, you might be back next week.' Maud looked up at her daughter, who was also trying not to cry.

Betty hugged both the children again and then let them go. She tapped their bottoms lightly. 'Now go on, both of you, up to bed.'

Rene took them by the hand and left the room.

Betty sat in the chair and cried. Her mother was doing the same.

At seven the next morning, everybody in Glebe Street was standing outside their front doors as Rene and John walked with Hazel and Peter and the rest of the children and their parents who lived in the street. They were all making their way to the school.

The goodbyes and blown kisses from their friends and neighbours were a sad sight, as women wiped their eyes on the bottom of their pinnies. Mr and Mrs James from the dairy waved to them. Mr Houghton from the paper shop stood at his door.

Hazel walked along holding her father's hand. Miss Rose at school had told them that this was going to be an exciting adventure, but she didn't know if she was happy or sad. She didn't want to leave her mum and dad, or Gran and Auntie Betty, and she didn't want to cry as that made her mum cry and she didn't like that. The string of her gas mask box was across her shoulder, and the brown label that was tied to her coat had her name, address and the name of the school written on it. She was carrying her small attaché case that held her plimsolls, clean knickers and socks, a vest and a liberty bodice for when it got cold. They all had her name in them too. These were the things the government had told them to take. She was upset that she couldn't take her roller skates, but her father had promised that when he knew where she was, he would bring them to her.

Hazel looked at Peter, who was holding their mum's hand. He too had his gas mask and label and was carrying a school satchel with his clean clothes and his favourite bear. He couldn't sleep without Teddy.

As they approached the school, the number of parents and children was overwhelming, and when they turned into the street where the school was, they stopped and stared at the line upon line of double-decker buses.

'Bloody 'ell,' said John. 'Not seen nothing like this before.'

'Well, mate, we ain't been through this before,' said a man who was carrying his young daughter on his shoulders.

'That's true,' said John, as he gave his name to one of the women standing at the gate.

'Morgan. The M's are over there.' She pointed her pencil at a line of parents and children, many of whom were crying.

16

'I don't wanna go,' said Peter tearfully, pulling his mother back.

'You must,' said Rene.

'Why don't you love us any more?'

Rene bent down and scooped her son into her arms and held him close. 'Of course we love you; that's why we're sending you somewhere to be safe.'

'But what if you die?'

Rene couldn't answer that.

Hazel went and held her brother's hand. 'Don't worry, you've got me and I won't let anything nasty happen to you. We'll always be together; I promised Mum and Dad.'

Rene went and buried her head in John's shoulder. This was getting all too much for her.

The parents helped their children on to the right bus and hugged and held them for as long as they could. When they had to leave them, the children banged on the windows, and as the buses began to move away, the tears and waving began in earnest.

Everybody stood and watched as the convoy slowly moved out of sight. They all knew that inside was a very precious cargo.

Very slowly the crowd began to disperse.

John put his arm round Rene's shoulders and tried to comfort her.

'Will we ever see them again?' she sobbed.

'Course we will, love.'

'They looked so sad.'

'It's a big step for them.'

'They're too young to be going to stay with strangers. What if Peter wets the bed?'

John couldn't add any words of comfort.

'What if they're sent to Scotland? We'll never see them again.' Rene was regretting giving their consent for their precious children to be sent away. 'What if they get ill treated?'

'They won't. There's people there to look after their welfare.'

'Yes, but will they? What if they want to come home?'

'I'm sure Hazel will write to us as soon as she can, and she'll let us know if things don't work out all right for them.'

Chapter 3

SOME OF THE boys on the bus were laughing, shouting and playing about despite the conductor, who was there to keep order, telling them to sit down and be quiet. Most of the girls and the younger children just sat and stared out of the window; many had tears running silently down their cheeks.

'I wanna go home,' said Peter, still holding Hazel's hand.

'We can't. The government said that all children have to leave London.'

'Why? There ain't a war on.'

'I know.' Hazel looked out of the window as the bus moved past some of the places she knew, places she'd been with her mum and dad. They went past the cinema that their gran sometimes took them to, and there was the cottage hospital where she'd gone with her mum when she fell over and cut her knee. They passed the park that they all loved and had had many a happy time in. Would she ever see these places again? She sniffed back a tear; she mustn't let Peter see her cry.

There wasn't any traffic, as the roads had been cleared to get the buses with the children to the various railway stations, but it seemed for ever before the bus that Peter and Hazel were on turned in to Victoria station.

There were hundreds of children in the station and the teachers made them stand in line. After a while, they were told which platform they had to march to. The trains, with smoke puffing out of their engines, were waiting, and the children were shown which one to get on. Hazel found a seat for her and Peter. They quickly sat down with their luggage and their gas masks on their laps. Four other boys and two girls came and sat in their carriage, and a teacher joined them. They didn't know any of them, and the teacher looked very stern. Peter quickly took hold of his sister's hand.

A woman with a clipboard came in and asked all the children's names and what school they came from.

'Where we going, miss?' asked one girl, who was wearing a very stained and dirty blue coat.

'I'm afraid I don't know,' replied the woman.

'Well I 'ope they've got a proper bed. I ain't ever slept in a proper bed.'

The teacher looked at the girl and smiled.

To Hazel it seemed like they were never going to move, then suddenly the guards started shouting and slamming doors and a whistle was blown. After a lot of clanking, banging and jerking, the train slowly pulled out of the station. Crowds of people were on the platform, waving and saying goodbye to children who must have lived close by. It was very sad. Hazel was trying hard not to cry. She didn't want to go away. She didn't want to leave London without her mum and dad and Gran and Auntie Betty. When would she see them again? Where were they going?

When Rene and John turned in to Glebe Street, it suddenly looked very empty and quiet with no children and none of the usual noise.

As they went into Maud's kitchen, her mother called from the scullery, 'They got orf all right then?' She came into the kitchen carrying the teapot, which was covered as usual with the multicoloured crocheted tea cosy. The cups and saucers were already laid out.

'Well we only saw them on to the bus,' said John. 'We've no idea what station they were going to. If we had known that, at least it would have given us some idea where they were being sent.'

'The school wouldn't tell you?'

'No. We've just got to wait.'

'Why's that, then?'

'Don't know. A form of security, I suppose.'

'So it could be anywhere in the whole of the country?'

'Yes,' said Rene, brushing away another tear. 'We'll just have to wait till Hazel writes.'

'She's a good girl,' said Maud.

Rene could only nod in agreement.

For the rest of the day, in every home, people were wondering where their children had gone to, and if they were all right, and whether they'd done the right thing.

After a while Hazel and Peter started to eat their sandwiches and began to relax.

Two boys were playing a noisy game of snap, two were reading and one of the girls just stared out of the window. The girl with the scruffy coat told them that her name was April.

'That's 'cos I was born in April,' she said proudly. 'What yer got in yer sandwiches?' she asked Hazel.

'Fish paste.'

'I like fish paste,' she said.

'And where are your sandwiches?' asked the teacher.

'Ain't got none.'

'You were told to bring them.'

'I know, but me mum couldn't be bovvered.'

'I'll go and see if I can find you some.'

'Cor, fanks, miss.'

'Where d'yer live?' asked April, when the teacher had gone.

'Rotherhithe,' said Hazel.

'Me mum says it's a bit posh round that way.'

Hazel didn't think it was any different to anywhere else, and certainly not posh.

The teacher came back with a packet and handed it to April.

'Cor, fanks.' She tore open the parcel and quickly began eating the sandwich. 'I like cheese,' she said with her mouth full, spitting some of the contents over the boy next to her.

He brushed the crumbs off his smart navy blue blazer and said, 'Ain't you got any manners?'

'Cor, you're stuck-up.' With that, April burst out laughing.

Peter moved closer to his sister. He didn't like this girl. She looked rough and would pick a fight with anyone.

April settled back and said, 'Looks like I'm gonna be with a lot of posh people.' The next moment she leaned forward in excitement as they passed some cows and sheep, and the teacher began telling her about them.

After a while they all sat back, and with the steady rhythm of the train and after the early start, eyelids slowly began to close.

When the train stopped, everyone jumped up and tried to pull at the leather strap that would let the window down.

'Where are we?' asked the boy in the smart blazer. He poked his head out. 'Can't see any name plate.'

A woman in the corridor opened the door to their carriage and said to the teacher, 'Miss Hooper, this is our destination. Would you kindly gather all the children from your school and see that they stand on the platform in an orderly manner. We don't want the local people to think that we don't have any discipline over our students.'

'Yes, Miss Andrews.'

April burst out laughing. 'I ain't ever been called a student before.'

Hazel prayed that she wouldn't be living anywhere near April; she didn't like her.

'Where are we, miss?' asked the boy in the posh blazer.

'Billingshurst,' said Miss Andrews.

'Where's that?'

'Sussex. Now come along.'

It was a very small station, and outside were a lot of buses.

'Why are the buses green?' asked Peter.

'Don't know,' said Hazel. 'Might be 'cos we're in the country.'

'And they ain't got no upstairs.'

'Would all the children from Silwood Street School come along with me,' said Miss Rose, Hazel's teacher.

One of the other teachers was putting them into twos and they were marched along the platform. Outside they climbed on to buses, and the next part of their journey began.

They were a while on the bus, and Peter said, 'I'm hungry.'

'So am I,' said Hazel. 'P'raps when we get to the person who's going to look after us they'll give us something to eat.' It seemed a long time since they'd had their sandwiches on the train.

Hazel was looking out of the window. It was very green everywhere, and people were standing at the side of the road just staring at them.

The sun was beginning to set when the bus stopped outside a large hall. Once again they were told to walk in an orderly manner as they went inside. Miss Rose was in charge, and she was bustling around talking to various women, some of whom were wearing a green uniform. The other teachers were all talking together and glancing across at the children. Hazel was worried.

Why were they looking at them like that? What was wrong?

A lot of people were sitting on seats, and there was a line of tables down one side of the room.

'First you have to go into that room at the end, then you go and stand on the stage,' said Miss Rose.

The children filed into the room.

Peter was clutching Hazel's hand. 'Don't leave me, Haz,' he said with tears in his eyes.

'You'll be all right. I'm with you.'

When it was Hazel and Peter's turn, they had their coats taken from them and powder puffed over them, then a nurse puffed the powder in their hair and inside the front and back of their clothes.

Some of the children were crying.

'What's this for?' shouted out an older boy. 'Just 'cos we comes from the East End don't mean we're lousy.'

'It's just a precaution,' said the nurse.

Hazel was bewildered. Her mum would go mad if she found out that these people thought they were lousy.

Hazel grabbed Peter's hand and they went and stood on the stage. She watched as people came up one by one and took children away. They then went to a table, and the woman behind it wrote something down and gave them a brown paper carrier bag.

'Hallo,' said a tall woman standing in front of them. 'And what's your name, little girl?'

'Hazel. And this is me brother Peter.'

'Oh. I see. Would you like to come and live with me?' she asked.

'Dunno,' said Hazel.

'I don't want the boy, but you can come.'

Peter looked at his sister and tears filled his sad blue eyes. 'Don't leave me, Haz. Please.'

She held on to his hand. 'I ain't going anywhere without you. Remember, I promised Mum.'

The woman walked over to talk to one of the teachers and pointed to Hazel and Peter. The teacher said something to her, and the woman went and sat down again.

Many women came to look at them, but they only wanted to take Hazel.

Some of the men who looked like farmers took boys.

Peter's legs were aching and he sat down on the floor. 'What we gonna do if nobody wants us, Haz?'

'Don't know. Go back home, I suppose.'

'That's good.'

A short, plump woman stood in front of them. She had a rosy face and her brown hair was covered with a headscarf. 'I've been watching you two. How would you like to come and live with me?'

'Only if you take Peter too.'

'Course. Now come on, let's get registered. By the way, I'm Mrs Jacobs.'

'I'm Hazel, and this is Peter.'

'Very nice.'

They went to a table and Mrs Jacobs filled in a lot of forms, then Peter and Hazel were each given a brown paper carrier bag. When they looked inside, there was a tin of condensed milk, a packet of biscuits, a packet of tea and a bag of sugar.

'What's this for?' asked Peter.

'It's to give your new family a start,' said the lady behind the table.

Hazel didn't want a new family; she just wanted her own mum and dad.

'Someone will be round to see you in a few days, just to make sure you are settling in. Be good now.'

Mrs Jacobs took Hazel's hand and they made their way outside.

'It's very dark,' Hazel said as she took hold of her brother's hand.

'No streets lights here, you're in the country now.'

'Where are we?'

'A lovely little village called Osborne.'

Hazel was none the wiser.

Chapter 4

HAZEL AND PETER followed Mrs Jacobs as she began walking along the road. Hazel was frightened. There weren't any pavements and the high bushes looked creepy. Where were they going?

'Is it very far to your house?' she asked.

'Not too far, just a couple of miles.'

Although she didn't know how far a couple of miles was, it sounded a long way for her and Peter's tired legs.

'We'll be passing the school shortly; that's where you'll be going.'

'Have you got any children?' asked Hazel, still worried about the thought of walking a couple of miles and trying to keep up with Mrs Jacobs.

'No, not yet, but I will have after Christmas.'

29

Hazel was bewildered. Did she mean she was having more evacuees?

A little further along, Mrs Jacobs said, 'That'll be your school.' She crossed the road. 'Come and have a look.'

'It's ever so small,' said Peter, looking at the outline of the building.

'It's big enough for the children round here. It's got three classrooms. One's for the little 'uns, then one for the middle lot. Then there's a class for the big 'un's 'fore they leave. Most of the boys work on the farms here even before they leave.'

'Have you got a farm?' asked Peter.

'No, but me and my husband work on one, and that's where we live. Come on, let's be off. They've got lovely stoves in the classrooms, and in the winter you can take a potato to school with you and have it baked for your lunch.'

'Can't we come home?' asked Peter. 'Well, not home, but to your house?'

'No, it's much too far for you to walk there and back in the time.'

Hazel had been very quiet. This wasn't what she'd expected, and she didn't want to still be here in the winter. 'Will me and Peter be in the same class?'

'I don't know, love. The teacher will sort that out tomorrow.'

'We got ter go to school tomorrow? But it's Sunday, and in London we're still on holiday,' said Hazel.

'I'm only telling you what the woman at the church hall told me: that it's to be opened just for the evacuees. I expect it's so you can get used to it and the teachers can see what class you need to be in.'

'Will we have to do a test?' asked Hazel.

'I would think so.'

'I don't like tests,' said Peter.

'Well how's the teacher going to know what class to put you in?'

'Dunno,' said Peter. 'Is it much longer to your house?'

'A little way yet.'

'Me legs are tired.'

'Sorry about that, but I can't drive and me husband didn't want you, so he wasn't gonna be much help. Perhaps I should 'ave got one of the WVS ladies to take us home.'

Hazel stopped. 'Why are you taking us to your house if your husband don't want us?'

'We have to. The government said that as we've got a spare room, we have to take evacuee kids. I told 'em come Christmas we wouldn't have a spare room. But would they listen? No. Now come on.'

'We'll go home if there's no war,' said Hazel.

'Well, we'll just have to wait and see,' said Mrs Jacobs.

Hazel and Peter were very tired, and Peter began crying.

'Now come on, stop dawdling. And stop that whining.'

'I want me mum.'

'Well you can't have your mum.'

'We had to get up very early this morning, that's why Peter's so tired.' Hazel didn't like this lady.

'I had to get up very early as well. We all do when there's a farm to run.'

Hazel took Peter's bag and held on to his hand. 'Come on. Be brave.'

'I don't want to be brave. I want Mum.'

The woman turned off and began to walk down a small lane, and Hazel wondered how much further they had to go.

'That's where we live,' said Mrs Jacobs proudly, pointing to a house at the side of the road.

It looked very small, with tiny windows.

She pushed open the door. 'Coo-ee, Walter, we're home,' she called out.

'I was getting worried about you,' said the tall, red-faced man who came out of the room in front of them. 'So one of these is the kid we've got to look after?'

'Yes. This is Hazel, and Peter. We've got 'em both.'

The two children stood perfectly still. This man frightened them.

'I thought you was only going to get one?'

'I was, but they looked so sad, I couldn't separate them. But just think, we'll get twice as much money and that'll help.'

'Yes, but it also means twice as much work and food.'

'Don't worry about that. Right then, kids, I'll show you where you're going to sleep.'

They followed Mrs Jacobs up a very dark, narrow staircase. At the top were three doors. 'That's the bathroom and lavvy,' she said, pointing to one that had a window over the top. 'This is me and me husband's room, and this is yours. It's only got one bed, but you can share.'

They stepped inside a very small room, and as Mrs Jacobs switched on the not very bright light, they could see that there was just a single bed pushed up against the wall, and that was all. The tiny window was very high up, in the roof.

'I'll bring you up a chair for you to put your things on. But first take your coats off, then come down and I'll make you a cup of cocoa.' She went back downstairs.

Peter went to Hazel and clutched her tightly. They both clung to each other as the tears fell.

'I want to go home,' sobbed Peter.

'I know, and so do I, but we can't.'

'Why did Mum and Dad send us away? Don't they love us any more?'

'Course they do.'

'But there ain't a war.'

'I know.' Hazel didn't know what else to say. 'Look, let's not worry about it tonight. Tomorrow when we go to the school we'll tell Miss Rose we want to go home.'

'It's a long way to that school.'

'I know.' Hazel felt very alone, but she knew she had to be strong for Peter; after all, she had promised their mum she'd look after him. 'Now come on, dry your tears and let's go and get a drink.'

'All right.'

Rene tossed and turned. Eventually she got out of bed. 'I'm sorry, John, but I can't sleep.'

'I know, love.'

'D'you think they're all right?'

'Course they are. I expect they're tucked up in bed, fast asleep. Now come on, come back to bed.' Although John sounded very confident, he too was worried about his children. Where were they? Was someone looking after them? What if there was a war and he was called up? He felt sick with worry. They were so happy, and all this could be taken away from them. Although not a religious man, he silently prayed for his family.

The rumble of thunder made Rene jump.

'Come on, love, get back in, it's only a drop of rain.'

Rene got in beside John and he held her close. They both knew that this was going to be a long, sleepless night.

'What was that?' asked Peter as he clung to his sister.

'It's the rain beating on the window.'

'I don't like it. It's ever so dark.'

'I know. Give Teddy a big hug and close your eyes.'

'I want ter go to the lav, but I can't see.'

'All right, I'll take you. I'll put this light on and you wait here till I put the bathroom light on.'

'All right. But don't be long.'

'I've only got to go across there,' she said in a hushed tone, pointing to the bathroom door.

They both got out of bed, and after Hazel found the switch, she carefully made her way to the bathroom. This was the only good thing about this house: at least they didn't have to go outside or wee in the pot.

The door of the other bedroom flew open. 'And where are you two going?' Mr Jacobs filled the doorway.

'Peter wants a wee.'

'That's all right then. Don't leave the light on.'

'No, we won't,' said Hazel.

Was this going to be their home if there was a war?

She stood outside the door and waited for Peter. She just wanted to go back to London and her mum and dad.

Chapter 5

HAZEL WAS DISORIENTATED when she woke up. Where was she? And what was Peter doing in her bed? When she looked towards the window, she realised she wasn't at home, and once again the tears fell. Peter was holding her tight and she was almost falling out of bed. Carefully she moved his arm and he quickly sat up.

'Where are we, Haz?'

'We're at Mrs Jacobs' house, but I don't know where that is.'

'What do we do now?'

'I don't know; go and see if we've got something for breakfast, I suppose. Then we've got to find that school. Come on, get up.'

Hazel went to her small attaché case and took out

her clean knickers. Her mother always said she must have clean knickers on every day. But who would wash them for her? She never had to think about that at home.

Slowly they crept down the stairs.

'It's very quiet. I wonder what the time is?' said Hazel.

She opened the door to the small kitchen.

'Hello. Sit yourselves down and I'll make you some toast,' said Mrs Jacobs. 'Did you sleep all right?'

They didn't answer.

Hazel looked round the room. She hadn't taken a lot of notice of it last night, as she was too tired. It was very pretty, with flowery curtains that were the same pattern as the cushions on the two armchairs.

'There was a lot of rain in the night. I hope it didn't keep you awake.'

'No,' they both said together.

'That's good. Now when you've had your toast, you can start to walk to school. You must go straight there and don't play about on the way. Understand?'

They nodded.

They sat quietly eating their toast, and when they'd finished, Mrs Jacobs took them to the end of the lane and showed them which direction to go in. 'You'll see the school. Now go on. Be off with you.'

'Can't you take us?' asked Hazel.

'No. I have work to do. The chickens and pigs want

feeding, and besides, you're a big girl. You've come all the way from London on your own, so I'm sure you can find your school. I'll see you when you get back, then we can sort things out.'

They started the long walk to school.

'What did she mean when she said "sort things out"?' asked Peter.

'I don't know.'

They passed a field that had cows in. They stopped and the cows came to the hedge to look at them.

'I don't like them,' said Peter, backing away. 'They're ever so big.'

'I know.' Hazel didn't like the look of them either. The only large animals they ever saw were in the zoo, or the horses with the men who came round the streets asking for rag and bones. As they walked on, Hazel remembered the time she'd been given a goldfish for some of Auntie Betty's old clothes, but the fish had soon died.

After a while they saw the school. A lot of children were waiting outside.

'Miss Rose said we've got to wait here till she tells us where to go,' said Eve Ward, a girl at their school.

'Hazel! Hazel Morgan!' screamed out another girl as she rushed towards them.

'Sue! Sue Johnson!' yelled Hazel as they fell into each other's arms. 'I didn't see you on the train,' she added.

'No. Me mum and dad had a row. Mum didn't want me to come but Dad said I had to. I missed the train so one of the teachers brought me down in her car. Hello, Peter. Where are you two staying?' Sue was a little older than Hazel, and she also had two grown-up sisters, so she was very knowledgeable and the other girls always listened when she told them things.

'I dunno. It's some little place miles away. We had to walk here as Mrs Jacobs had to feed the pigs and chickens.'

Sue began to laugh.

'What's so funny?' asked Hazel.

'You two on a farm.'

'So where are you?'

'In the village.'

'Whereabouts?'

'Just up the road with the sweetshop lady, but it's only till they find someone who'll have me for good.'

'For good!' said Hazel. 'You gonna stay here for good?'

'I'll have to if there's a war.'

Just then Miss Rose came out of the school with the other teachers. She clapped her hands. 'Children, come here.'

Slowly the children gathered in front of her. Some of the teachers were dabbing at their eyes.

'Now, children, please listen to me very carefully,' continued Miss Rose, softly. 'I'm sorry to have to tell you that Mr Chamberlain has just told us that this country is at war with Germany.'

'Does that mean we can't go home?' asked one boy.

'I'm afraid so.'

Peter grabbed Hazel's hand and began to cry. 'I don't want to stay here.'

Hazel held him close. 'Nor do I, but I think we have to now.'

'But what about Mum and Dad?'

'I don't know.'

'Now, children, I want you to march in an orderly line into the school and find a desk to sit at. Then you are to write a letter to your parents telling them where you are and who you are staying with. There is paper, pencils and envelopes on every desk.'

Hazel quickly put up her hand.

'Yes, Hazel?'

'Please, miss, I don't know where we are.'

'When you're settled at a desk, I'll come and give you your address.'

'Thank you.' Hazel took hold of Peter's hand and went into the school.

All over the country, people like those who lived in Glebe Street were listening to the wireless. When Mr Chamberlain told them they were at war with Germany, many of the women began to cry.

John and Rene were sitting downstairs with Maud and Betty. John put his arm round Rene's shoulders.

'What do we do now?' she sobbed.

'Dunno, love. Just wait to be told, I suppose.'

'When will we see the kids again?'

'Dunno,' he said again.

'I'll put the kettle on,' said Betty, going quickly into the scullery, where she buried her head in her pinny and cried. She didn't want a war. They were all happy with their lives.

Among the many leaflets full of advice and instructions that every family had been given was one telling them about the air-raid warnings and what to do when they heard one. They had been told about the up-and-down noise the siren made, and when it started up on that sunny Sunday morning, everybody rushed outside to see what was happening.

Hilda and Ron were at their door. 'Maud, what d'we have ter do?' Hilda asked her friend with a bewildered look on her face.

'I told her we've got ter make our way ter the shelter,' said Ron.

'I ain't going there.'

There had been an air-raid shelter erected a few streets away for a block of flats.

'Look, I think we all should go and sit under the table,' said John.

'That ain't very safe if the Germans start ter bomb us,' said Maud.

'They might just be testing the siren,' said Mr James from the dairy as he walked across the road with his hands tucked under his apron. He joined the small crowd that was now gathering.

Everybody looked very worried as they gazed up at the sky.

'Could be,' said John.

'Have you found out where your two are?' Mrs James asked Rene.

Rene shook her head. She too looked up at the sky. She was concerned that everybody was still standing in the road and nobody seemed to know what to do. They could be bombed at any minute.

'They say we're gonna have air-raid shelters put out back,' said Ron.

'Well they bloody well better get on with it,' said Maud.

'I ain't standing out here to be blown to kingdom come. I'm going inside to sit under the table,' said Betty.

'I'll come with you,' said Rene.

They went inside just as the long note of the all-clear sounded.

'See, I told you they was just testing it,' said Mr James.

After a lot of talking, the crowd slowly dispersed.

'I'll see to the dinner,' said Maud.

'Don't know if I can eat anything,' said Rene.

'Well you'd better, after I've spent half the morning getting it ready.'

Rene looked at her mother and gave her a warm smile. She knew Maud was only trying to make things as normal as possible.

That afternoon, Maggie and Tom arrived.

'Oh Mum, we just had to come over and make sure you're all right.' Maggie was hugging her mother.

'Rum do, this,' said Tom to John.

'It certainly is.'

'Did you let the kids go?' Maggie asked her sister.

'Yes, we felt we had to.'

'It's gonna be hard for you not having them around.'

'I shall miss 'em,' said Maud.

For the rest of the afternoon they sat around talking and drinking tea. Each with their own thoughts about the war.

Hazel sat at a desk and looked around. This was a funny little classroom. There were a lot of drawings on the walls of children running away from some kind of fireworks. Was this supposed to be the Londoners running away from the bombs exploding around them? The teacher's desk was between the blackboard and rows of desks. Cupboards were wide open and stacked with papers; there was a fat round black stove in the corner, and she guessed this was where the kids put their potatoes.

Miss Rose walked into the room. 'Have you all started your letters?'

A chorus of 'Yes, Miss Rose,' went up.

Hazel looked at her paper. On it she'd written: *Dear Mum, Dad, Gran and Auntie Betty. We are very unhappy. Please come and get us. Love Hazel and Peter.*

Miss Rose stopped and looked over Hazel's shoulder. 'You can't write that.'

For the first time in her life Hazel answered her teacher back. 'Why can't I?'

'It will only upset your parents.'

'I don't care.' Tears were running down her face. 'Come on, Peter, let's go home.'

Peter looked bewildered as he followed his sister out of the room.

Chapter 6

'WHERE WE GOING?' asked Peter once they were outside the school.

'Home,' said Hazel, taking hold of Peter's hand.

'What, all the way home? To see Mum and Dad?'

'Yes.'

'But we ain't got no money for the train fare.'

'Hazel Morgan, come here.'

Hazel stopped, sat down on the ground and burst into tears.

'Come along, Hazel, this isn't like you. Dry your eyes, and you and Peter come with me.' Miss Rose was standing over them; she ruffled Peter's hair fondly.

Hazel did as she was told and they went back into the school.

Miss Rose took her to a smaller room and sat behind

a desk. 'Now please sit down and tell me what the problem is.'

'We just want to go home.'

'I'm afraid you can't, not now that war has been declared.'

'But we don't like where we've gotta live.'

'Why not?'

'It's a long way away. A long walk to school.'

Miss Rose looked at the piece of paper she was holding. 'Dairy Lane Farm. So you're on a farm?'

Hazel didn't react.

'I would have thought that would be very exciting. What seems to be the problem?'

'We have to sleep in the same bed.'

'A lot of children would be very happy to share a bed.'

Hazel thought about the girl on the train who said she'd never slept in a proper bed, and felt guilty.

'It's all very strange and upsetting for you at the moment, but I'm sure that in a couple of days you will have settled down and then things won't look so bad. Now come back into the classroom and write a nice letter to your mother and father. After all, they are already worried about you, and if you ask to come home right away, that's going to make them very sad.'

Hazel stood up and Peter quickly took hold of her hand. He felt safe holding his big sister's hand.

'Good girl. Now this is where you are staying.'

Hazel took the piece of paper and said out loud, 'Dairy Lane Farm. Osborne. Sussex. But it ain't got no road or number.'

'That's all you need here.'

'But will Dad be able to write to us?'

'Of course. Now come with me.'

They went back into the classroom.

On Tuesday morning Rene rushed into the kitchen waving the letter she had just received. 'Mum. Mum. We've got a letter. I heard the postman and . . .' She was busy tearing at the envelope. 'It's only a page.'

'Give 'em time. They ain't been there long enough to get their bearings. Well, come on. What they got to say?'

Rene quickly scanned the letter. 'They're on a farm in Sussex and had to go to school today.' She looked up. 'That was written on Sunday. They've been told there's a war on and can't come home.' Once again tears ran down her cheeks.

'At least they're safe, love. And on a farm. That'll be different.'

'They don't say if they're happy or if there's other children.'

'Give 'em a chance, they ain't been there five minutes.'

'Mum, I'm worried. What if someone was telling them what to say? How would we know?'

'Now stop getting yourself in a state. Look at the time; you'd better be off ter work.'

'I know, but making shirts ain't gonna help the war effort, is it?'

'Not yet, but you might soon be making shirts for the forces.'

'Could be, I suppose.' Rene kissed her mother's cheek and, grabbing her handbag, called out, 'Bye,' and left.

'Bye, love.' Maud sat in the chair and picked up the letter that was lying on the table. 'Poor little buggers.'

Maud was hanging out the washing when Hilda came out of her lav.

'Hallo, love. Everything all right?' she asked, coming up to the coal bin that separated their yards.

'Not too bad. Rene had a letter from the kids this morning. They're on a farm in Sussex somewhere.'

'That's nice.'

'At least it's not up in Scotland or somewhere hundreds of miles away.'

'If they was in Scotland they could stay with my Adam and his boys. Mind you, from what I can gather, those boys are a bit of a handful.'

'I've got the kettle on. Fancy a cuppa?' said Maud as she hung the last pillowcase on the line.

'Why not? Ron's got his head buried in the paper and carrying on at the news. I told him, you can't change things, what's done is done.'

Hilda came through the gap ready for tea and a chat.

That evening, the family was sitting round the table discussing the children.

John said, 'As I said to Rene, they don't seem to be that far away, and I reckon that later on we could get down to see 'em.'

'I want to go next Sunday,' said Rene.

'I think we should wait a while. Let's find out where they are first and give 'em a chance to settle in. I'll get a map from work tomorrow and then we can see where they are.'

'I'll start getting a few bits together for you to take to them,' said Betty.

'Thanks,' said Rene.

Suddenly everyone's mood was lifted.

On Monday, Hazel, Peter and the rest of the children from London had their first proper day at their new school. They weren't very happy. All playtime the local kids had been taking the mickey out of their accents.

'Why do you talk funny?' one boy asked Hazel.

'We don't talk as funny as you,' she replied.

Sue Johnson came over. 'He giving you trouble,

Haz? Take no notice. They're just a bunch of country yokels; they've never been to London or seen the world.'

'I bet you ain't seen the world,' said the boy.

'We've seen a lot more than you. Come on, Haz.' Sue tucked her arm through Hazel's and they walked away with Peter trotting behind and grinning.

'What did Miss Rose say to you when you run out the class yesterday?'

'Told me to come back and write me letter. I didn't see you when we went . . .' Hazel stopped. She couldn't say 'home', because it wasn't her home.

'No, I know. Miss Rose told me to get me things 'cos I was being moved.'

'So where are you now?'

'In with a Mrs Miller. She's a lovely lady, her husband's a farmer and she's got two daughters, Mary and Donna. They're grown up like my sisters, so I'll feel as if I'm at home.'

How Hazel envied her friend.

Back in class, Hazel sat and thought about yesterday. When she and Peter had got back to the farm, nobody was about. They'd wandered into the kitchen and out back.

Hazel had taken a deep breath. It was just a big open space with lots of funny old buildings and fields in the distance; there was no fences or garden. This must be what a farm looked like.

'Hello, you two,' said Mrs Jacobs. 'Had a good day at school?' She'd put down the pail she was holding and tucked a strand of her dark hair under her big hat. 'Just feeding the chickens; come on and have a look.'

Peter had held on to Hazel's hand and they'd followed Mrs Jacobs as she went round the back of one of the buildings.

There were chickens flying about all over the place. Hazel was frightened and ran away screaming when they came towards her flapping their wings. Peter was right behind her.

'Hazel, come back here,' called Mrs Jacobs. 'They won't hurt you. They know it's feeding time. Very intelligent, chickens are. Grab a handful of feed and throw it.'

Very slowly and reluctantly they came back and did as they were told, throwing the feed as far away as they could.

Mrs Jacobs laughed. 'This could be your job, so you'd better get used to them.'

Peter looked at his sister with horror written all over his face.

They moved away from the chickens, which were now busy eating.

'Come on, I'll give you a walk round and show you the farm. This is the piggery. We've only got two at the moment, but you'll love it when we have the little 'uns.'

They went inside the smelly building and a large pig jumped up at the low wall round the pen, making the children leap back.

'Down, Flora.' Mrs Jacobs pushed the pig on the nose.

'Why did you call her Flora?' asked Hazel, who didn't like the look of this animal any more than the chickens.

'All our animals have names, even the cows. Come on, let's go and see Mr Jacobs. He's started the milking.'

Reluctantly they followed Mrs Jacobs into another smelly building full of cows tied up. Mr Jacobs was sitting on a small stool, milking one of them.

'All right, love?' he asked when they walked in.

'Yes thanks. Just showing 'em around,' Mrs Jacobs said, smiling.

He looked up at Hazel and Peter and said, 'Just remember all the time you're here that I don't want you getting up to no good, and I don't want to find you near the animals. Understand?'

They both nodded vigorously. Hazel knew they wouldn't be going anywhere near these animals.

'Right, come on and I'll give you something to eat,' said Mrs Jacobs.

Later that evening, in the kitchen, Mr Jacobs said, 'Looks like we're stuck with you two for a while. Yer knows there's a war on now, don't you?'

53

They nodded.

'Well just make sure you behave yerselves, and don't worry the missus.'

Hazel and Peter went to their room.

'I don't like him,' said Peter.

'Nor do I. But now Mum and Dad know where we live, they might come and see us and take us back home.'

'I hope so.'

That evening when John arrived home, he took a map from his jacket pocket and laid it out on the table. 'This is where the kids are,' he said to Rene. He pointed to a spot that had a big ring round it.

'It's ever so small and looks like it's miles away from everywhere,' said Rene.

'I know. But at least it's on the map, and don't forget, they are on a farm.'

'I've been worrying about that. Hazel don't like dogs, so how's she gonna get on with pigs and cows?'

John laughed. 'I don't think they let 'em milk cows or feed the pigs.'

'I hope not.'

'You never know, young Peter might end up being a farmer.'

'Don't talk daft.'

'I'm hoping that Holden will let me have a car in a week or two. The few he hires are all out at the moment, but he said as soon as they come in I can have one.'

'That'll be wonderful. Let's go down for dinner and tell Mum.'

As Rene went to open their kitchen door, John pushed it shut and took her in his arms. 'Rene, whatever happens to all of us in this war, I want you to remember that I'll always love you.'

'I know that. What's brought this on?'

'I'm expecting to be called up.'

Rene looked shocked. She had been so busy worrying about the children that she had almost forgotten that her husband, who she loved so very much, might be going away. 'Please, John. Don't say that. I couldn't bear it if you went as well.'

'I think I'll have to.' He knew that at the age of thirty-six he was of call-up age. He held her close and kissed her long and hard.

Rene closed her eyes. The thought that was running through her mind was that if only they didn't have to go downstairs for their dinner, she could think of much better things to do than eat.

Chapter 7

HAZEL AND PETER were over the moon. They were on their way to school, and Hazel was reading out the letter they had received that morning. 'Dad says that perhaps later on, when we've settled in, they might be able to come and see us.'

'Will they take us home?' asked Peter.

'I hope so.'

'Well they ain't had any bombs drop on 'em, have they?'

'No. But the war's only been on for a little while.'

'I'm going home. I'm going home.' Peter ran off in front, chanting.

'Peter, come back here.' Hazel stopped. 'Now you listen to me. You mustn't say anything to anybody.

56

D'you hear? I don't want Miss Rose to know, or the Jacobs. They might try and stop us.'

'They can't do that, can they?'

'I don't know.' She knew Peter wasn't happy here, but what could she do? Miss Rose made all the children show her the letters they had written. She said it was part of their lessons and she had to check their spelling, but Hazel knew it was to see if they had said something that might worry their mums and dads.

As they wandered on, Hazel looked all around her. The gentle breeze was making the golden corn sway, and she had to admit to herself that it was lovely here, with all the fields and trees, so different from London, though she didn't like the animals or chickens. If only their mum and dad were here, it would be perfect.

Yesterday, Mr Jacobs had told the two children to sweep the yard.

'This will be one of your jobs, and no mucking about and chasing the chickens. Got ter keep yer busy,' he'd said, giving Hazel a large stiff broom.

By the end of the week, Rene was getting restless. 'Look, John, don't you think we could go by train to see them? Perhaps we could go one Sunday.'

'You know I'd love to, but I've been thinking, and I'm a bit worried we might upset them.'

In many ways Rene knew that John was right. They'd had a leaflet telling parents not to bring their children back to London just yet. It still broke her heart every time she thought about them. What made it worse was that she had heard that some parents had been to see their children, and a few had even brought them back with them because the children had been so unhappy.

When they were downstairs discussing it that evening, her mother said, 'Well I feel the same way as John. Let 'em settle in a bit before you go racing down there.'

Rene began sulking. 'It sounds like to me that you don't care about them and don't want them around.'

'Rene,' said Betty. 'How can you say that?' She went into the scullery. She was very angry with her sister and knew that if she stayed in the room she would say something she would regret.

Rene followed her out. 'I'm sorry, Bet, but I feel so helpless and I want to see them so much.'

As the tears ran down her face, her younger sister held her close. 'I know you do. We all do.'

John was the next to come into the scullery. 'Look, how about we go to the pictures tomorrow night?' he said. 'It'll do you good to have an evening out.'

Rene gave him a smile. This wasn't like John. They didn't often go to the pictures together, only to see a Western or a war film; she usually went with Betty, as they both liked the musicals. 'All right. Betty could come with us.'

'If you want.'

'Thanks,' said Betty.

They had sat through the B film and the news, and now they were watching one of the government information films that were shown during every programme.

'Parents. Don't bring your children back home,' said the voice-over. 'You may think they are unhappy, but take a look at these.' They were looking at children laughing and playing in fields. They had rosy cheeks and looked so healthy. 'So please remember, no schools are open in the towns and cities, and although life may be the same for you at the moment, it could all change. So keep them safe.'

When the lights went up, everybody sat very quietly.

On the way home Rene said, 'I wonder if those kids were really evacuees and not actors?'

'Dunno,' said John.

'Surely the government wouldn't tell lies about that?' said Betty. 'Would they?'

'Dunno,' said John again.

At the end of the month, John was reading an official-looking letter he'd received that morning.

'John, are you listening to me?'

'Sorry, Rene.'

Her face was suddenly filled with fear. She put her hand to her mouth. 'Oh no.'

'I'm afraid so, love. I've got to go for my medical.' He placed the letter on the table.

'When and where?' she asked.

'Saturday. At the church hall.'

'I'd heard they were doing them there. Old Mrs Porter at work said her son had his there.'

'Has he gone yet?'

Rene nodded. 'He left last week.'

John grinned. 'Don't let's count our chickens yet. You never know, I might not pass. I might have flat feet.'

On Saturday afternoon, Rene hurried home from work and watched from the front-room window till John came walking down the street. She heard him pull the key through the letter box and stood at the top of the stairs waiting for him.

He looked up. 'Everything all right, love?' he asked, as he made his way upstairs towards her.

She nodded. 'Just waiting for you,' she said, holding up her cheek for his kiss. 'Well?'

'I think I've passed.'

'Oh.'

'You sorry?'

'In some ways.'

'I know how you feel.' He took his jacket off. 'Some

of those that were there were only kids. I felt really old. How about a cuppa?'

'Kettle's on.'

He followed her to their small scullery. 'Rene, some of 'em were saying that it might only be a couple of weeks till we get called.'

'Oh John.' She went into his arms. 'I don't want you to go. It's bad enough not having the kids here, but you as well.'

'I know, but there's not a lot we can do about it. We must go and see the kids before I go.'

Rene wiped her eyes. 'I'd like that.'

John kissed her, and she responded.

'Now I've passed as fit, can I prove it to you?'

'Why not.'

He took her hand and they made their way to the bedroom.

'This is something we couldn't do when they were around,' said John, as between kisses he undid Rene's blouse and skirt.

'How would you like to help out in the fields next weekend? The men will be gathering the stacked corn now it's dried and ready for threshing,' said Mrs Jacobs.

'Dunno,' said Hazel.

'We could pay you.'

'Both of us?'

She nodded. 'It won't be much, but it'll give you

something to do, and you'll be able to meet some of the other people who live round here. We all get together and help each other out at this time. It can be good fun helping to build a haystack.'

'Could do, I suppose.'

'Hazel, I know you and Peter aren't happy here, but we do try to do our best.'

Hazel looked down at her feet. She suddenly felt guilty. She hadn't been rude to Mrs Jacobs, but she hadn't ever been very friendly. 'All right.'

'I'll sort out some clothes for you to wear. You don't want to spoil your school things. There's a jumble sale at the village hall on Monday. I'll go along and perhaps get you some shorts and sun hats.'

Peter was standing listening to all this, and once they were in bed he said, 'I don't wanna go and help in some field.'

'Why not? We'll be getting paid, and we can put that towards our running-away money.'

'S'pose so.'

'Besides, it might be good fun, and much better than sweeping that yard with those rotten chickens chasing us. And she said she'd get us some shorts.'

'They better not be big baggy ones down ter me ankles.'

For the first time in a long while, Hazel laughed a genuine, hearty laugh. Tears were running down her face.

'Wot yer laughing at?'

'The thought of you running about wearing long baggy shorts.'

Peter joined in with her, and they rolled around on the bed.

The following Saturday, Peter and Hazel followed Mrs Jacobs into one of the fields, where there were already a lot of people working.

There were stacks of corn, and a tractor was going along collecting them. The children watched as men threw them on to the back of the tractor. It looked like heavy and dusty work.

'Hello, Jenny,' called a woman in khaki dungarees and a coloured scarf tied round her head. 'How are you?'

'I'm fine thanks, Beth,' called back Mrs Jacobs. 'This is Hazel and Peter, they've come to give us a hand.'

'That's good. Now, Jenny, you be careful. We don't want you to go lifting anything.'

'I won't,' she called back.

Jenny Jacobs bent down and took hold of Hazel's hand. 'Now, you see that table over there?' She pointed to the far side of the field. 'If you go over there, you'll find Mrs Miller from up the road. She'll tell you what to do. All right?'

They both nodded and quickly made their way to Mrs Miller.

'My, don't you two look smart,' said Mrs Miller as they stood in front of her. 'And I see those shorts and tops fit you well. They belonged to my two girls years ago. Remember to keep your sun hats on all the time. This sun can be treacherous.'

Again they nodded.

Hazel felt good in her red shorts and white top, and Peter looked just as nice in his khaki shorts and blue top. They both had little sun hats and had been very pleased with the clothes Mrs Jacobs had given them.

'Thank you,' said Hazel when they'd tried them on, surprised at how nice they were.

'Well it's dusty work up in the fields, and I don't want you mucking up your nice clothes.'

'Right,' said Mrs Miller. 'I want you to take bottles of drinks over to the workmen. There's water, lemonade and ginger beer. That will keep you busy all day. Take as many as you can carry, and be careful of the tractor.'

They both picked up two bottles. They were very heavy, and walking over the stubble was hard work.

'Hazel! Hazel!' Someone was calling her, and Hazel stopped. She was very surprised to see her friend Sue come running up to her. 'What are you doing here?' she asked.

'I'm helping Mrs Miller. I told you, she's the lady I'm staying with. Her daughters are over there; they're helping as well. Isn't this fun?'

Hazel couldn't believe her luck. Suddenly the day seemed a lot brighter.

All morning they worked and laughed together. At lunchtime, someone came along in a tractor and brought a box full of sandwiches and cakes.

'Hazel, Peter and Sue,' called Mrs Miller. 'Come and sit yourselves down and have a sandwich. I expect you're hungry after all the work you've done this morning.'

They plonked themselves on the ground and took the sandwiches that were offered.

'They'll taste real good,' said Mrs Miller. 'Get yourselves a drink, too.'

Hazel and Peter had flushed cheeks.

'Well you both certainly look a lot healthier now than when you first came here,' said Mrs Jacobs, who was sitting on a chair. She turned to Mrs Miller. 'They looked such sad little things when I first saw them. I know Walter didn't want two, but I couldn't part 'em, and they're no trouble.'

'Will you be able to keep 'em when . . . ?' Mrs Miller nodded her head towards Mrs Jacobs.

'Don't know.'

Why had Mrs Miller said that? Hazel wondered. Were they going to be moved?

For the rest of the day they were busy, and when it was time to leave, Hazel didn't want to say goodbye to Sue.

'Come on, Sue,' said Mrs Miller. 'You can see Hazel and Peter tomorrow. Look, why don't you both come and have a bit of lunch with us? Would that be all right, Jenny?'

'I don't see why not.'

'I'll meet you at the school, then I can show you where I'm staying,' said Sue, who also had bright red cheeks.

For the first time in weeks, suddenly Hazel felt a lot happier. She was looking forward to tomorrow, and seeing her friend again.

Chapter 8

A FTER MEETING S UE at the school, Hazel and Peter went with her to Mrs Miller's house. Both her daughters were home.

'Hello, kids,' said Mary Miller, when they walked in. 'Did you enjoy yourselves yesterday?'

'Yes thank you,' said Hazel.

'And you look really smart in my old shorts. I didn't know me mum had kept those after all these years. They look better on you than they ever did on me.'

Hazel stood looking at Mary, who seemed to be moving about the kitchen all the time she was talking.

'How d'you fancy a walk in the woods? We'll take some bowls and collect blackberries. Then Mum can make us an apple and blackberry pie.'

'Mary, give them a chance to get their breath back.

Let them have a drink first. It's a bit of a walk from the Jacobs' for those little legs,' said Mrs Miller. 'Donna, get them a glass of lemonade.'

'Go in the garden and I'll bring it out to you,' said Donna.

In the garden, drinking their lemonade, Hazel looked around her and said softly to Sue, 'You're ever so lucky living here.'

'I know.'

'We going in the woods?' asked Peter.

'Mary will take us, she likes going for walks. It'll be fun in the woods; it's a bit early but if we're lucky we can collect conkers.'

'What's conkers?' asked Peter.

'They fall from the trees, and Donna showed me how to thread them on a piece of string and play a game. We don't get conkers in Rotherhithe, more's the pity.'

'D'you like it here?' asked Hazel.

'I should say so. The school's much easier and I just feel happy.'

'Don't you miss your mum and dad?'

'Yes, of course I do. But my dad told me that if I was unhappy, he'd be here like a shot and take me back. Since I've moved in with the Millers, I'm fine.'

How Hazel envied her friend.

Mary came out to them. 'I'm glad you've not got your school clothes on. Have you finished?'

She pointed at their glasses.

'Yes thank you,' they all said together.

'Right, off we go.'

They laughed and ran and climbed the small trees and collected blackberries and even found some conkers and had such a happy time.

When they got back to the Millers' house, Mr Miller was sitting in the bright sunny kitchen drinking tea and reading his newspaper. 'Hello, you lot. Enjoying yourselves?'

They all nodded. Hazel and Peter weren't sure of the rosy-faced man with the shock of white hair. He was smiling, though.

'See you've got a nice lot there.' He looked at the bowls of blackberries they had brought in and put on the table. 'And by the look of your faces, I'm guessing you've already eaten a few. I see you've got some conkers as well. We'll have to get them strung for you.'

'Sue, take them outside to the washroom and all wash your hands, and you'd better give your faces a wipe round. I don't want Jenny telling me off 'cos you've gone back covered in blackberry juice,' said Mrs Miller. 'Then come back and we can have a bite to eat.'

They followed Sue.

'You wait till you taste Auntie's dinners.'

Hazel stopped. 'Why do you call her Auntie? She ain't your aunt.'

'I know, but she said it was easier than to keep saying Mrs Miller.'

'Well I'd never call Mrs Jacobs Auntie.'

'Nor me,' said Peter.

Hazel looked around her. This was a happy place; she wished she could live here.

They were very tired as they made their way back to the Jacobs'; it had been a wonderful day. They had laughed a lot when they were learning to play conkers, and Sue was right about Mrs Miller's dinner: it was lovely, just like Gran made. Suddenly Hazel was very homesick. Why couldn't they be with people like the Millers?

'Have you had a nice day?' asked Mrs Jacobs as they walked in.

'Yes thank you,' they said together.

'Mrs Miller sent these for you.' Hazel put a bowl of blackberries on the table.

'Did you pick them?'

They nodded.

'Well now I'll have to make you a nice pie.'

Mr Jacobs looked up from his paper and gave them a quick nod.

'Now, go and have a wash and get ready for bed, and then come down and have some milk and a biscuit. I expect you'll be tired; it's been a very busy weekend for you.'

They left the room and did as they were told.

Later, when they were in bed, Peter said, 'I wish we could go and stay with the Millers.'

'So do I,' said Hazel. 'So do I,' she repeated sleepily.

It was November, and a tearful Rene was telling her mother that John had received his call-up papers that morning.

'Oh no, love. When's he gotta go?'

'Friday week. He's going to Catterick, wherever that is.'

'How's he gonna get there?'

'By train. He's got a travel warrant. Oh Mum, first the kids, now John. Bloody Hitler. I'd like to cut his balls off.'

'Rene!' said her mother, clearly shocked at her daughter's outburst.

'Sorry, Mum. It's just that I feel so angry that someone could disrupt so many people's lives.'

'I know, but think of all those poor buggers abroad that have been killed.'

'I know.'

'Will he get a chance to see the kids before he goes off?'

'Yes. We're going to see them on Sunday.'

'You won't have a chance to write and tell 'em.'

'No, but perhaps it's better if we just turn up. Don't want 'em sitting at the window all day waiting.'

'You're probably right.'

On Monday, when they arrived at the school, Sue came running over to Hazel and said, 'The Millers really like you and Peter, and Donna was wondering if you'd like to go to Worthing with us on Sunday.'

'We'd love it. Anything to get away from the farm. But why Worthing? Where is it and what's there?'

'It's at the seaside, and Donna said she's going to meet a girlfriend of hers who's going into the air force and I think Donna wants to join as well. And she said that if you two come with us she could get on and talk to her friend and not worry about me. Is that all right?'

'I should say so.'

'Will your lady let you go?'

'I would think so.'

'Good.'

When the bell went and they made their way into their classes, Hazel felt a lot happier.

'So is that all right?' she asked when they got back to the farm and she told Mrs Jacobs about the trip to Worthing.

'I think it would be lovely for you. But you'll have to wrap up. The wind can be very cold.'

That evening, when they were in bed, Peter said, 'Wish it could have been a Saturday and the shops open, then we could buy something.'

'We are not using our going-home money on silly things, so there.'

'Oh all right.'

On Sunday morning, Rene and John set off for Osborne. They had comics, chocolate and sweets for the children.

Rene felt sick with anticipation and excitement as they made their way to Victoria station. 'I hope I don't cry when I see them,' she said.

'I hope you don't, and don't tell them I'm going in the army on Friday, it might upset them.'

The platform was full of people saying goodbye, and Rene could see by the many who were crying that their friends and menfolk were going away. This upset her, as she knew she and John would be facing the same thing on Friday.

The train was very crowded but they found a seat, and finally they left the station behind and were on their way.

'How we gonna know when we get there, now they've taken all the railway signs away?' asked Rene.

'The stationmaster will call out the name of the station, so we'll have to listen carefully.'

'Well if you ask me, I think that's a daft thing to do. They take the names away but still call out the station. Is that supposed to fool the enemy?'

'Don't ask me.'

They settled back and let the rhythm of the train take them towards their children.

It was a crisp, clean morning as Hazel and Peter made their way to the Millers' house. They were very excited about going to Worthing with Donna.

'Can we have a paddle?' asked Peter.

'I would think so, but it'll be very cold and you'll have ter dry your feet on your hankie.'

'What we got in our sandwiches?' asked Peter.

'I think it's cheese,' said Hazel. She was pleased that Mrs Jacobs had done them some sandwiches. 'And you've got to wait till we get there before you eat them.'

'We going on a train?'

'Dunno.'

'I like trains.'

'You'll just have to wait and see.'

When they arrived at the Millers', Sue said excitedly, 'Donna's taking us in the car.'

When they'd got settled on the back seat and were on their way, Donna said over her shoulder, 'I'll leave you three by a little café I know. It's just on the sea front. If you wander off, make sure you get back there by three o'clock. There's a clock, so you'll know the time.'

Hazel squeezed Peter's hand. This was going to be a lovely day out.

When they arrived at the front, the children were disappointed to see that there were rolls of barbed wire all along the beach.

'We can't go and throw stones into the sea or go for a paddle,' said Peter.

'I'm really sorry, kids,' said Donna. 'I didn't know they'd done this.' She looked around for her friend. 'Look, you can get on to the beach just here near the wall.' There was a small space.

'We can collect stones and build a tower or something,' said Hazel.

'Yes, why not,' said Donna.

When Donna's friend arrived, the two girls went off arm in arm.

'Is Donna going to join the air force?' Hazel asked Sue.

'She wants to. Her mum don't want her to, but her job ain't . . . I think they called it a reserved occupation, or something like that.'

'What does that mean?' asked Hazel.

'It means it ain't helping the war effort. She works in a shop in Horsham.'

Hazel thought about her own mum and dad. Were their jobs helping the war effort? Or would they have to go in the forces? If they did, would she ever see them again? Despite having such a good time, suddenly Hazel felt very sad. She wanted to go home. She wanted to be with her mum and dad.

Chapter 9

WHEN THE PORTER shouted that they had arrived at Billingshurst, Rene and John got out of the crowded train. On the platform, they looked around. Apart from a few people hurrying about their business, the station seemed almost deserted.

'How we gonna get to Osborne?' asked Rene, beginning to panic.

'I don't know, love. I'll go and ask the porter.'

'Sorry. I can't say I've ever heard of Osborne,' he said, and walked away.

'What we gonna do?' asked Rene.

'Let's find a pub and ask; someone in there must know.'

They walked a little way and saw a pub on the corner.

'Are they open yet?' asked Rene.

John looked at his watch. 'I would think so.'

He pushed open the door, and three pairs of eyes looked up from a game of dominoes. John went up to the bar with Rene close behind.

'Yes, sir,' said the big man with a bushy moustache behind the bar. 'What can I get for you and the lady?'

'Nothing, thank you. We were wondering if you could tell us the way to Osborne.'

'Sorry. I'm afraid I've never heard of it. Mind you, there's lots of tiny hamlets round this way.'

One of the men sitting playing dominoes said, ''Tis a long way away.'

'D'you have a car?' asked the landlord.

'No. We've just come from London to see our kids. They're staying at Dairy Lane Farm.'

'It's a long walk,' said another of the domino players.

'Is there a bus?' asked John.

'Not all the way on Sundays,' came back the reply.

Rene's face began to crumble. 'How we gonna get ter see the kids?'

John turned to the barman. 'They've been evacuated down here and I want to see them before I go in to the army on Friday.'

Rene was trying very hard not to cry.

'Here, missus, have a drink.'

'No thank you.' She brushed the rogue tear away. 'What we gonna do, John?'

'I dunno. Is there a taxi?' he asked.

'Don't get a lot of call for taxis round here.'

'There's old Bert,' said one of the domino players. 'He does a bit of running around. He might take yer.'

'Where can I find him?' asked John.

'The missus will know,' said the barman. 'I'll go and get her.' He disappeared through a door behind the counter.

A few minutes later he returned followed by a large woman.

'What seems to be the trouble, pet?' she asked. 'Morning, boys,' she said to the players, who nodded back to her.

'We've got to get to Osborne to see our kids,' said John.

'You'll have to catch the bus. I think it stops at Osborne.'

'Where do we get this bus?' asked Rene, wiping her eyes.

'Up the road. It runs every hour on a Sunday. It's on the hour.' She looked up at the clock. 'I think there's one due at twelve.'

'But they said there wasn't any buses that went all the way to Osborne,' said Rene.

'Silly buggers they are. They don't know much; they just sit there playing dominoes all day and never go anywhere. You just go up the road to the bus stop. I'll show you.'

'Thank you,' said Rene as they left the pub with the woman.

'So you're going to visit your kids. How's the little 'uns settling in?' she asked.

'We don't know. We've only had a couple of short letters from them,' said John.

'That's kids for you. Get you all worried and I expect they're fine. Me husband said you're off to the army on Friday?'

'Yes. I wanted ter see 'em before I went.'

'Bloody awful thing, war. Let's hope it don't last too long.'

They continued for a short distance in silence.

'Right. This is it.'

'Thank you so much,' said John as he shook her hand.

'Thank you,' said Rene.

'Now when you come back, pop in for a drink. I'd like to know how you got on.'

'Thank you,' said John again.

The woman turned and walked back.

It seemed for ever before a very old bus came along and the conductor told them that they did stop at Osborne.

Rene was getting more and more anxious. 'I wonder how far from the bus stop it is?' she whispered as they sat down.

There were just two other passengers on the bus.

'It'll be almost dinner time before we get to see them.'

'Don't worry, love,' said John as they made themselves comfortable.

'But we'll have to get back tonight. And with these buses . . .' She stopped. 'You'd better find out what time the last one leaves Osborne.'

John was shocked when the conductor told them that the last bus went at four. 'But get to the stop a bit early, as we don't stop if nobody's there.'

Rene wanted to cry.

'How long before we get to Osborne?' asked John.

The conductor looked at his watch. 'It takes roughly an hour, hour and a half. We should arrive somewhere round about one, but a lot depends on what's on the road. Sometimes it can be cows, sheep or tractors, and that can really hold us up.'

Rene squeezed John's hand. At least they were on their way.

John gave Rene a slight smile. He was still wondering how far away from the bus stop Dairy Lane Farm was.

Donna took the children into a café for an ice cream.

'Well, kids, have you had a good day?'

'Yes thank you,' they said together.

'That's good.'

'Has your friend gone?' asked Sue.

'Yes. She has to go back to camp.'

'Will you see her again?'

'I don't know.' Donna sat with her elbows on the table, clutching her cup of tea. 'I shall miss her.'

'Would you like to go in the air force?' asked Sue.

'Yes I would, and if this war carries on for too long, then everybody who isn't married or hasn't got kids will have to go.'

'Will our mum have to go?' asked Hazel.

'No, she has you two.'

'But we don't live with her now.'

'I don't know the answer to that. Everything is in a mess these days.'

'Come on, let's make our way back home.'

Hazel and Peter very reluctantly got into the car. They'd had such a lovely day, they didn't want to go back to the Jacobs'.

Peter held his sister's hand and whispered, 'I wish we was going to stay with Sue.'

'So do I,' came the soft reply.

When the bus stopped at Osborne, Rene and John got off and watched it disappear down the road.

'Where do we go now?' asked Rene.

'I don't know.'

They stood looking around them. On one corner was a shop that had a post office sign outside, but that was shut. There was a large house on another, and as they approached that, they could see the sign cut in the wall that told them it was the village school.

'It's so small. Surely that can't be the school they both go to?' said Rene.

'I don't know, love. Look, there's a garage over there.' John pointed to another corner. 'And a pub there.'

'So this crossroads must be the village?'

'Looks like it.'

'So which way is Dairy Lane Farm?' asked Rene.

'We'd better ask in the pub,' said John.

'We can't hang about there,' said Rene. 'We've got to find the kids.'

'I know that, but at least let's find out which road we have to go down.'

'S'pose so,' said Rene reluctantly.

When they walked into the pub, all the men stopped talking and looked at them.

John went up to the bar with Rene close behind him.

'Good morning, sir,' said the barman. 'Ain't never seen you round here before. What brings you to this part of the country?'

Everybody was looking and waiting for the answer.

'We've come to see our children. We're from London and they've been evacuated down here.'

The barman smiled. 'Thank goodness for that. We thought you might be spies.'

The chatter started up again.

'We want to know what road we have to take to get to Dairy Lane Farm?'

'It ain't a farm, it's just a smallholding,' said the barman.

'Is it very far?'

'Nah, just a couple of miles. You take the road opposite and just keep walking till you come to a rough track. You can't miss it, it's the only house down there.'

'Thanks,' said John. They moved towards the door.

'He said it was a couple of miles,' said Rene.

'I know,' whispered John. 'But you know what these country yokels are like. It might not be that far.'

'But what if it is? Peter can't walk two miles a day to school.'

'Now don't start getting yourself in a state till we see them. If we think they're unhappy, then we'll bring them home.'

For the first time Rene smiled. 'Could we, John? Could we really bring them home?'

'We'll see.'

The children were all singing along with Donna as she drove them home.

After a while she said, 'Sue, don't mention to Mum that I might be joining the air force, will you?'

'No. Course not.'

'Good. Now, do you two want me to take you straight home, or would you rather come back with us? I expect Mum has got enough dinner for you both.'

'Please. Could we go to your house?'

'I don't see why not.'

Sue hugged Hazel. 'I like it when you're at our house.'

'So do we,' said Peter.

Chapter 10

'I̶T'S A BLOODY long way,' said Rene as she stopped again and adjusted her shoe.

'If you ask me, it's a bit further than a couple of miles,' said John.

'Those poor kids. Do they have to walk this far to school every day? That's it, John. We're taking them home.'

'Let's see if they want to come first. For all we know there may be a school bus or something.'

'I hope so.'

After a while they saw a dirt road.

'D'you think this is it?' asked Rene.

'Dunno. You wait here and I'll go along and see if there's a sign or someone I can ask.'

Rene sat on a gate and watched John go off. She felt

so helpless. Why had she let the children go? What if they didn't want to come home? Suddenly she caught sight of John waving at her to come. She hurried along. Her spirits were uplifted. She was going to see her children.

He was standing at the end of the track. 'I think this is it.'

Rene looked at the house. It was very small, with tiny windows, and in the yard at the side they could see some chickens running around. 'Looks like they could be having plenty of eggs.'

They made their way to the front door and John knocked.

'I've told you kids enough times to go round the back,' a man shouted. He opened the door and stared at them, surprised. 'Yes. What d'you want?'

Rene and John stood looking at this tall, well-built man. He had a shock of dark hair and needed a shave.

'We've come to see Hazel and Peter Morgan.'

'And you are?'

'Their parents,' said Rene hastily.

'Oh. Jenny, come down here,' he called out. 'You'd better come in,' he said to Rene and John.

'Are they about?' asked John, looking round him.

'No. They're out with a friend.'

A woman waddled into the room and held out her hand. 'Hello. I'm Jenny Jacobs. I was just at the top of the stairs and I heard what you said. This 'ere is Walter, me husband.'

Rene was very surprised to see that Mrs Jacobs was pregnant. 'When will the children be back?' she asked.

'Don't rightly know. When they get to the Millers', they stay for a while. Been out all day, they have. I think they've been to Worthing with one of the girls. Nice family, the Millers.'

Rene and John were clearly devastated to have missed the children.

'Look, why don't you sit down and I'll make you a cup of tea.'

'Thank you. That would be very welcome,' said Rene as she tried to take in her surroundings. This was a small room and sparsely furnished, with just a table and four chairs, two armchairs and a dresser against one wall. The window didn't let in a lot of light.

Mrs Jacobs went into another room, which Rene thought must be a kitchen of sorts.

'Is this your farm?' John asked Mr Jacobs.

'We look after it,' came back the answer.

'Have you got many animals?'

'Enough to keep us all right.'

John could see it was going to be hard work talking to this man. 'Wouldn't mind having a look round. Don't see many animals in Rotherhithe.'

'Have yer tea first.'

Mrs Jacobs came back in carrying a tray. Rene jumped up to help her and put it on the table.

'Thank you.'

'I hope Hazel's helping you,' she said.

'She tries.'

'How are the kids with the animals?' asked John.

'Not too good. They don't like chickens and they mustn't go in the cow shed when Walter's milking.'

Rene didn't know what to say. 'Have you got a toilet I could use?' she asked, dreading the thought of going outside where the chickens were.

'Upstairs. The door on the left.'

Rene was taken aback. The Jacobs had something they didn't have. A toilet inside.

She went up the narrow staircase and was surprised when she opened the door to see a small room with a lav, a basin and a small bath. When she came out, she looked at the other two closed doors. Which one was her children's room? She would have loved to look in, but knew she would probably pick the wrong one and get caught.

When she went downstairs she said, 'Well, Hazel and Peter must be very pleased not to have to go outside to the lav. We ain't got such luxuries.'

'The owner had that put in when he lived here; that was before he bought the big farm and house further over,' said Mrs Jacobs.

John looked at his watch. 'We have to catch the last

bus at four. It's getting on for half past two now, and it took us over half an hour to walk here. Do you think they'll be much longer?'

'I couldn't say. It's a pity you didn't let them know you was coming.'

'It was a bit of a spur-of-the-moment thing,' said John.

Rene was beginning to panic. She didn't really like these people; there was something about them that made her feel uneasy. 'Is that school at the crossroads the one they go to?'

'Yes,' smiled Mrs Jacobs. 'I think they like it.'

'It's very small.'

'There's not a lot of children round abouts. The farms are very scattered.'

'It's a long walk for Peter's little legs.'

'He's a strong lad,' came back the answer.

'I've brought them some comics and sweets. Can I put them in their bedroom?'

'You can leave them on the table; they'll be all right here.'

'When's the baby due?' asked Rene.

'The new year.'

'Won't having our two be too much for you with a new baby?'

'I don't think so.'

'Babies can be hard work.'

'I expect Hazel will be helpful.'

They sat in silence for a while, then John said, 'Are they very far away? Could we go and find them?'

'It's a fair walk. It's the other side of the village.'

'I think we should go and try to find them,' said Rene. She wanted to get away from this place.

'You might meet them walking back.'

'Well we'll be off then.' John stood up and they quickly left the house.

As they walked up the lane once again, Rene let her tears fall. She felt so unhappy. What had started out as a day full of hope and joy was gradually turning out to be a disaster. 'What have we done, John? Why did we let our kids come to a place like this?'

'We'll try and find them and then we can take them home.'

Hazel and Peter were happy at the Millers'.

'Come into the kitchen and I'll get you a drink,' said Donna.

They sat at the table with Mary and Sue and talked about Worthing.

'It was a nice day but the bit of beach we was allowed on didn't have sand,' said Peter. 'I like sand best; you can build some smashing sandcastles.'

'It's much better to walk on as well,' said Mary.

'I ain't ever been to a beach with sand,' said Sue. 'We used to go hopping, though,' she said proudly. 'I loved hopping.'

'We ain't been hopping,' said Peter. 'Was it good?'

'Yes,' said Sue. Her face was beaming.

'Did you help pick the hops?' asked Mary.

'Yes. It was hard work pulling 'em off the bines and we had to put 'em in a big trough fing. And we had to sleep on straw that prickled a bit. But me nan and me mum put a lot of our furniture on the lorry that took us, so we had a table and chairs, and of a night we'd sit round the fire and sing songs. D'you know, someone even used to bring a piano.'

Mary laughed. 'What if it rained?'

'We took it all into a barn.'

Hazel was surprised that Sue had had such an exciting time. She felt a little bit put out and she had to ask: 'Didn't yer mum and dad ever take you to the seaside?'

'No.'

'We went with our mum and dad to Ramsgate once,' said Hazel.

'The sands there were smashing,' said Peter.

'I've only played in the sand at the sand pit in the park.'

Hazel felt a bit sorry about what she had said to her friend, and added, 'Still, it was nice of Donna to take us today.'

'There's some cake there,' said Mary, pushing a plate in front of them.

'Thank you,' said Hazel, who had been looking at

the cake longingly. 'I like your mum's cake. She's very clever.'

Mary smiled. 'I'll go and tell her that.'

Mrs Miller came into the kitchen smiling. Hazel thought she always seemed to be smiling. 'I should have asked Jenny if you could stay for a bit of dinner.'

'Thank you. We would have liked that,' said Hazel.

'That's what I like about you two: you are always so polite. Perhaps another time. I don't want to upset her and Walter.'

Hazel looked at Peter. They were very disappointed that they wouldn't be staying to dinner. 'Perhaps we should be getting back.'

'I'll get Donna to run you home; after all, it's been a long day for you, and you do have to get up for school in the morning.'

When Rene and John got back to the village, they stood looking around them. It was empty. Not a soul in sight. Which way was it to the Millers' house?

'Who can we ask?' said Rene.

'Don't know, love. The pub's shut. I suppose we could bang on the door.'

'We'll have to if we want to see the kids. Oh John, what a mess.'

He put his arm round her shoulders. 'I would have thought there was a church round here. These places always have a church, and as it's Sunday there could be people in there. Look, you have a seat and I'll have a hunt round.'

'I don't think I can walk much further. Me feet are killing me.'

'I'll have a scout round.'

Rene watched her husband go off. If they didn't find the children today, this time next week she would be without both her kids and her husband.

It wasn't long before John returned. He was smiling.

Rene jumped up. 'Which way?'

'I don't know. There's a hall just up there,' he pointed along the road, 'and I can hear singing. I thought I'd come back for you before I went in.'

Rene had a spring in her step as they made their way up to the door. John turned the big handle and walked in.

There were about ten people singing, and John and Rene stood at the back and waited. John looked at his watch. It was a quarter past three. They had just three quarters of an hour to find the kids.

When the singing finished, a man came up to them. 'Welcome to our place of worship. You're new to our village and you are most welcome.'

Everybody turned to look at them.

'Thank you, but we are looking for the Millers' house. You see, our children have been evacuated here and we would like to see them before we have to get the bus back to Billingshurst.' John said all this in a rush.

The man turned to his congregation. 'Would that be Sally and Tom's place?' he asked.

'Yes,' said the woman next to him. 'But she's only got one little girl; her name's Sue. What are the names of your children?'

'Hazel and Peter. They're with the Jacobs at Dairy Lane Farm and they've been out with the Millers' daughter today.'

'I reckon that'll be Donna,' said the woman, smiling. 'Nice girl, Donna.'

'So could you tell us where they live?' asked John, who was having a job to control his patience.

'Yes, it's down the road between Bert's garage and the school house.'

'Thank you,' said Rene and John together.

'Is it very far?' asked John.

'About a mile,' came back the answer.

When they got outside, Rene asked. 'What we gonna do?'

'I don't know, love. I don't know.' They walked back to the crossroads. 'If we go down there, we'll miss the last bus, and there's nowhere to stay or get a taxi.' He sat on the seat that Rene had been sitting on and held his head in his hands. 'Sodding war.'

Chapter 11

'HELLO THERE, KIDS. Did you see your mum and dad?' asked Mrs Jacobs as soon as the children walked in.

'No,' said Hazel, looking bewildered. 'Mum and Dad was here?'

'Yes, this afternoon.'

'Where did they go?'

'They went looking for you. You must have passed them when you were in the car.'

'We didn't see anybody,' said Hazel as tears began to well up. 'What can we do? Will they be back?'

'I shouldn't think so. They had to catch the bus back to Billingshurst.'

Hazel began to cry.

'They've left you some comics and sweets.'

'Can't we go back to the village?' asked Peter, wide-eyed and confused.

'The bus goes at four. It takes all of three quarters of an hour to get there, and it's a quarter to four now.'

'What if we run all the way?' asked Peter.

'You still wouldn't get there in time.'

'Would Mr Jacobs take us in his truck?' asked Hazel, trying desperately to think of ways in which she could see her mum and dad again.

'Not now he's started the milking.'

Hazel sat and cried.

'Now come on, it's not that bad. They'll be back another time.'

But Hazel wanted to see them now, today.

As soon as they'd finished their meal, Hazel and Peter went to their bedroom. They sat on the bed and began looking at their comics.

'I can't believe Mum and Dad was here. Why didn't they write and let us know they was coming? We could have met the bus,' said Hazel.

Peter sat cuddling his teddy. 'I want to go home. I want to see Mum and Dad and Auntie Betty and Gran.'

'So do I.' Hazel put her arm round her brother and let a tear plop into her lap. 'We could have been all ready to go back with them.'

'What we gonna do, Haz?'

'I don't know.'

'Could we go and stay with that nice Mrs Miller?'

'I wish we could, but you know she's got no room.'

They both sat with tears running down their cheeks, thinking about home.

When Rene and John finally arrived home, it was dark. As they went to pull the key through the letter box, the front door flew open.

'Well?' asked Betty. 'I saw you coming down the road. How are they? Are they all right?' Betty closed the door. When the blackout curtain was in place, she switched on the light and saw her sister's tear-stained face. She quickly put her hand to her mouth. 'Oh my God. What's happened?'

They made their way along the passage and into the kitchen.

Maud stood up when they walked in. 'Did you see them?' she asked.

Rene shook her head. 'They was out.'

'I told you you should have let them know. Anyway, what's the place they're staying at like? Is it clean?'

'We didn't see a lot,' said John. 'The bloke's a bit cagey; can't say I like the look of him.'

'Why?' Maud looked alarmed. 'He wouldn't hurt 'em, would he?'

'He'd better not,' said John.

'The woman's having a baby in the new year and they've only got a very small house,' said Rene.

'But I thought it was a farm?' said Betty.

'It's just a small farm,' replied her sister. 'And I'm a bit worried that Hazel will end up being a skivvy. I'll have to try and get down there on me own.'

'I'll come with you,' said Betty.

'It'll have to be in the week. The buses are awful on Sundays. And I'm gonna bring 'em home.'

John didn't say anything. He knew his wife was right, and he knew that he might not be here to help her.

Hazel woke with a start. The sheet was wet and cold. She jumped out of bed. 'Peter. What you done?'

'I'm sorry, Haz,' sobbed her brother. 'I couldn't help it. I didn't know I'd done it.'

'You ain't wet the bed for years.'

'I'm sorry,' he said again, tearfully.

Hazel shivered.

'What we gonna do?' said Peter, standing next to her.

'I don't know. Get dressed.' She pulled the bed-clothes back and stood looking at the wet patch. How could she tell Mrs Jacobs? She suddenly remembered that on a Saturday morning when she'd helped her mum make the beds, they'd always put the top sheet on the bottom and the clean one on top. 'Look, what I'll do is to put the bottom sheet on top. It might still be a bit damp tonight, but at least it'll be dry to lay on.'

'You gonna tell Mrs Jacobs?'

'Course not. She don't make our bed anyway.'

'What about me jammies?'

'You might have to sleep in damp ones tonight.' She started to strip the bed.

Peter went up to her and held her tight. 'Thank you, Haz. I love you. You're so nice.'

Hazel stopped what she was doing and sat on the bed. 'And I love you, Pete, and we have to look after each other now.'

Rene was up early on Friday morning. She was determined to go with John to see him off.

'Rene, I keep telling you I don't want you to come with me.'

'I know. But I want to.'

'You know I can't bear to see you crying. Look, why don't you go to work?'

'I don't want to.'

Although John wanted her to be with him, he knew it was just prolonging the agony, and he had seen how drawn she was beginning to look since Sunday.

He held her close. 'Please, love, go to work. When I leave here, I'll be able to think of you all the way to wherever I end up, and when I've finished me training, I'll be back and we can go and see the kids. How does that sound?'

Rene knew it made sense. She kissed him long and passionately. When they broke apart she said, 'I love you, and don't ever forget me.'

'I love you too. And I will never, ever forget you.' He kissed her again and then picked up his small case.

Downstairs, Maud and Betty were waiting in the passage.

'Bye, son,' said Maud softly as she held him tight.

Betty kissed his cheek. 'See you soon, soldier, and don't worry about Rene. She'll be all right.'

He opened the door and they stood at the gate and watched him walk away. At the bottom of the road he turned and waved, and Rene burst into tears.

At the end of the month, the children got a letter and a parcel from home. The letter told them that their dad had gone into the army.

'Dad's in the army,' said Peter as Hazel read it out to him. 'Does that mean he's got a gun?'

'I don't know. I expect so.'

'Hope he shows it to me when we see him.'

'Mum says that when he's finished his training, they're coming to see us.'

'When will that be?'

Hazel shrugged. 'They don't say.'

'Why can't Mum come and see us?'

'She says she can't get time off from work now they're making uniforms.'

Hazel was very disappointed that it could be weeks before she saw her mum and dad again.

'Come on, let's get to school.'

'I don't wanna go to school,' said Peter.

'You've got to.'

'I don't feel well.'

'You're all right. Besides, you don't wanna stay here all day on your own, do you?'

'You could stay with me.'

'And what would Miss Rose say?'

Peter looked down at his shoes. 'Dunno.'

'So that's it. Right, put your coat on and we'll be off.'

'But it's pouring with rain.'

'I know.'

'We'll get wet.'

'Peter, shut up. D'you know, sometimes you can be a right nuisance. We'll have to dry ourselves out at school. It's a good job they've got the big stove. Now come on, let's go. Besides, we're gonna be making Christmas decorations today, so that'll be fun.'

'If you say so.'

They arrived at school very wet.

'After you've hung your coats up, take off your wet shoes and socks and dry them in front of the fire. Not too close, mind, you don't want to burn them.' The teacher was fussing round the children, making sure they would be sitting in dry clothes all day. 'You've got your plimsolls in your locker. When you've put them on, you can put your potatoes in the basket and they will be ready for you at lunchtime.'

Hazel and Peter did as they were told, but all day Peter was sniffling.

At the end of the day Miss Rose said to Hazel, 'You'd better not bring him to school tomorrow if he's not well. I don't want him giving his cold to all the other children.'

Hazel looked worried. 'But will Mrs Jacobs let him stay at home?'

'I'll give you a note to take back with you.'

'Thank you.'

It took them a long while to get back to the farm, and Peter looked really poorly when they walked in.

'My goodness, what's wrong with you?' asked Mrs Jacobs.

'He's got a cold.'

Mr Jacobs was sitting in his chair as usual, waiting till it was time for him to go and milk the cows. He looked up. 'That's all we need, a snivelling kid around. Well you'd better keep out of our way; we don't want to catch it. Not with the work we have to do to make a crust.'

Hazel and Peter scurried up the stairs and Peter fell on to the bed and cried, while Hazel just sat and looked at him through her tears and sobs. She had never heard Mr Jacobs say so much all the time they had been here.

The following morning Hazel turned over and looked at Peter. She quickly sat up.

'Peter. Peter. Talk to me. Are you all right?'

He opened his eyes to a squint. 'I don't feel very well.'

'You're all red. You ain't been eating any of those berries we see on the way to school, have you?'

Peter slowly shook his head. 'Me throat's ever so sore.' He could hardly get the words out.

'I'll have to get Mrs Jacobs.'

Peter held on to her arm. 'No, don't.'

'I must.' She pulled away and left the room.

In a short while she was back, with Mrs Jacobs puffing behind.

'Now what's the trouble with you, young man?' Mrs Jacobs said as she walked into the room. She stopped suddenly. 'Oh my God.'

'What is it? What's wrong with Peter?'

'I'm not sure, but I'll have to get Walter to go and fetch the doctor. He won't be very pleased about this.'

Hazel frantically held on to her arm. Tears were running down her face. 'What is it? What's he got?'

'I'm not sure, but it looks like scarlet fever.'

'What's scarlet fever?' asked Hazel.

'It's very contagious.'

'What does that mean?'

'You can catch it from him and if he's got it he will have to go to hospital.'

Hazel looked at Peter and burst into tears. She went up to him and held him tight. 'I won't let you go anywhere without me.'

'I'll go down and get Walter. And you should stay away from Peter.'

'He's me brother, and I told Mum I'd never let anyone take him from me.'

Mrs Jacobs left the room. She was very worried. If it was scarlet fever, what about her unborn baby? She knew her husband would be very angry. He hadn't wanted evacuees in the first place.

Hazel could hear Mr Jacobs shouting. She sat holding Peter and trembling. What was going to happen to them? If only they could tell their mum.

She heard the old truck drive away. It wasn't long before it was back again and she heard two men's voices. The heavy footsteps on the stairs told her that the doctor had arrived.

A well-rounded older man opened the door and

came in. He had a ruddy face and a lot of untidy white hair when he took off his black trilby. 'Well, young man, what have you been up to?' He took a stethoscope and thermometer from his black bag and proceeded to take Peter's temperature and listen to his chest. He also pressed on his arm.

'I'm afraid it does look like scarlet fever to me. I'll send for the ambulance.'

Hazel was crying. 'Where you gonna send him?'

'He'll have to go to Worthing hospital.'

'What about me? Can I go with him?'

'I'm afraid not.'

'I ain't letting Peter go.'

'I'm afraid you have to. I'll see about the ambulance, then I'll have to speak to the billeting officer who's in charge of the evacuee children round here.' He turned to Mrs Jacobs, who was standing in the doorway. 'I will also have to get in touch with the milk board.'

'Why?'

'I see from the churns outside that you sell milk, and you can't sell it if there is a contagious disease on the premises. Today's milk will all have to be thrown away and this room fumigated. And you can't sell any more till you are told.'

Mrs Jacobs looked stunned. 'What? You can't mean that. It's our livelihood.'

'I'm very sorry.'

'Not as sorry as Walter will be when he hears about this.' She stomped down the stairs.

Hazel looked at the doctor. 'What will happen to us?'

'Peter will go to the hospital, and as I said, I will have to see about you. You can't stay here on the farm in case you have it too.'

Hazel began to cry again. 'I don't want him to go.'

'He must.'

'Can't we go home?'

'No. I'm sorry.'

'Mr Jacobs will hit me.'

'No he won't.'

'Yes he will. He don't like us.'

'I'm sorry, Haz,' said a sad, soft voice from the bed.

'Peter, it ain't your fault.'

The doctor put his arm round Hazel's heaving shoulders. 'Come on now, love. It'll all be all right, you wait and see.'

But Hazel knew it wouldn't be. 'Can Peter take Teddy with him?' She was very sorry about the milk and knew that Mr Jacobs would take it out on her. 'Who will have me?' she asked pathetically.

The doctor's face softened and he sighed. 'Don't worry. I'll take you home with me till we find you somewhere to stay. Now come along, pack up your things, while I go down the road and make a phone

call to my wife. She can put all the wheels in motion.'
He smiled at Hazel and patted the top of her head.
'Whatever Peter takes with him I'm afraid will have to
be left at the hospital, and that includes Teddy.'

Chapter 12

HAZEL WAS SITTING in the back of the doctor's car, crying. She could see Mr Jacobs arguing with him. Mr Jacobs was shaking his fist at the ambulance. Earlier she had watched Peter being wrapped in a big red blanket and gently lifted from the bed by a strong ambulanceman, who had told him that he wasn't to worry, and that he would be all right and should be back here in about three weeks. Now her brother was inside the ambulance and was being driven away from her. Her world had just collapsed. She had no home, no brother, and she couldn't tell her mum and dad what had happened. She watched the doctor begin to walk away from Mr and Mrs Jacobs. She could see that they were very angry.

The doctor opened the car door. 'Sorry about that,' he said to Hazel as he got into the driver's seat. 'I'm afraid Mr and Mrs Jacobs aren't very happy.'

The doctor had stood and watched as they poured the milk down the drain. Hazel wanted to run away. This was all their fault. Why did this have to happen?

'Why did they have to throw the milk away?' she asked as they got nearer the village. 'We wasn't allowed anywhere near the cow shed.'

'It's just a precaution. It might have been contaminated, and that could start an epidemic.'

Hazel wasn't really sure what he meant.

It wasn't long before they arrived at the doctor's house on the other side of the village.

'Here we are, my dear.' He stopped the car close to the front door, and it was immediately opened by a very well-dressed, tall, upright lady, her grey hair neatly cut. To Hazel, she looked very regal.

The doctor got out and opened the car door for Hazel. 'Hazel, this is my wife, Mrs Hyland. Rosa, this is Hazel.'

'Hello, Hazel.'

Hazel stood back. She was worried. Should she shake the lady's outstretched hand or not?

The doctor must have sensed her dilemma and he gave a little laugh. 'You can shake my wife's hand. You won't give her scarlet fever. Besides, as a doctor's wife, like me she comes into contact with all sorts of things. Now, shall we go inside? It's beginning to get a little chilly out here.'

Hazel picked up her small case, and with Mrs Hyland's hand on her shoulder, she was ushered into the spacious hall.

'You can hang your coat up here.'

Hazel did as she was told.

'Now we will go along to the kitchen. I think Mrs Vincent has made the tea, and there's some cake.' Mrs Hyland gave Hazel a smile.

'I'll just go into the office, dear, and write up my notes.'

'Of course, William. I'll bring in your tea. Come along, Hazel.'

Hazel followed Mrs Hyland into the large kitchen. It was bright and warm. There was a long wooden table in the middle with chairs round it, and the big stove against the wall had a kettle bubbling on top.

Mrs Hyland said to the lady who was pouring out the tea, 'Mrs Vincent, this is Hazel. She'll be staying with us for a few days till the doctor gets her settled somewhere.'

Mrs Vincent gave her a smile, and suddenly Hazel couldn't stop herself, she burst into tears.

'There, there, my lovely,' said Mrs Vincent as she went to Hazel and held her close to her ample bosom. 'You have a good cry.'

'It has been a very traumatic day for her,' said Mrs Hyland.

Gradually the tears subsided and Hazel moved away.

'Now, my lovely, you sit yourself down and have a cup of tea and a piece of my nice home-made cream sponge.'

'Thank you,' said Hazel tearfully.

'The doctor will get all the paperwork sorted out,' said Mrs Hyland.

'Can I go home?' Hazel gave another dry sob.

'I don't know.'

'I don't want to go back to the Jacobs'.'

'You won't have to do that.'

'Can I stay here with you?'

'You will for a week or so, just till we make sure that you haven't got scarlet fever. The doctor will write to your parents and tell them what has happened.'

'Me dad's just gone in the army,' Hazel said softly.

'Oh my dear,' said Mrs Hyland. Her heart went out to this poor child, who had been taken from her home. Now her brother was in hospital and her father was in the army. Her poor mother. What a dreadful war this was. She smiled at Hazel. 'When you've finished your tea, Mrs Vincent will take you up and show you your room.'

'Thank you,' said Hazel.

When Mrs Vincent pushed open the door to a bright room, Hazel stood in the doorway.

'Here we are, my lovely. Just you put your things in that cupboard.'

'I ain't got much.'

'Not to worry.'

'Is this room all fer me?'

'Yes.'

Hazel looked at the pretty cover that was over the bed and the dark-coloured table and wardrobe. 'It's lovely,' she said, giving Mrs Vincent a slight smile. 'I hope I can stay here till Peter comes out of hospital, then me mum can take us back home.'

'Well you can for the moment, but this house will have to be used for soldiers when they come back from the front and out of hospital. They will stay a short while waiting to be rehabilitated.'

Hazel wasn't sure what the front was, or rehabilitation.

Later, after they had finished a lovely meal and had settled down for the evening listening to the wireless, the telephone rang. The doctor had to leave as he had been called out to a patient. Earlier he had told Hazel that he had written to her parents and told them about Peter and given them her new address.

'Will Peter be all right?' she had asked.

'Of course.'

'If Mum comes here, can we go and see him in hospital?'

'I'm afraid not. You should write to them as well and tell them that everything is all right. It will help to put their minds at rest.'

When Mrs Hyland took Hazel up to bed, she sat with her for a few moments. 'Hazel, for the short time you'll be here, I want you to be happy. You can't go to school for a little while, but I'm sure Mrs Vincent will find the odd job for you to do. Would that be all right?'

Hazel nodded.

'That's good.' She tucked Hazel in, and at the door she turned and blew her a kiss. 'Good night.'

'Good night,' said Hazel. As soon as the door was closed, she began to cry. Her thoughts were of Peter. Was he all right? She did so want to see him. Would he get told off if he wet the bed? What if her mum came to see her; would she take her home? Although the doctor and his wife and Mrs Vincent were very kind, she was so unhappy and homesick.

'Mum.' Rene burst into the kitchen clutching a letter. She was crying. 'Mum,' she said again.

'My dear girl, what is it? Whatever's the matter?'

'It's Peter. He's in hospital.'

'What?'

'He's in Worthing hospital. He's got scarlet fever.'

'Where the bloody 'ell did he get that from?'

'I don't know. This letter's from a Dr Hyland; he's got Hazel.'

'Is she all right?'

Rene nodded. 'I've got a letter from her as well. She says they are ever such nice people and she can stay there till they make sure she ain't got it and then they'll see about finding somewhere else for her to stay. I've got to go and see them.'

'You won't be allowed to see Peter.'

'That's what the doctor says. He said he'll let me know how he is.'

'Those poor kids. How long will he be in hospital?'

'The doctor reckons about three weeks, that's if there ain't any complications.'

'Oh my Gawd. Did he say what they can be?'

Rene shook her head.

Maud sat at the table and read the two letters her daughter passed to her.

'John'll go mad when he hears about this.'

'You can't tell him. You know what he's like. He'll bunk off camp to go and see them, and then he'll finish up in prison. Life's a bloody mess.' Maud looked at the clock. 'Look at the time, you'll be late for work.'

'I don't feel like going.'

'Rene, pull yourself together. They're not gonna let you have time off to see yer kids and you ain't gonna do yourself any good moping about here. Now go on, be off with you.'

Rene knew her mother was right. Reluctantly she picked up her handbag and left.

Maud sat looking at the letters. After a little while she went next door. She had to confide in someone, and Hilda and Ron were always good listeners and they made a decent cuppa.

'Hello, love,' said Ron when Maud walked in. 'You come about that letter?'

'What letter?'

'The letter we had this morning.'

'I've come about a letter, but it's the one Rene's had from Hazel.' She sat down at the table just as Hilda came in from the yard.

'Hello, love. Looks like we're going to be in fer a right old mess.'

'What you talking about?'

'The letter we've had from the government this morning.'

'Oh, another one. I leave them till later. Can't be bothered with them.'

'You should have read this one,' said Ron. 'We can't have Anderson shelters 'cos we've got a water main that runs through our yards, so we've gotta have brick ones.'

'And yer knows what that means, don't yer?' said Hilda, folding her arms across her bosom. 'All the bleeding bricks, sand and cement coming through the house. I wish we had a back way into the yard.'

Maud looked shocked. 'When's this gonna happen?'

'Seems we've got an ARP bloke and he's gonna tell us. They're doing one road at a time.'

'Well I ain't sleeping in no brick shelter,' said Maud.

'You will if that bastard sends his bombers over,' said Ron.

'D'you think he will?' asked Maud.

'Pretty sure of it.'

They were silent for a moment or two.

'Anyway, what was you saying about a letter?' asked Hilda.

Maud showed them the two letters.

'Poor little buggers,' said Hilda, passing them to Ron. 'What's Rene gonna do about 'em?'

'I don't know.'

'Will she be bringing 'em home fer Christmas?'

'Dunno. Ain't been giving Christmas that much thought.'

'Well let's face it, there ain't that much ter get excited about is, there?' Hilda picked up the letters again. 'Poor little buggers.'

Chapter 13

A WEEK LATER, Hazel was thrilled to receive a parcel of comics and sweets from her mum. She was sitting at the table telling Mrs Vincent the contents of her letter. 'Mum says that when she can, she's going to see Peter.'

'Will she come and see you?'

'She don't say. But I expect she will.' Hazel liked sitting here talking to Mrs Vincent; she was a homely woman.

'That will be lovely for you.'

'Mum says that Nan's having a brick shelter built in the yard.' Hazel gave a little giggle. 'And she says that Nan's ever so cross at all the stuff coming though the house and the men tramping on her clean lino.'

'What, through the house?'

'We ain't got a back way.'

'I wouldn't like that,' said Mrs Vincent.

'Did you know that the doctor says I can go to school on Monday?'

'He did say. I shall miss you helping me.'

Hazel gave her a smile.

Mrs Vincent went up to her and gave her cheek a little squeeze. 'You're a good girl, Hazel.'

The first morning Hazel was allowed to go back to school, her friend Sue came running up to see her.

'Mrs Miller told me about your Peter. Is he all right?'

'The doctor said he was.'

'They was all saying about the milk that had to be chucked. I bet you had a laugh about that.'

'No. I felt very sorry for the Jacobs.'

'Auntie Sally said that they had to fumigate your bedroom. Was that true?'

Hazel nodded.

'Did you have to stay there and be fumigated as well? Like we was when we first came here?'

'No. Dr Hyland said they puffed some stuff in there and then they had to put sticky tape all round the door and seal it off.'

'Oh,' said Sue as she tucked her arm through Hazel's. 'What's it like staying with the doctor?'

'Nice. I wish I could stay there all the time, but it seems I'm gonna be moved again now I ain't got scarlet fever.'

'Where yer going?'

'Don't know.'

'I hope you stay in the village.'

Hazel suddenly stopped. She was gripped with fear. 'Could I be sent away?'

'Dunno.'

That evening, Hazel asked Mrs Hyland if she might be sent away from the village.

'I'm afraid I don't know. I think it all depends if there is anyone around here who is willing and has the room to take you. The doctor will let you know, so please don't worry too much. I'm sure it will all work out fine.'

But Hazel couldn't help worrying. She was aware that more evacuees had arrived since they'd come to the village. What if she was sent miles away from here? What about when Peter came out of hospital? Some of the kids had been nasty to her, running away when she got near them, but she was pleased when the teachers told them off.

The following week, the occupants of numbers 36 and 38 and many more in Glebe Street were gathered in James's dairy to get their few groceries. The talk was all about the shelters being built in the back yards.

'The bloody mess those blokes have made,' said Hilda. 'My Ron had a right go at 'em.'

'Did it do any good?' asked Mrs James as she took

two rashers of bacon from the slicer and wrapped them in greaseproof paper.

'Humph,' said Hilda, pulling her coat round her. 'Not likely. The sods accidentally on purpose dropped a bag of cement in me passage and it split. You should 'ave seen the bloody mess. It went everywhere. I could 'ave cried. I'm still clearing it up.'

'It's the mud on their boots that gets me,' said Maud. 'That yard's like a quagmire.'

'How much longer they gonna be?' asked Mrs James.

'Dunno,' said Hilda. 'The sooner they finish the better.'

'You know butter and bacon's gonna be rationed next month, don't you?' said a woman who lived further up Glebe Street and was watching Mrs James give Hilda her bacon.

'I know,' said Mrs James. 'We get enough paperwork about it, and there's talk about rationing sugar and meat as well. I tell you, all the forms we have to fill in are a nightmare, and we have to make sure you lot are registered with us. It looks like we could be in for a right miserable Christmas.'

'It will be for us, what with John away and Peter in hospital, and this morning Rene heard from the authorities that Hazel is being moved to Worthing.'

'I'm surprised that Rene ain't brought her home. After all, there ain't any air raids,' said a woman who was holding a baby.

'Not yet there ain't, but old Wally was saying that some bombs have been dropped in Scotland,' said Maud.

'Bloody 'ell,' said Hilda. 'Me son lives up there.'

'Scotland's a big place,' said Mrs James. 'Besides, how does Wally know?'

'Now he's been made an air-raid warden, he reckons he knows everything,' said Hilda.

'A right jumped-up little Hitler he is. You should have heard him shouting at us the other night 'cos we was showing a bit of light,' said the woman with the baby.

'Well you ought ter know by now that yer can't show any,' said Hilda.

'I know. But I was just seeing ter me baby.'

Gradually the women dispersed. As Hilda and Maud made their way across the road, Hilda said, 'Come in fer a cuppa, Maud.'

'Okay.'

'What was you saying about Hazel being moved to Worthing? Will she be near Peter?'

'Dunno. Rene had a letter this morning. It just told her that she would be moved next week.'

'Poor little cow,' said Hilda. 'So if Peter's still in hospital, Hazel'll be all on her own for Christmas.'

'I know. Well you can imagine the state our Rene's getting herself into. I can see that as soon as she gets an address, she'll be going down there and bringing 'em both back.'

'How long's Peter gotta stay in hospital?'

'Dunno. Where's Ron?'

'Out looking at the shelter.'

'Whatever for?'

'He reckons he's gonna put a door on it, and a shelf, and a bit of lino on the floor,' she laughed. 'And 'e's talking about having a couple of chairs in there as well.'

Maud laughed. 'That's the funniest thing I've heard fer weeks. It's gonna be like home from home.'

'Don't let him hear yer laughing. He's dead serious.'

'Surely he don't think we're gonna sit in that thing?'

'He says he's being like Mr Churchill; he tells us we've got to be ready for anything.'

Maud was still laughing when Ron came in. 'Any more tea in that pot?'

Hilda put milk in a cup. 'I was just telling Maud here what yer up to.'

'Come out and have a look and I'll show you what I'm gonna do. As soon as it's dried out I can make a start, and it'll look really good. I'm even thinking of distempering the walls, as it'll be bloody dark in there.'

'You'll have a light, though, won't yer?' asked Maud.

'Yer. I've got a hurricane lamp and a load of candles.

When I've done ours, if yer like I'll come and sort yours out.'

'I dunno. Can't see me sitting in there.'

'Don't you be so sure, me gel. Don't you be so sure.'

Maud knew that tonight she'd have something funny to tell the girls. Hopefully it would bring a smile to Rene's sad face.

'I don't wanna go to Worthing.' Hazel sat at the kitchen table in the doctor's house. She was crying.

'There, there, my lovely,' said Mrs Vincent, cradling Hazel's head against her chest in a comforting way.

Hazel looked up. 'Why can't I stay here with me mates?'

'There's no room, my lovely.'

'It ain't fair. Why can't I go home?'

'I wish I could take you in.' Mrs Vincent felt so helpless as Hazel clung to her. The poor child was being sent away again. What was her mother going to say about this? In the short while Hazel had been here, she felt she had got to know the whole family.

Mrs Hyland came into the kitchen. 'I'm so very sorry, Hazel. I really do wish we could keep you, but it's out of our hands. The WVS lady will be here at twelve, and she's going to take you in her car.'

'I don't wanna go.'

'I know. Dr Hyland asked them to keep you in the

village, but only a few people can take evacuees and they are all full. Believe me, he has tried.'

'I'll do you up some sandwiches,' said Mrs Vincent. 'And I'm sure we can find you some lemonade.'

Hazel didn't answer; she was too upset.

Sharp at twelve, the WVS lady knocked on the door. She gave Mrs Vincent a warm smile. 'I'm here to take Hazel Morgan to Worthing.'

'This way.'

Hazel was still sitting at the table. 'I don't want to go.'

The WVS lady looked taken aback. 'I'm sorry, but I do have my orders.'

Hazel turned her head away and continued to look at her comic.

'Now come on, Hazel. This isn't like you. Be a good girl,' said Mrs Hyland.

Hazel looked up, tears running down her cheeks.

The WVS lady sat on a chair next to her. 'I'm taking you to a Mrs Morison. She has two girl and two boy evacuees already and she is going to take Peter when he comes out of hospital.'

Hazel looked at her. 'Will she really?'

The woman nodded. 'Yes. It's all arranged. Now come on, be a good girl and let's get you settled in before it gets too dark.'

Hazel slid off her chair and smiled for the first time

that day. 'Me and Peter are going to be together again.'

Mrs Vincent hugged her.

'The doctor said he's sorry he can't be here to say goodbye, but he's thinking of you.' Mrs Hyland also hugged her.

'Thank you for having me.'

'It's been our pleasure. I only wish it could have been for a lot longer.'

They all walked to the car.

'Give Peter our love when you see him,' said Mrs Hyland.

'I will.' Hazel sat in the front seat and held on to her little case.

'You can put that in the back,' said the WVS lady.

As they drove away, Hazel waved. This was going to be another change in her short life. But at least she would be seeing Peter soon.

Chapter 14

IT WAS DARK, cold and raining when the WVS lady stopped the car. 'Wait here while I pop into this paper shop and find out where Eric Road is. I won't be long.' She got out and slammed the door shut.

Hazel rubbed the inside of the car window with her gloved hand, but she couldn't see very much, as everywhere was blacked out.

In a short while the woman came back.

'Thank goodness it isn't too far away. Are you all right?'

Hazel only nodded.

It wasn't long before they turned into a road. The WVS lady was driving very slowly and peering through the windscreen wipers trying to see house numbers.

126

'Well that's number eight, so ten should be next door.' She stopped the car. 'Wait here and I'll find out.' Once again she left Hazel sitting looking at the outline of the house. It had a house joined on to it on one side; on the other side was a gap.

The front door opened and Hazel could just about make out two figures talking and the WVS lady turning and pointing at the car. Hazel was frightened. She didn't want to be here. What would this woman be like? And what about all the other kids? Would they gang up on her?

The WVS lady came back and opened the car door. 'Come along, Hazel. Quickly. Mrs Morison is expecting you.'

Hazel got out of the car, clutching her little case. She was very nervous as she approached the house.

'Come on in, love. Don't be shy.'

As soon as the front door was closed and the blackout curtain pulled across the door, Mrs Morison switched the light on. Hazel found herself in a hall that had a table with a mirror over and a line of shoes underneath. Further along the wall hung various coats on hooks. She followed the thin woman who was wearing a wraparound floral overall and a brown woolly hat, down a passage and into a room where four children were sitting at a table. As they entered, they all looked up and stared at Hazel.

'June, Pattie, Terry and Alf, this is Hazel, she's come

to live here with us,' said Mrs Morison.

'You the one that's got scarlet fever?' asked Alf. He had ginger hair and squinty eyes, and he looked to be the oldest.

'No. It's me brother Peter, and he's in hospital.'

'Well I hope he ain't coming here,' said June. She had long dark hair. 'We don't wanna catch it.'

'You won't catch it,' said the WVS lady. 'When he gets here, he will be better.'

Pattie, who had short dark hair, wore glasses that had a piece of white elastic round the back of her head to keep them on. The other boy, Terry, just grinned at Hazel.

Hazel didn't like the look of any of them.

Hazel had been with Mrs Morison for two weeks. Today she had been told that Peter was coming out of hospital, and she had been standing at the window all morning waiting.

'You should be helping us, not gawping out the window,' said Alf.

Hazel now knew that Alf was twelve. Terry was eleven, June was also eleven and Pattie was ten. Mrs Morison was a widow. She had a daughter who lived round the corner and came to see her mother nearly every day. The girls slept in one bedroom and the boys in another. June and Pattie slept in a big bed, while Hazel was on a camp bed. Peter was also going to be on a camp bed in the boys' room.

Alf ruled the roost. Hazel didn't like him. He was always telling the others what to do. Mrs Morison expected the children to help round the house. This Saturday morning they were polishing the furniture in the front room. Alf had been shouting at them to mind the ornaments. They had to make their own beds, and change the sheets every week. Mrs Morison wasn't a bad cook, but Hazel knew the food wasn't as good as her gran's. They always had to wash up. The school was much bigger than the one at Osborne, and as Hazel didn't know anyone, she wasn't very happy. She was longing to see Peter again.

Rene was sad when she got the letter from Hazel telling her about the place where she was now living.

'She don't sound very happy, Mum. Should I go down there?'

'I dunno, love. What good will it do? Besides, she's only been there five minutes.'

'I just want to see 'em.'

'Of course you do. But you can't see Peter, and you might upset Hazel too much.'

'You're right. I'll wait till he's out of hospital, then I'll go down. I'm still in two minds as to whether to bring 'em home or not.'

Her mother looked sad. 'It'll be funny this Christmas without 'em.'

'I can't believe it's only a few weeks away.' Rene choked back a sob.

'Perhaps John will be home by then.'

'God, I hope so. I couldn't bear it if they were all away.'

'When does he finish his training?'

'Should be soon.'

Just after Rene got Hazel's letter, a letter from John lifted her spirits. Now it was Saturday half-day and she was hurrying home from work. She had been in a state of excitement all morning. John should be home by now. For her this was the best news since this war had begun.

'Hello, love,' said her mum as she opened the door for her. 'He's upstairs.'

Rene raced up the stairs. John was standing in the doorway waiting for her. He took her into his arms and kissed her cheek and then her lips. It was a long, passionate kiss. She finally came up for air.

'It's smashing to see you again, love,' he said, holding her close.

'Oh my God. What they done to your hair?'

'Regulations, I'm afraid.'

She began to laugh. 'Wait till the kids see you. And you look like you've lost a bit of weight.'

He patted his stomach. 'It's all the exercise. How are the kids? Is Peter still in hospital?'

Rene took off her coat and hat. 'Yes. He should be out this weekend and he's being moved to the house with Hazel. At least they'll be together, so that's a good thing. The woman they're with will have six evacuees then.'

'She must be making a bob or two. Just as long as she don't make 'em work.'

'Don't say that. That's been going through my mind ever since I heard they were moving Hazel.'

'So you've had a couple of letters, then?'

Rene nodded.

'And?'

'She seems all right.'

'Is that it? Just all right?'

'The last letter's there on the dresser, so you can see for yourself.' Rene sat down and began to take her shoes off. 'What did you want me to do, go racing down there to see for myself? Look at the performance the last time.'

'I'm sorry. It's just that I worry about them.'

'And don't you think I do?'

'Please, Rene, don't let's argue.'

'I'm sorry. It's just that I'm worried about you all. In fact my life is one long worry.'

He pulled her to her feet and took her in his arms, and holding her close whispered, 'I'm sorry.'

She held up her tear-stained face and he kissed her.

'Well I'm here now, so that's one worry less.'

'How long for?'

He broke away and moved over to the dresser. He picked up Hazel's letter. 'Her writing don't improve much, does it,' he said with a faint laugh.

'John. How long a leave have you got?'

'Don't let's worry about that for the moment.'

'John. I want to know.'

'Why? You want to see the back of me?'

'Don't be so damn annoying.'

He sat at the table. 'Well if you must know, I'm on embarkation leave.'

'What? Does that mean you're going abroad right away?'

'In a couple of weeks.'

'But most blokes spend a bit of time in a camp over here.'

'Well we've heard on the grapevine that they're short of mechanics in France, and that's where we'll be heading.'

'Bloody French. Why can't they fight their own battles?'

'Don't let's worry about that. Let's make the most of our time together.'

'Will you be here for Christmas?'

He didn't answer.

Rene let the tears trickle down her cheeks. 'Not Christmas Day?'

'I'm sorry.'

For a moment or two Rene didn't know what to say. 'Could we go and see the kids while you're here?'

'I don't see why not.'

'I need to see them. I want to know if they're safe.'

'Of course you do. So do I.'

'We can go on Sunday.'

'Right then, it looks like we could be off to Worthing. That should be a lot easier to get to than Osborne.' He pulled her to him and kissed her again.

Rene wiped her tears away. 'We'd better get down to dinner.'

'Rene, when this lot's all over, I promise you that we are going to get a little house just for us, somewhere in the suburbs.'

'I shall keep that promise with me for the rest of this war.'

He kissed her cheek and playfully slapped her bottom. 'Come on. Dinner awaits.'

Chapter 15

A S SOON AS the car drew up outside the house, Hazel rushed out to greet Peter. She was very surprised when she saw him get out of the car. He didn't look like her brother. He looked thin, and his hair was long. She ran to open the front gate, and when he walked up to her, she held him close and cried.

The other children had come to the door to look at the new arrival.

'Now come on, Hazel. You should be happy at seeing your brother,' said Mrs Morison.

'I am, but he's so thin and he looks ill. Are you all right?'

He only nodded.

Mrs Morison looked at this lad, with his sallow skin and sunken eyes with the dark circles underneath. He

134

didn't look at all well. 'I think we'll have to start to fatten you up, young man.'

Peter quickly held on to Hazel's hand.

'Take your brother upstairs and put his nice new clothes away.'

'Why's 'e got new clothes?' asked June.

'All his old clothes had to be destroyed,' said the WVS lady who had brought him.

'Oh,' she said, looking at Peter. 'Has he still got that scarlet fever?'

'No.'

'Me mum won't be happy at him being 'ere.'

'Well you can write and tell her he wouldn't be here if he was still infectious.'

June laughed. 'I can't spell that word.'

'Come on, Peter. I'll take you upstairs,' said Hazel. She could see this talk was worrying him.

Mrs Morison watched the sad little lad follow his sister and knew he wasn't going to be any trouble.

'I want to go home, Haz,' Peter said as soon as they were in the boys' bedroom and alone.

'I know you do. Are you all right?'

He nodded. 'They took me teddy and burnt it.'

'Who did?'

'The nurse. She said everything had to be burnt.'

'Oh Peter.' She held her brother's hand. 'We'll get you a new one.'

'I can't sleep without Teddy.'

135

'I know. This is a nice coat.' She held it up.

'I've got all new clothes.'

As Hazel took his things from the bag, she commented on the contents. 'And you've got a school tie and jumper. You'll look very smart when you go to school.'

'Will I be with you?'

'No. The girls and boys are in different buildings.'

A tear trickled slowly down his cheek. 'Why can't we go home?'

Hazel sat on one of the beds. 'I'm gonna write and tell Mum we ain't gonna stay here.'

'What are these kids like?'

'I don't like 'em. Alf's a bully and June's a know-it-all.'

'Where will I sleep?'

'In here with the boys. You're on the camp bed.'

'Hazel. Peter. Come down here,' Mrs Morison was calling them.

'Come on, we'd better do as we're told.'

'Does she hit you?'

'No.'

Mrs Morison was at the bottom of the stairs. 'Say goodbye to the WVS lady.'

'Goodbye,' said Peter softly.

The woman turned to Mrs Morison. 'If you need us, just get in touch. Now I think that's everything. You've got his ration book, and Peter has his identity card and gas mask. Your allowance will be in the post.'

'Thank you,' said Mrs Morison, smiling as she shut the door behind the woman.

Then she turned to Peter. 'Well, young man. What are we going to do with you?'

He looked at his sister with fear in his eyes. 'I don't know.'

For the rest of the day Peter followed Hazel about. That evening when Mrs Morison went out, Alf declared himself to be in charge. When it was time for bed, Peter reluctantly hung back.

'Come on, you, you're the youngest so you gotta go ter bed first,' said Alf, pushing him towards the door.

'I don't wanna go.'

'Cor. Listen, everyone. He can speak.'

Peter hung on to Hazel, who said loudly, 'Leave him be.'

'If I say bed, then bed it is.'

'You ain't in charge here.'

'I am when old Morison goes out.' He put his face close to Hazel's. 'And as yer know, that's most nights when she's round her dear daughter's or up the pictures.' He turned and grinned at the rest of the kids, who were watching this with open mouths. Nobody stood up to Alf.

'Come on, Peter,' said Hazel. 'I'll read you a story.'

As they left the room Alf shouted out, 'And don't keep us awake snoring.'

Great shrieks of laughter from the other kids followed that.

In the bedroom Hazel helped her brother to get undressed. 'These are nice pyjamas.'

'Can't I come in with you?'

'No, I've only got a camp bed.'

'I don't wanna stay in here with him.'

'I'm sorry, but I can't do anything about it.'

'Can't we bring this bed into your room?'

'There ain't space. Peter, stop being such a baby.'

With that he burst into tears. 'I ain't got Teddy and now you're telling me off,' he sobbed.

Hazel hugged her brother. 'I'm sorry, but what can I do?'

'I want Mum.'

'Of course you do, you ain't been well. But I'm sure Mum will come and get us when she can.'

Peter looked at his sister and wiped away the tears with the flat of his hand. 'D'you think she will, Haz?'

Hazel smiled at him. 'I'm sure she will.'

They sat together for a while, and when Hazel heard June and Pattie come up the stairs she said, 'Come on now, Peter, into bed.'

Reluctantly he did as he was told.

'What yer doing in the boys' bedroom? You know it

ain't allowed. You ain't still worrying about 'im, are yer?' asked June, pointing at Peter.

'It's all strange to him.'

'It was all strange to us once.'

'I know, but he's been ill.'

'You'd better get outta there, before Alf and Terry come up.'

'Good night.' Hazel kissed her brother's cheek. 'Shout if you need me.'

'I will. Night, Haz.'

Hazel woke with a start.

'Leave me be.'

She could hear Peter shouting, and she jumped out of bed.

'What's wrong? What's the matter?'

Peter was standing by his bed crying, and Alf was standing next to him.

'What's wrong? What you done to him?'

'I ain't done nuffink. The dirty little sod's gorn and piddled the bed.'

'Oh no.' She turned on Alf. 'How do you know?'

'He woke me up with his grizzling and shuffling about, trying to take the wet sheet off. Wait till old Morison finds out about this; she ain't gonna be best pleased. Yesterday was clean sheets day.'

'Roll the sheet up and I'll get one off my bed,' said Hazel to her brother.

'Don't leave me, Haz.' He held on to her arm.

She brushed him away. 'I've got to go and get you a sheet.'

June and Pattie were sitting up when she went back into her bedroom.

'What's going on?' asked June.

'Nothing for you to worry about,' said Hazel as she began to pull the sheet off her bed.

'Your brother piddled the bed?' asked June.

Hazel didn't answer as she rolled up the sheet and took it next door.

She had just made up the bed when Mrs Morison came to the door. She was wearing a dressing gown and slippers and had a pink hairnet over her pipe-cleaner curlers.

'What's going on in here?'

If Hazel hadn't been so upset, she would have laughed.

'He's piddled the bed,' said Alf, grinning.

'He couldn't help it,' said Hazel.

'And what are you doing in here, young lady?'

'I came to take the sheet away.'

'Did you? And where was you going to hide it?'

'I wasn't. I was gonna put it on my bed.'

'Well, you'd better carry on. 'Cos I ain't washing sheets on a Sunday.' She turned and walked away. 'And keep the noise down. I want me lay-in.'

Hazel made up Peter's bed and told him to get in.

'Just try and sleep. It's ever so early.'

Peter squeezed his eyes shut tight.

Hazel took the wet sheet and put it on the top of her blanket; she didn't want the wet sheet next to her.

'I wouldn't do that fer my brother, if I had one,' said June.

Hazel didn't reply. She just wanted to get away from here.

Later that morning, when they were all having their breakfast, Alf kept looking at Peter and grinning, and every time he passed him he'd say out loud, 'Who's piddled the bed then?'

Hazel was angry. 'Leave him be.'

'You know I reckon we should all club tergever and buy him some nappies,' said Alf.

Shrieks of laughter came from the other three.

'Who'd put 'em on 'im?' asked June.

'His big sister.'

'And who would wash 'em?' asked Terry.

'His big sister,' said Alf again.

Peter was looking terrified.

'Leave him be,' repeated Hazel. 'He ain't been well.'

'That still ain't no excuse fer piddling the bed. The dirty little bugger. You'd better not do it ternight, otherwise I'll chuck yer downstairs with the mice that run about all night.'

'Come on, Peter.' Hazel took his hand and they left the room.

'He'll be wanting yer to wipe his bum next,' shouted Alf after them.

The screams of laughter made Hazel angry as they went upstairs.

'I'm sorry, Haz.'

'What you gonna do tonight?'

'I don't know.'

'Well don't drink too much before you go to bed.'

'All right.'

Rene cuddled up to John. It was so lovely having him next to her. His gentle breathing told her he was asleep. Next Sunday they would be going to see the kids, and she had made up her mind she was going to bring them home, although she hadn't told John yet. She would write to Hazel and tell her they were coming to visit, as she didn't want to miss them again. The war had been going on for months and nothing had happened here, but even if it did, at least they would all be together. The thought of the children being here for Christmas excited her, but she knew that John wouldn't be here and that upset her. Christmas was always very special in their house.

John moved, and she kissed his back.

'You shouldn't do things like that,' he said, turning over.

'And why not?'

'You know what that will lead to.'

'I hope so.'

'Do you know, Rene Morgan, you are nothing but a hussy.'

'I hope so,' she said again.

Chapter 16

HAZEL HAD BEEN awake for most of the night, listening for any little sound that would tell her that Alf and Terry were laughing and taking the mickey out of Peter. Her brother was a shy boy, and she was afraid Alf would enjoy bullying him. She knew that Peter was unhappy and afraid of Alf; she had written and told her mother how much he was missing his teddy bear, though had tried to make things sound all right, as she knew her mum would be worried about them.

In the morning, when she woke after a fitful sleep, she waited till she heard Alf and Terry go downstairs. Going into the boys' bedroom, she was relieved to find Peter smiling and proudly telling her that his bed was dry.

As they all got ready for school, Peter was his usual quiet self. He looked very sad as Hazel took him for his first day at the new school. She left him with a teacher, and although she had told him he mustn't cry, she could see that his bottom lip was quivering, and she quickly walked away.

At the end of the day, he was waiting outside the gate for her.

'What was it like?' she asked as they walked along.

'All right.'

'Well that's your first day over.'

As they passed the shops on the way back to Mrs Morison's, Hazel felt sad to see the Christmas decorations some of them had managed to put up.

'Can we go home for Christmas?' asked Peter.

'I hope so.'

'Will Father Christmas know that I'm living here?'

'I hope so. Peter, don't tell Alf that you know there's a Father Christmas, otherwise he might write and tell him not to come to you.'

'All right.'

Hazel could remember how upset she'd been when a girl at school had told her that there was no Father Christmas. That day when she'd got home from school, her gran had comforted her, telling her that it was like believing in fairies: 'Anything's possible if you believe.'

Hazel thought about past Christmases. She loved

being with Gran and Auntie Betty. They always had such a lovely time, playing games and opening their presents. Would they still be here at Christmas? She knew she had to be brave for her brother, but she just wanted to sit and cry; like him, she was very homesick.

It was Wednesday when Hazel got the letter from home telling her that her mum and dad were coming to see them on Sunday. She was running round the room waving her letter.

'Will they take us back home?' asked Peter.

Hazel looked at Pattie, who was in the room with them. 'I don't think so,' she said carefully.

'What time will they be here?' asked Peter.

'I don't know. But we ain't going out this time.'

'Your mum and dad been ter see yer before?' asked Pattie.

Hazel nodded. 'But we didn't see 'em, as we was out.'

'That was a shame.'

'Yes, it was. They would have . . .' Hazel stopped. She didn't want the other kids to know that they could be going home.

'Will Dad bring his gun?'

'I don't know if he's allowed to bring it home.'

'I wanna carry it for him.'

'You'll just have to wait and see.'

'I wish I knew what time they was going to get here,' said Mrs Morison when Hazel told her her news. 'It would have been nice to get a bit of dinner for 'em.'

'Mum said the trains are all over the place so they could be here at any time.'

'I reckon she's right.' Mrs Morison went over to the stove and began stirring something that was bubbling on top.

'I expect they'll take us out somewhere,' said Hazel. She didn't want her mum and dad to stay here; she wanted to be with them on their own.

At last Sunday was here. Hazel and Peter were up very early and beginning to get anxious. They had spent the morning looking out of the window.

At the same time, Rene and John were almost fighting their way on to a train. The station was very crowded with servicemen and women in a colourful array of uniforms. Some had kitbags thrown over their shoulders and were looking sad, while others looked happy and were searching the crowd for familiar faces.

It wasn't till one o'clock that Hazel screamed out and ran to the front door. She had spotted her mum and dad as they turned the corner. She ran up to them with Peter following behind.

First her dad picked her up and twirled her round

and round, at the same time covering her face with kisses. Then he turned to Peter and did the same. Rene bent down and held them both at once; she had tears running down her face.

'How are you both?' she said when she managed to control her emotions.

'We're all right,' said Hazel.

'Looks like you could do with a haircut, young man,' said John, ruffling Peter's hair. 'I can see I'll have to take you back to camp with me and get it done properly like mine.'

Peter looked horrified at the thought. 'I don't want my hair like yours.'

His dad only grinned.

'Are you better now, Peter?' asked Rene.

'Yes,' he said, holding on to her hand tightly as they walked back to the house.

'Is the lady treating you all right?' asked John.

Hazel nodded. 'But we wanna come home.'

John looked at Rene.

'Let's get inside,' said Rene. 'I hope Mrs Morison will give us a cup of tea.'

'She said that if she knew what time you'd get here, she was going to give you some dinner.'

'That was nice of her.'

Hazel pushed open the front door. The other kids were all standing in the doorway of the front room.

'Hello,' said Alf. 'I'm Alf. This 'ere is me mates

Terry and June and Pattie. We all live here with Peter and Hazel.'

'That's nice,' said Rene, just as a smiling Mrs Morison came out of the kitchen wiping her hands on the bottom of her floral pinny.

'From the commotion Hazel made I guessed it was you. Kettle's on. I daresay you fancy a cuppa after yer journey.'

'Thank you, that would be very nice,' said Rene.

'Hazel, bring yer mum and dad inter the kitchen. It's warmer in there. I 'spect it was perishing on the train.'

'We were all so tightly packed we could hardly move, so that kept us warm,' said Rene.

'How's school?' asked John.

'Not bad,' said Hazel. 'Are Gran and Auntie Betty all right?'

'Yes, love,' said her mother. 'And they send you their love.'

'I wish we could see them,' said Peter.

Rene looked at John and said quickly, 'It's a bit too much of a journey for your gran.'

They were trying to make polite conversation, but Rene could see that Hazel and Peter were getting restless.

After a while John stood up. 'Thanks for the tea, but would you mind if we took the children out and looked for somewhere for dinner?' he said to Mrs Morison.

'No. I thought you might want to. Our dinner's ready anyway. Wrap up well, kids, it's bitter out there.' She turned to Rene and, giving her a smile, added, 'If you're walking along the front this time of year, that wind can go right through you.'

As soon as they were outside, Peter grabbed his mum's hand and said, 'I wanna come home.'

'So do I,' said Hazel as she skipped along holding on to her dad's hand.

'Well I reckon that wouldn't be a bad idea,' said John. 'Yer mum will need looking after while I'm away.'

'Where you going?' asked Hazel.

'I don't know yet.'

'Can we come with you?' asked Hazel.

'I'm sorry, love, but I don't think so.'

'So can we come home today?' she asked.

'I don't see why not.' Rene felt so happy being with her children, and she had made up her mind that she wasn't going to let them go away again. 'We will have to collect all your things and your ration books, and then we can go home.'

Hazel and Peter's faces were a picture of joy.

'But you can't take them back to London,' said Mrs Morison.

'Nothing's happening there,' said Rene. 'And we miss them so much.'

'Well if you ask me, I think it's all wrong. The government has spent a lot of money getting these children settled.'

'Yes, I know. But we miss them, and we all want to be together.'

'Well, please yourself.' Mrs Morison pulled her beige cardigan tighter round her. 'I suppose you'll want their ration books?'

'Yes please.'

They were a very happy family as they made their way to the station. Rene decided that whatever happened, she would not let the children be sent away ever again.

Chapter 17

A FTER A LONG and tiring journey, with many stops and starts, they finally arrived at 38 Glebe Street.

'What are those funny-looking silver things in the sky?' asked Hazel.

'They're barrage balloons, silly,' said Peter, full of confidence and jumping about to get a better look. 'Seen 'em in me comics. There's wires that come down from them and the German planes get all tangled up in 'em and then come crashing down.'

'They look ever so pretty.' Hazel stopped at the top of the road. 'Everything looks different.'

'That's because it's getting dark and there's no street lamps alight. It all looks very different in the dark,' said Rene.

'Does Gran know we're coming back?' asked Hazel when they reached their gate.

'We did tell her that you might want to come home,' said Rene as she pulled the string though the letter box and opened the door with the key.

'Well,' said Maud when Rene pushed the kitchen door open.

'Gran! Gran!' yelled Hazel, and she threw herself at Maud, quickly followed by Peter.

Hazel was hugged, and her tears fell. 'I've missed you so much.'

'And I've missed you.' Maud had a job to keep her own tears from flowing. 'Come here, Peter, and give me a cuddle.'

Peter was locked in his grandmother's arms, and for the first time in months he felt safe and happy.

Then it was Betty's turn to hug and kiss the children. 'We've missed you so much.'

When they finally took stock of the children, Maud said, 'You don't look very well, Peter. Are you all right?'

He nodded.

'Mind you, all that hair don't help,' said Rene. 'John's taking him to the barber in the morning.'

'I don't wanna haircut like Dad's.'

'I don't think you'll get one like that,' said Betty.

'I'm starving,' said Peter.

'Sure sign he's home,' said John.

'I'll do something on toast, Mum,' said Rene.

'Ain't you had anything to eat?'

'We went in a café and had a sandwich, but it's out of season down there and most places are shut. You two, take your things upstairs.'

'Would have thought the lady they were staying with would have got you something to eat,' said Maud.

'She said she would have if she'd known what time we might have got there,' said Rene.

Slowly the children went upstairs. To Hazel it seemed funny being home after all this time; she still couldn't believe it, and hoped it wasn't just a dream and she would wake up back at Worthing.

She pushed open the door and gave a little squeal. 'Look, there's a teddy on your bed and a new doll on mine.' She rushed over and picked up the doll, which had a pretty china face and was beautifully dressed. 'I bet Auntie Betty made this frock. It's lovely.'

Peter was grinning fit to bust as he clutched his new teddy.

'Come on, let's go and thank 'em,' said Hazel.

They ran down the stairs, laughing. This was the best day of their lives, and it wasn't a dream.

The next morning after their mother had gone to work, they spent time with their dad and gran exploring the brick shelter in the yard.

'Will we have to sleep in here?' asked Peter, all wide-eyed.

'I hope not,' said his gran.

'I want to,' he said. 'Can I?'

'It's a bit cold, and what about all the spiders?' asked Hazel.

'I whitewashed the walls, and Ron from next door made these bunk beds and put the door on and put this little shelf up,' said their father. 'Auntie Betty put the plant on it. It looks nice, don't it?'

'Will it die?' asked Hazel.

'No, it's not real,' said Maud.

'Dad, will we really have to sleep in here?' asked Hazel.

'I don't know, love. I hope not. Come on, let's get indoors, it's cold in here. When we've had a cuppa, we'll go and get Peter a haircut.'

Early afternoon on Saturday 23 December, the family stood at the gate and waved goodbye to John. He had told them that he didn't want them to walk to the end of the road with him. Before he turned the corner, he stopped, turned and blew a kiss. Rene was crying, and so were the children. Betty was holding Peter's hand, while Maud stood with her arm around Hazel's heaving shoulders.

'There, there, love,' she said, as much to comfort

herself as for her granddaughter's benefit. 'Come on inside, it's perishing out here.'

The sorry bunch all trooped into the house.

'It ain't fair. We've just got back, and now Dad's gone away. And he won't be here for Christmas. You should have let us come home before.'

'I'm sorry, love.'

'I don't think you really want us here.'

Rene just sat at the table with a blank look on her face at her daughter's outburst.

Betty looked at her sister and said to Hazel, 'That's not a nice thing to say. You can see your mum's upset at your dad going away.'

Hazel just sat sulking.

Betty felt sorry for her sister, but she was just one of millions; this scene could be happening all over Britain. She had some news herself, but decided to wait till after Christmas before she told her mother that she had signed on to go into the air force. That was if she passed her medical. As they needed something to do to lift the gloom, she suddenly said, 'Shall we go and get the tree?'

The children looked happier. 'Can we, Mum?' asked Hazel.

'I don't see why not. In fact I think that would be a very good idea.'

It had been decided last week that they would leave this job till after John had gone. If the children were home, it would give them something to do, and if they weren't, well they wouldn't bother, as it wouldn't be much of a Christmas without them anyway.

'Hazel, I think you should say sorry to your mum. Remember, she's just as upset as you.' Maud had been taken aback by her granddaughter's outburst.

Hazel looked down at her feet. 'I'm sorry, Mum.'

'Come here.' Rene hugged her daughter. 'You're forgiven. Now, let's go out with Auntie Betty.'

The bustle round the market was enough to lift anyone's spirits. Apart from the fact that there were so many men in uniform, you would never think there was a war on. The stallholders were still shouting their wares, although some of the stalls were beginning to look a little sparse, and the man was still roasting his chestnuts and selling his sarsaparilla, and the organ grinder was still playing his tuneless noise, though the monkey wasn't there. Someone shouted out that he'd had it for dinner a week ago. The light was gradually fading, and as no lamps would be allowed, the stallholders had begun to clear away.

'We'd better hurry up if we're gonna find some sort of tree,' said Betty.

'That bloke there's still got a couple left, but they look a bit ropy,' said Rene.

They stood in front of him and began to pick over what he had.

'How much?' asked Betty, holding up a sorry-looking specimen.

'You can have that one for a bob.'

'It's not very nice,' said Rene.

'You're not going to sell many more at this time o' night,' said Betty.

He looked at them and picking up another said, 'Give us a bob for the two of 'em then.'

'Done,' said Betty, opening her purse.

Hazel and Peter were in high spirits as they walked home carrying the trees.

'We can put these in a bucket. That way they won't look so sparse, and we can spend the evening decorating them,' said Betty. 'I managed to get some crêpe paper the other day, so we can put that round them. We'll make them look real good.'

Hazel and Peter loved their aunt; she was always so good at doing things and making them look nice.

'Good job we keep the decorations from one year to the next,' said Rene, pleased that her sister was around to brighten any sad days.

That evening there was plenty of laughter and squabbling as to where each bauble went, and by the time it was the children's bedtime the trees looked magnificent.

'Now come on, you two, time for bed.'

'I'm sorry, Mum. I didn't mean what I said.'

'I know you didn't.' Rene hugged her daughter and kissed her good night.

Once they were in bed, Hazel began to think about her dad. When would she see him again? Her mum had been doing a lot of crying, and she felt really sorry for being so cheeky.

Peter must have been thinking about his dad as well, as he said softly, 'Haz, will Dad be in the fighting?'

'I don't know.'

'He told me his gun is nearly as big as me. I wish I could go in the army.'

'Don't talk daft. Now go to sleep.' Hazel turned over and said her silent prayers.

When Rene went to bed, her thoughts were all about John. She knew he was going abroad and she worried about him. She let her tears fall. She loved him and her children so much that all she wanted was for the family to be together, but how long would it be before that happened? She didn't even let her thoughts go in any other direction.

They tried to make Christmas Day a happy one. Maggie and Tom came over for dinner, and in the evening Hilda and Ron came in. A fire had been lit in the front room, and the aspidistra had been spirited upstairs and the tree brought ceremoniously in to stand proudly in its place.

They sat around talking. Hilda, Maud and the girls had their port and lemon, while Ron and Tom had a bottle of beer.

Maud overheard Ron talking to Tom, who was confiding that he was waiting for his call-up papers. Did Maggie know, or was this something she was keeping from her mother? Suddenly everybody seemed to have secrets.

'Will the schools be open after Christmas?' Hilda was asking Rene.

'I don't know. Mrs James in the shop might know, but I'll give 'em a little while before I pack 'em off.'

'Well it's all quiet round this way,' said Maud. 'Mind you, it's the shortages that are beginning to get me down. Whenever you go to buy something, they tell yer it's out of stock.'

'Shoved under the counter, if yer ask me,' said Hilda.

'I find that being at work all day, I've not got time to go traipsing round the shops,' said Maggie.

Maud looked round at her family. One had gone; how many more would have flown the nest before too long? 'I'm just going to get a few bits,' she said.

'D'you want a hand, Mum?' asked Maggie.

'No, it's all right.'

When she came back, she was carrying a tray of glasses.

'What you brought them in here for?' asked Betty.

Maud put the glasses on the table and went to the sideboard. 'Right, now come on, cheer up. I've got a little something put away.'

The talking stopped and they all looked at Maud.

'What have you been up to, then?' asked Betty.

With a flourish, she brought a bottle of whisky out of the cupboard.

'You crafty old . . .' Ron stopped before he said a naughty word in front of the children.

'Where did you get that from, Mum?' asked Rene.

'Your husband gave it to me and told me to tell you all to have a drink on him.'

Once again Rene's tears fell.

Hazel went to her mother and scrambled on to her lap. Peter did the same.

Maud poured out the drink and everyone stood up.

'To John,' they all said.

'And may we all be together soon,' added Maud.

But deep down each of them had their fears about what the future would bring.

Chapter 18

THE NEW YEAR came in very cold and damp, and as the months went on, the news from around the world grew worse. Rene was worried that there was a lot of fighting in France. Was John there? The few letters she'd had from him didn't tell her where he was. At home, every day brought more problems for housewives, with the shortages and longer queues.

Butter, sugar and bacon were now on ration, and there was talk of meat going on soon. James's dairy had become a meeting place, and most mornings people came in with their own tales of woe.

Because of the shortage of teachers, the men being called up and the women evacuated with their schools, there weren't any schools open in London, so the children had to amuse themselves.

Rene was now making parachutes and Betty was waiting for her medical. Maud was almost beside herself when her youngest daughter told her that she had joined up.

Maggie's husband Tom was waiting to go into the army, and Maggie had been moved to another office. She said it was to do with the War Office and was all very hush-hush.

Everybody's lives were being upset, but Hazel and Peter were enjoying being at home and not having to go to school. Rene, however, was worried about their education, so when she had the time, she and her mother would try to help them with their sums and reading.

February the twenty-fourth was Hazel's eleventh birthday. She was upset when she didn't get a letter or a birthday card from her father. 'I think he's forgotten me,' she said.

'Hazel, be fair. He probably don't even know where he is, let alone what the date is.' Rene was as upset as her daughter, but not about the card. It was just that she was worried and missing John so much.

Gradually the weather was turning warmer. Betty was now in the air force and they were waiting to hear from her and find out where she was stationed. They hoped that she would be near and could get home now and again. Maggie came to see them a few times, but she said she didn't know how often she would be able to get away from work, while at the weekend she just wanted to go home and sleep. She didn't have any set hours now, and could be on duty all night. Many more children had returned to London and were playing in Glebe Street, and Maud was concerned that Peter was becoming a bit wild. He and his friend Billy were racing round the streets, pretending to be soldiers, firing imaginary guns.

Hitler was marching across Europe, and Rene worried constantly about John. His letters took a while to get to her. One morning she was very excited, as she received three.

'Don't he ever give you any hint of where he is, then?' asked Maud.

'He can't. If he does, it's blanked out by the censor. They read all our letters.'

'I can imagine what some of 'em put in 'em, then.'

'I don't suppose they turn a hair, I expect they're thick-skinned.'

'I suppose they have ter be.'

At the end of May, everybody sat intently listening to the wireless. France had fallen and they were bringing the troops home from Dunkirk. Rene went to the pictures and sat looking for John on the newsreels of the soldiers who were lucky enough to be rescued. But she never saw him.

'P'raps you'll hear soon,' said Maud, trying to comfort her daughter. 'He might be on his way right now.'

'I pray he is, Mum. I'm worried stiff.'

'Of course you are, love, it's only natural.'

On June the eighteenth Peter turned eight. Rene had managed to get him a book about planes, and he was becoming very knowledgeable about anything to do with the war. He and his friends would study books and comics and could name all the planes. To his grandmother's distress, he was also beginning to get very cheeky.

Rene hadn't had any news of John for months. She had dark circles under her eyes through lack of sleep.

'Mum, what if he's dead?' she said one evening as they sat and talked after the children had gone to bed.

'You mustn't think like that.'

'But how will I know?'

'I'm sure you would have been told by now. Perhaps he's been taken prisoner.' Maud patted her daughter's hand, as much for her own comfort as for Rene's.

'He won't like that,' said Rene. 'And it could be for the rest of the war. Sod Hitler. I'd like to string him up.'

'You and thousands of others, love.'

When Rene had the letter from the Red Cross telling her that John was a prisoner of war, she was relieved to learn that he was alive, but sad because she knew she wouldn't see him again till the war was over.

'Will he be able to write to us?' asked Hazel.

'I don't know,' said Rene. 'We shall just have to wait and see.'

'P'raps he'll try to escape,' said Peter.

'I hope not. He might get shot,' said Maud.

'Mum, tell Peter not to say things like that.'

'I only thought . . .'

'Well don't think,' said Hazel, turning on her brother.

Throughout August there had been air raids over Britain. The dairy now had metal bars along the front of the window, and every night Mr James would slip planks of wood into them to stop the window shattering and the glass flying about if they got bombed. Everybody was becoming aware of what danger could lie ahead. When the sirens did sound and enemy planes came over, much to Peter's delight the Spitfires intercepted them. The sky was full of vapour trails and he wouldn't stay in the shelter but stood outside excitedly naming the planes.

'Peter, get in here,' shouted his gran.

'I'm all right. They ain't bombers, they're fighters.'

'I don't bloody well care what they are. Get in here.'

'Peter, you wait till Mum gets home. She'll take you down to the warden's post to Mr Hunter and he'll give you a clip round the ear,' said Hazel.

Reluctantly Peter did as his gran and sister told him. Wally Hunter put the fear of God into all the boys with tales of what he could do to them if they got out of hand.

September the seventh was a lovely sunny Saturday. Maud was talking to Hilda and Ron out in the back yard. Once again the air-raid siren went, and once again people took their time getting into the shelters.

The low drone of planes made everybody look up. The sky darkened and seemed to be full of menacing-looking black planes.

'Bloody 'ell,' said Ron. 'I don't like the look of them.'

No sooner had the words left him than the scream of bombs came whistling down, and one after the other the explosions made them all gasp.

'The kids,' shouted Maud. 'The kids.' She ran through the house as fast as her legs would carry her, but she felt as though she was running through treacle.

The front door burst open and Hazel ran into her arms. 'Gran. Gran. I'm frightened.'

'I know you are, love. Where's Peter?'

'Peter!' screamed Hazel. 'Come in here.'

Peter rushed in and shut the door behind him.

'Now quick, both of you in the shelter.'

As they shut the door behind them, a bomb fell close by and shook the shelter.

With fear in her eyes Hazel asked, 'Will Mum be all right?'

'Yes, love. They've got shelters near the market.' Maud hoped her daughter would be safely inside.

The thud of bombs falling made the children sit close together on the bottom bunk and put their hands over their ears.

'I don't like it, Gran,' said Hazel.

'Neither do I.' Maud was so afraid of dying or being maimed. Was this shelter strong enough? How was Rene? She would be worried stiff.

For an hour the whistle of falling bombs and the earth gently lifting after an explosion made them all cling together.

After a while it began to quieten down and the explosions moved further away, then at last the long single note of the all-clear sounded. Very slowly they emerged from the shelter, not sure what they would find.

'You all right, Maud?' shouted Ron from next door.

'Yes thanks,' she replied. 'What about you two?'

'Hilda's a bit shook up.'

'I'm not surprised. Bloody 'ell. Look at that.' Maud was pointing in the direction of the docks, where a great pall of thick black smoke was rising in the air over the rooftops.

'Christ,' said Ron. 'That looks pretty bad. I'm going out front to get a better look.'

He was followed by Hilda, and next door Maud and the children made their way out on to the road too.

Everybody in Glebe Street was looking towards the docks. Flames were shooting up and oil drums were exploding. The thick black smoke was darkening the sky.

'I don't like to be a Jonah,' said Mr James. 'But that's gonna be a right beacon for tonight.'

'What with that and the railway lines at the end of this road, we could be in for a very bad night,' said Ron.

Hilda looked as pale as a ghost. 'Ron, what we gonna do?'

'Get ourselves organised for a long sleepless night. Have you got enough candles, Maud?'

She nodded, not taking her eyes off the pall of smoke.

'Take bedding into the shelter, and a couple of flasks of tea and some sandwiches. We don't know how long we'll be stuck in there.'

'I'll do that now,' said Maud. 'Come on, kids, you can help me.'

There wasn't any protest as they followed their gran inside.

When Rene left the shelter in the market she ran all the way home. What would she see? Were her family safe? She could have cried when she turned into Glebe Street and saw that every house was still standing.

'Mum. Mum!' she cried out as she ran inside.

'Mum,' shouted Hazel, running down the stairs to meet her. 'We was ever so frightened.'

'So was I. But you're all right?'

'Yes. We sat in the shelter with Gran.'

'Where is Gran?'

'Getting the shelter ready for tonight.'

Rene took her daughter's hand and they made their way outside.

'What you doing, Mum?'

'Thank God you're home,' said Maud. 'I'm getting ready for tonight. Ron reckons we're in for a bit of a pasting. He said to bring the bedding in and make a couple of flasks of tea and some sandwiches.'

'I'll give you a hand.'

'We've got plenty of candles. But bring in a change of clothes for you and the kids.'

'Why?'

'Well, we don't know what might happen.'

Rene could see that her mother was bustling about to take her mind off what could happen to them tonight.

'And don't forget to put your policy bag in there as well. I ain't been paying a penny a week all these years to lose out.'

Rene smiled and kissed her mother's cheek.

Maud touched her face. 'What was that for?'

'I never tell you how much you mean to us.'

'Don't talk daft. Now go and get that bedding.'
Maud was very touched at such a simple gesture.
There must be thousands of other households all over
London doing the same and preparing for tonight. But
how many of them would see tomorrow? She quickly
brushed a tear away with the bottom of her pinny. She
mustn't let them see how upset she was.

'Maud, Maud, are you there?' Ron was calling her
from next door. She popped her head out of the shelter.
'What is it?'

'Here, take this.' He handed her a bottle.

'What is it?'

'It's whisky. Have a drop before you all settle down
for the night. It'll help yer sleep.'

Maud laughed. 'Bloody hell. We'll be had up, being
in charge of the kids while drunk and incapable.'

'See you in the morning,' said Ron.

'God willing,' replied Maud.

171

Chapter 19

COME SIX O'CLOCK that Saturday evening, most Londoners had settled into air-raid shelters, or under the stairs of their homes. At seven, the long moan of the air-raid warning began.

At 38 Glebe Street, two chairs had been brought into the shelter, and Maud and her family sat tight-lipped waiting for the inevitable. As the sound of the siren filled the shelter, they all looked up from what they were holding but not really concentrating on. The children were looking at comics and Rene was reading a book. Maud was knitting, and the click, click, clicking of her needles grew faster, but nobody said a word. Almost as soon as the siren stopped, the sound of planes and falling bombs filled the air.

As the evening wore on, suddenly amongst the

whistling and exploding of the bombs a new and different noise assailed their eardrums.

'What the bloody hell's that?' asked Maud. Fear was written all over her face.

'That's a gun that's pulled along on the back of a lorry, Gran,' said Peter. 'We've seen 'em in the park, and the soldiers can drive round the streets with 'em.'

'Well I wish they'd go away from our road,' said Rene, trying to make herself heard over another loud bang, bang, bang, bang that filled the shelter.

Peter was sitting wide-eyed, while Hazel just sat staring at the floor as it gently lifted and subsided again as a nearby bomb exploded. 'I don't like it, Mum. I'm frightened,' she said, jumping every time there was an explosion.

'I know you are, love. We all are. Shift up,' Rene said as she sat between her children on the bunk bed and put her arms round them, holding them close. The thought that was filling her mind was: would they all still be alive in the morning?

Maud, who could almost read her daughter's mind, leaned forward and patted her knee. 'We'll be all right.'

Rene had a job to keep the tears back, but she knew she had to be brave for the children. Why had she brought them home to this?

Some of the bombs were beginning to drop very close, and they could hear glass breaking mixed with the clattering of roof tiles sliding down and hitting the ground. Bells from fire engines and ambulances was another new noise that added to the cacophony, which seemed to be endless.

Would it ever stop?

Hazel put her hands over her ears. 'I'm frightened.' She began to cry.

Peter leaned across his mother and held his sister's hand. 'It'll be all right, Haz. Remember how frightened I was when I went inter hospital? You told me I'd be all right, and I am.'

Rene kissed his cheek. How proud she was that they were growing up into caring people. But how much more growing up would they be allowed to do?

'I know, let's sing a song and drown old Jerry out,' said Maud.

'What shall we sing?' asked Hazel.

'I dunno. What d'you know?'

'What about "Run Rabbit Run"?' said Peter.

'That's a good one.'

Very half-heartedly they began to sing. They had only got through the first verse when there was a terrific explosion and the door of the shelter blew open. A gust of wind showered them all with dust and blew out the candles.

Hazel screamed. Rene jumped up and after a struggle managed to close the door.

'That must have been a close one,' said Maud, her face colourless.

'We'll put this chair in front of the door just in case it happens again,' said Rene.

'I wonder who copped that one?' said Maud.

'Well it wasn't us,' said Rene. In the few seconds it had taken her to close the door, she had seen in the light of the fires all around that their house was still standing.

The noise went on for hours. After a while the children began to feel drowsy.

'Look, why don't you two put in those earplugs the government gave us? That might help to quieten the racket.'

The children did as their gran said and cuddled together.

'That drop o'whisky you put in their warm milk must be having an effect,' Maud whispered, smiling as Rene covered them with a blanket.

'I'll be had up for encouraging me kids to drink.'

'It's medicinal.'

'I think it's having the same effect on me.'

'Well why don't you get your head down as well?'

'How can I?'

'Go on, love, try to shut your eyes for a little while.'

Rene woke with a start. She stood up. Her legs were stiff. 'I must have dozed off. What's happened?'

'It's gone a bit quiet,' said Maud.

Rene walked round the tiny space rubbing her legs. 'I'm dying for a wee.'

'I think the kids have nearly filled the bucket.'

'Could I risk going to the lav?'

'Dunno.'

They sat for a while straining their ears for the slightest noise.

'I think I'll risk it. After all, it is just outside. I won't shut the lav door.'

'Well I don't think anybody will see you sitting on the pan. But be careful.'

When Rene stepped outside, the dawn was just breaking and light from the fires gave everywhere a lovely rose-coloured glow. She wanted to cry. The sky looked so beautiful, and they were all still alive. She crunched over broken glass and tiles as she made her way to the lav. What would they find indoors when they finally came out of the shelter?

At five o'clock the long, sweet note of the all-clear came and everybody emerged to look at the damage.

'Maud, Maud, are you all all right?' shouted Ron.

'Yes thanks,' said Maud. 'How about you two?'

'We're okay. Just been indoors to look at the damage. We ain't got no winders and the roof looks a bit dodgy.'

'We ain't been in yet.'

'Well just be careful. Don't let the kids in till you know it's safe. And watch yourself going up the stairs. Give me a shout if you're at all worried.'

'Thanks, Ron,' said Rene. 'I'll go in first. We need a cuppa.'

'I tried that. There ain't no gas.'

'Bloody hell,' said Maud. 'What we gonna do?'

'You'll have to dig out your old Primus stove.'

'That's a good idea.'

'Have you got any paraffin?'

'I think so.'

'You ain't kept it indoors, have you?'

'No. We keep it in the lav.'

'Thank Gawd fer that. You could all be blown up.'

'It'll take ages to boil a kettle,' said Rene.

'We've got ages,' said Maud.

Hazel and Peter stood at the door of the shelter.

'You two be careful as you come out.'

'We ain't got no winders,' said Peter.

'I know.'

'And look at Gran's nice lace curtain,' said Hazel. 'It's all torn.'

'It's a bit more lacy now,' said Maud, trying to make light of it.

Slowly they made their way into the kitchen. The lath and plaster ceiling was down, and everywhere was covered with grey dust. The windows were all broken and the curtains hung in torn strips. They went from room to room downstairs; they were all in the same state.

When Maud tried to open the front door, she couldn't. 'The door's stuck.'

Rene came and tried. 'I'll shout for Ron to give it a shove from the outside.'

She went out into the front room and yelled through the glassless window for Ron. He came over and pushed from the outside. When the door finally flew open, it almost knocked Rene flying.

'You wait till you see what's happened out here,' Ron said solemnly.

They all trooped outside and stood looking at the gaping hole at the end of the road that had once been a house.

'Oh my God,' said Maud. 'Are the Roberts all right?'

Ron shook his head. 'Wally said they got Freda and young Jimmy out, but they're still digging for Jim and Katie.'

'Are Freda and young Jimmy okay?' asked Rene.

Ron shook his head again.

Maud felt a tear trickle down her cheek. She had known Freda and Jim for years. Their children had grown up with her girls. Young Jimmy was a nice boy and at one time had been very sweet on Maggie. He wasn't in the forces as he had a withered arm.

Rene could see how distressed her mother was, and she came up and gave her a cuddle.

'Look at the dairy,' said Hazel. 'Where did all those planks of wood go?'

Mr James was looking at his shop front. The glass was still intact, but the blast had lifted the planks out of the metal bars he'd put across the windows and somehow spirited them away.

'Wally said the blast can do a funny thing. Well you can't get anything funnier than that,' said Mrs James, coming over to them. 'God only knows where our wood's finished up. What's your place like?'

'We ain't been upstairs yet,' said Rene. 'I'm dreading what I'll find.'

'I'll go up first if yer like,' said Ron.

'Thanks.'

Slowly they climbed the stairs, which were covered with bits of ceiling.

When Rene pushed open her kitchen door, she let out a gasp. 'We've got a bloody great hole in the roof.'

'Let me go in first,' said Ron.

One step at a time, they very carefully made their way across the room. All the furniture was covered with bits of tile, lath and plaster. The lovely glass lampshade Rene had always been so proud of had gone; the brown flex with the bulb still attached was hanging from a rafter and moving gently in the breeze. They could see the sky over the fireplace.

'What we gonna do if it rains?'

'Wally was saying that there's a lot of tarpaulins in a warehouse that they can put over the roof for the time being till they can get 'em fixed. I'll tell yer something, I'm really impressed at all the preparation that has gone on ready for this war.'

They slowly left the kitchen and made their way to the front room and the bedroom, where they were met with the same amount of damage.

When Rene joined her mother in the road, she related all they'd seen. 'We can't live up there.'

'You'll have to move downstairs,' said her mother. 'We can get a few blokes to help us bring the beds down and you can all sleep in the front room.'

Rene wanted to hug her mother. Ever the practical one she was.

The children were talking to their friends a little further down the road, when Peter came running over to his mother holding something.

'What have you got there?'

He opened his hand and Rene screamed out, 'Drop that! It might be a bomb.'

'No it ain't, it's shrapnel. Billy Walker said there's loads of it and they're all collecting it.'

'Well I don't like the idea of you picking up something that Jerry's dropped.'

'It might be from our guns. Oh go on, Mum, let me.'

'I think you'll find all the kids will be doing it,' said Ron.

'Oh all right then.'

'Peter, be very careful, don't pick up anything that looks suspicious. Just call a grown-up or an ARP warden,' said Ron.

Peter didn't reply. He just ran off to join his mates. To him this was a new and exciting game.

Chapter 20

FOR THE REST of the day, all that could be heard was sawing and hammering as people tried to board up windows and clear up the mess as best they could. Everybody was helping. The children thought it was a good game taking rubble from inside the houses in buckets and any other form of container that could be found and tipping it in the road. It helped to ease their fear and tension. Even Hazel managed a smile on her tired, worried face as the tin bath was taken from the hook in the yard and filled with rubble. It took a couple of women to lift it and tip the contents out; everybody was helping each other. Whenever any of them came out of their house and looked down the road at all the activity, they hoped and prayed that Jim and his beautiful daughter Katie would soon be found alive.

Most of the men who were still around were down there helping the wardens, police and firemen to move what was left of the house piece by piece. It was a sad sight, but now and again hope was renewed when the shout went up for everyone to be quiet, and they stood and listened for any sound that would tell them that someone was still alive.

All through the morning Maud and Rene cleared glass and pieces of ceiling from the downstairs front room, then with the help of some of the boys they moved the furniture around so that Rene's double bed could be brought down.

'When we can go back to sleeping in a bed again, we can all get in there,' said Rene.

Her mother didn't answer.

'Mum, you should see the state of me lovely dressing table.' Rene wiped a tear from her cheek. 'The mirror's broke and the glass is all sticking up in the lovely top that I've spent hours polishing.'

'Rene, it's only possessions. Think about poor Freda.'

'Sorry.' Rene felt guilty and went back upstairs. She got very angry when she stood in her front room and looked at John's pride and joy, his piano. It too had glass embedded in it, and was covered with bits of ceiling. The piano was the only thing they had ever bought on the never-never. She went downstairs. 'What can we do now?' she asked her mother.

'Dunno. I suppose we should go along to the kitchen and try and clear that.'

'We can have a go.'

Ron was at the front door and called out, 'Maud. Where are you?'

'We're in the kitchen,' she shouted back. 'What's the trouble?'

Ron came in and Maud quickly added, 'Have they found . . . ?'

He shook his head. 'Not yet. I just come to tell you that the WVS ladies are at the top of the road and they've got tea. Bring yer flasks and yer teapot; they're filling them up. Mind you, there's quite a queue.'

'What a wonderful idea. Someone's got tea. Me mouth feels like the bottom of a birdcage,' said Maud, bustling around and wiping out the brown china teapot.

Rene rushed out to the shelter and brought the flasks in. 'I'll go and queue up, Mum. You come along as quick as you can. I'll save you a place.' She quickly ran off.

'All right, love. Is Hilda up there?' Maud asked Ron.

'Yes,' he replied. 'I'm just going indoors to get our flasks. See yer in the queue.'

The cleaning had to stop when the water ran out. All morning there had been just a trickle, but an hour or two after it finally stopped, the water container came round and everybody rushed out into the street with buckets, kettles, saucepans and even vases. It was a sight to see all these people going back and forth carrying anything that could hold water.

'At least I'll be able to flush the lav,' said Mrs James. 'What is it with these blokes that causes such a stink?'

Rene only smiled. She would love to have John around making a stink. She hadn't had any more news, but at least she could hope he was still alive, she hadn't had that telegram that every wife and mother dreaded. He would be so worried if he knew what they'd been through, and they all knew that tonight wouldn't be any better, as the timber in the docks was still burning. She said a silent prayer as she went about clearing the dresser and putting all her mother's china in the cupboard underneath. If we are to go tonight, please let it be swift and painless. I don't want the children to suffer. Rene still felt guilty at bringing her precious children back to London. She sat back and thought about the future, and whether they had one. What if she and her mother were killed? Who would look after the children till John came back? That was it: they would have to go away again.

Her mother walked through the kitchen and Rene quickly dismissed her negative thoughts.

'I'm just going over the road to see if the dairy's got any milk. Don't like me tea without milk.'

* * *

Come evening, like everyone else, the family settled down to another sleepless night. And once again it was the same old routine: the siren first, followed by gunfire and bombs.

During a break Rene said, 'Tomorrow I'm going to see about getting you two evacuated again.'

'I ain't going,' said Peter.

'You'll do as you're told,' said Rene.

'I'll run away.'

'Hazel will be with you.'

'Can't you come with us?' asked Hazel.

Rene looked at her mother. 'Someone has to stay with your gran.'

'That's right, blame me.'

'I didn't mean it like that.'

'I don't need looking after. I ain't an invalid.'

'Well I ain't going away,' said Peter.

Rene knew that for the time being, that was the end of that conversation.

Noise from falling bombs, fire engines, ambulances and pom-pom guns disturbed them all night as they tried to get a bit of sleep.

The following morning everybody came out and inspected the damage. They were relieved to see that Glebe Street had escaped another direct hit. They were still mourning the loss of the Roberts family. The bodies of Jim and Katie had been brought out yesterday afternoon.

'Rene, you going to work?' asked Maud.

'I'll have to. No work means no money.'

'But what if the factory's gone?'

'Dunno. I'll have to go and find out if it's still there. I'll be back if it's not.'

'Well be careful.'

'I will. And Mum. Look after the kids.'

'Of course I will.'

Rene was worried about Hazel. She had been very quiet the previous evening and the look of fear on her face filled Rene with guilt as she left the house and made her way to work. What could she do to make Peter see that going away was the safest thing?

The factory was within walking distance, so she didn't have to worry about whether the buses were running.

As she turned the corner out of Glebe Street, everything looked so different. Everywhere there were great gaping holes where there had once been houses. It was an incredible sight to see the whole side of a house gone but the furniture still in place and even the beds neatly made. As she walked on over hosepipes and was directed down different roads because of unsafe buildings, unexploded bombs and huge craters, she found she was lost. This was a place she had known all her life, but now it looked so different, so odd. A policeman was talking to some firemen who were putting their hoses away; the house they had been attending was just a burnt-out shell. They looked very tired and dirty.

'Excuse me,' said Rene.

'Yes, love?' said the policeman.

'Could you help me? I'm lost. Lived here all me life, and now I can't find me way to Johnson's factory. That's if it's still there.'

'It's still there,' he said, pointing to her right. 'If you go down there, you'll see the dairy; that's still there but a bit of a mess. Milk was all over the place on Saturday night, so there'll be a few going without this morning. Be careful.'

'Thank you. I will.' Rene started on her way again. It upset her when she saw two bodies covered with sheets lying on the pavement waiting to be taken away. That was someone who yesterday was alive. How long would this last?

It was very quiet as she got nearer to the dairy, and when some rats ran across the road in front of her, she screamed.

'You all right, gel?' asked a man who must have been just behind his front door. These houses came straight out on the pavement.

'I've just seen two rats run across the road. Frightened the life outta me.'

'I've bin trying to swipe 'em all morning. D'you know, some are as big as cats.'

'Where they coming from?'

'The sewer at the dairy, it got the back blowed off last night. Bloody nuisance they are. The missus is scared stiff. She's terrified they'll come indoors.'

'So would I be.' Rene went to walk on.

'Be careful, love.'

'Thanks. I will.'

When she arrived at the factory, she stood for a moment just looking. Not a window had any glass left in it.

'Hello, Rene,' said a voice behind her.

She turned to see Tess, the forewoman who was in charge of her line.

'Bloody mess, ain't it?'

'What's it like inside?'

'They're all in there trying to clear it up.'

'Surely we won't be able to work in there?'

'Not till the electric's back on. You coming in?'

Rene nodded and followed Tess.

Inside it was very light. Rene was taken aback; sunlight was streaming through the windows.

'Makes a bit o' difference when the other buildings ain't there, don't it?' said her mate Joan, seeing Rene's surprised look. Joan worked on the machine next to her.

'Hello, Joan. You and your lot okay?'

'Yes thanks. What about you?'

'We're all right, though the old homestead's a bit battered.'

'Like mine,' said Joan.

'Do they reckon we'll be able to keep on working?' said Rene, looking around at the mess.

'Well Tess thinks they'll be taking the machines down into the basement. It should be safe down there.'

'I hope so.'

'After all, our boys must have parachutes,' said Joan.

Tess came up to them. 'Right, if you two can go downstairs and help the girls who are already down there to sweep the basement out. Ernie has got hold of a couple of blokes who are gonna take the machines and tables down later on.'

'Is there any lights on?' asked Rene.

'Yes. Don't ask me how, but Ernie managed to get a small generator put in months ago.'

When Tess had walked away, Joan said, 'Trust Ernie to make sure the work still goes out.'

The girls were very fond of Ernie, the shop foreman. He was very fair and understanding.

'It might be because we're doing an important job,' said Rene as they made their way to the basement.

'I don't like it down there,' said Joan, standing at the top of the stairs. 'Whenever I've gone down there for cloth I've seen rats.'

'Oh don't,' said Rene. 'I saw two of the biggest buggers I've ever seen this morning.'

Joan shuddered. 'Come on. We've got to do our bit to help with the war effort.'

'I suppose so,' said Rene as she followed Joan carefully down the concrete stairs.

Chapter 21

ALL DAY THE girls upstairs cleaned the machines and those downstairs swept the floors preparing the basement. At the end of the day, Mr Tucker, the owner of the factory, came in and thanked them.

'We hope to have the machines in place tomorrow to enable us to carry on working. You've done a great job, girls, and at least you'll be safe down here if Jerry starts coming over in the daylight.'

'That's comforting to know,' whispered Joan.

'Right, that's it for now. See you all tomorrow.'

'God willing,' said Joan.

He smiled and walked away.

As the girls left the factory, Joan said, 'I'm glad it's still light. At least I'll be able to find me way home.'

'I think I read somewhere that there's talk that we're

not putting the clocks back this winter, and next summer we're gonna have double British Summer Time. That means it'll be light till gone ten.'

'It'll be a job ter get the kids ter bed if it's still light,' said Joan. 'It's bad enough trying to get 'em in the shelter before us. Young Shirley won't have any of it.'

'I expect she's frightened,' said Rene, thinking about Hazel's sad and terrified look throughout the night.

'I expect so,' replied Joan.

Rene knew that Joan could have been evacuated with her children, as Shirley was just three, and her little boy Sam was only a year older, but she didn't want to leave her widowed mother-in-law alone. Joan's husband, who was an only child, was in the merchant navy, so in some ways Rene and Joan had a lot in common. Joan's mother-in-law looked after the children while Joan was at work, and when there was talk about children being evacuated, she had begged Joan not to take them away. She said she was worried she would never see them again. When Rene had wondered whether the old lady could go with them, Joan said she had refused, saying, 'I've lived here all me life and here I'll stay.' Joan was a bit upset about it at the time, but she loved the old dear like a mother, since hers had died years ago and her only other relative was an aunt who lived in Surrey somewhere.

As Rene walked home, her thoughts went over and over the last two nights. Was the shelter really safe?

Should she try and get all of them away? And would her mother go? Betty was stationed somewhere up north, and she must have read about what was happening in London. Would she be able to get leave and come and see them? Maggie was in an office doing important work, and she had been to see them a couple of times. Was she safe?

When she turned into Glebe Street, Peter came running up to her. He looked dirty and untidy.

'Mum.' His face was wreathed in smiles. 'You wait till you get indoors and see all the shrapnel I found today.'

'Look at the state of you.'

'I know. It don't matter.'

'You've torn your trousers.'

'I know.'

'How did you do that?'

'Me and Billy Walker was climbing over a bomb site and I got caught on a nail.'

'Peter, you shouldn't even be on a bomb site.'

'Why not? All the other kids are there.'

'What if there's an unexploded bomb in there?'

He laughed. 'It'll go whoosh.'

'Peter, that's not funny.'

Rene looked at her son. Although he was scared in the night, somehow he seemed to have grown up in just a few days. She pushed him gently through the open front door and walked into the kitchen. 'All right,

Mum?' she asked Maud, who was sitting at the table looked very tired. Hazel was next to her, reading.

'Nothing a good night's sleep won't cure. How was the factory? When you didn't come home, I guessed it was still there.'

'It's not too bad. The dairy's in a bit of a state.' She went on to tell them what they had done that day.

'So it looks like you'll still be working, then?'

'Looks like it.'

'Wally's been round. He wants you to go along to the warden's post.'

'Oh no. What's Peter been up to?'

'Dunno. He's been out all day and only comes in for something to eat.'

'Did Wally say what he wanted?'

'No.'

'Is dinner ready?' asked Rene.

'You've got time to go along to Wally if you want.'

'I suppose I'd better get this sorted.'

Peter was in the front room, carefully going through his shrapnel collection. Rene looked in. 'What have you been up to, young man?'

'Nothing. Why?'

'Wally the air-raid warden wants to see me.'

'Well it ain't nuffink I've done. Me and Billy and Jack have just been playing, that's all.'

'I hope you're right.'

Rene walked to the warden's post. It was in the

caretaker's office of the infants' school, which was just round the corner.

'Hello, Rene,' said Wally as he stood up.

'This is very cosy,' she said, looking around.

'We've got everything here. Kettle, gas burner and telephone.'

'Mum said you wanted to see me.'

'Yes. Take a seat.'

Rene sat in one of the two armchairs. 'Is it about Peter?'

Wally looked surprised. 'No. What makes you say that?'

'It's just that he told me he's been playing on a bomb site.'

'All the boys are there, can't stop 'em. It's a bit of an adventure for them. No, I've been told to recruit some fire-watchers, mostly from the younger women that are still around. If I don't find enough volunteers, then I'll have to enlist 'em.'

Rene laughed. 'You can't do that.'

'Yes I can. You'd be surprised what powers I've got. So, will you be a fire-watcher?'

'I don't know. What do I have to do?'

'You'll go about in pairs and just look out for fires.'

'What, in an air raid?'

'You'll have a tin hat, an armband and a whistle.'

'Oh, thanks. That'll stop me being blown to kingdom come.'

'Someone's got to do it.' He offered her a cigarette.

Rene shook her head. 'Would I have to do it every night?'

'No. I'll draw up a rota. The more people I can recruit, the less hours you'll have to do.'

Rene looked at a map on the wall as Wally drew out a shape with his finger.

'This is the area you'll have to patrol. What do you say?'

'Ain't got a lot of options, have I?'

'Not really. If you come along here later on tonight, I'll get your tin hat sorted and give you a bit of training with the others on what to look out for and how to use a stirrup pump. I'll also be able to tell you who you'll be working with, and what nights.'

Rene stood up.

'Thanks, Rene.'

She left the post and walked back home. She couldn't believe it: now she was a fire-watcher.

'You a fire-watcher? Will it be dangerous?' asked her mother when Rene told her her news.

'I hope not.'

'Mum, I don't want you to do it.' Hazel looked at her mother; her eyes had black rings under them.

Rene patted her hand. 'I'm afraid I have to, love. But don't worry, I'll be careful.'

'Cor,' said Peter. 'Can I come out with you?'

'No you can't.' Rene couldn't believe the difference

in her two children in such a short while. Hazel had always been the strong one, while Peter had relied on his sister. Was it because Peter could see no danger?

'Get yerself sorted out and I'll dish up the dinner. Mrs James let me have a tin of corned beef. I had a few taters and so I've made a corned beef pie. Thank Gawd the gas come on this afternoon. Those blokes must have a right job trying to get things working again.'

The thought that went through Rene's mind was: would it all happen again tonight?

It did happen that night, and every night for weeks after. It became almost like second nature to have to go to the shelter armed with flasks and sandwiches as soon as the evening meal was over.

Twice a week Rene donned her tin hat and made her way to the warden's post. The family thought she looked silly in the grey steel hat. She was on duty with Ted Andrews, a tall, quiet man who lived in the next street. He was a widower with two daughters who lived up north with their children.

On the first night they went out together, he told Rene about his daughters and grandchildren. 'They want me to go up there. I love ter see 'em, but I couldn't be stuck in the middle of nowhere. Lived here all me life. Besides, I couldn't leave Sally.'

'I thought Wally said you were a widower.'

'I am. Sally's me dog. And before you ask, I ain't in the army 'cos I've got a dickey heart.'

When Rene told her mother all this, Maud said, 'Well let's hope he don't have a heart attack when you're out together.'

As the weeks went on, Rene found out that Ted was a caring man who took his job very seriously. He always made sure Rene was all right and tried to keep her out of harm's way when the air raid started. He kept his eyes peeled for planes and the red-hot shrapnel that fell all around them. Sometimes, as they stood in a doorway and stared at the sky, it looked quite beautiful, with the searchlights sweeping back and forth picking out the silver barrage balloons. If aircraft came over, though, then all hell would break loose. Gunfire filled the air, and when the shells burst, it looked like a wonderful, deadly firework display.

One evening when they were on duty things were pretty hairy, and Rene was very nervous as they walked the streets looking for any fires that had been started by the falling bombs. Suddenly a screaming whistle came towards them. Ted pushed her into a doorway and fell on top of her just as a loud explosion filled their ears and made the ground heave and shake.

Rene felt the rush of air as the blast went past them, knocking the wind out of them and covering them with dust. They could hear a nearby building falling and they lay still for a few moments getting their breath back and coughing, before Ted got to his feet.

'Are you all right?' he asked, helping her up.

'Yes thanks.' Rene straightened her tin hat.

'Sorry about that.'

Rene was brushing her coat down. 'That's all right.'

'Did I hurt you?'

'No. I'm fine. But I've laddered me stockings.'

He gave her a smile. 'That was a close one. I think we'd better go and see if we can be of any help.'

'Do we have to?'

'I would think so. Are you worried about what we might see?'

She nodded.

'Don't be. Remember, someone might just want a shoulder to cry on.'

She gave him a weak smile and brushed some dirt from her face, then together they made their way to where they thought the bomb had dropped.

Chapter 22

RENE WAS VERY nervous as they hurried along in the direction of where the bomb had dropped. Although she wanted to help, she didn't want to see people who had been blown to pieces. She knew she wouldn't be any use if she just stood there crying.

'Come on, love, get a move on,' said Ted, stopping. He had been rushing ahead of her.

'Sorry,' she said, trying to keep up with him.

'Rene, you'll have to wear some more sensible shoes, you know that, don't you?'

'Sorry,' she said again as she trotted along behind him. She winced every time she heard and saw the red-hot shrapnel pinging off the rooftops.

As they got closer, they could hear shouting and

banging, and an ambulance with its bell ringing raced past them.

When they turned the next corner, they both stopped. Where there had once been a pub was now just a mass of tangled metal, bricks and wood.

Scrabbling over the rubble were all sorts of people in many different uniforms, as well as civilians digging with anything they could find.

'We ain't got no shovels, but if you could give us a hand taking some stuff out the way, that would be a help,' said a policeman to Ted and Rene as they joined the crowd.

They started digging and throwing lumps of masonry behind them.

'Are there many trapped inside?' asked Ted.

'Don't know. A lady who lives in the next road said she thought the landlord and his family were in the basement, but we can't get to it just yet,' said the policeman who was directing the operation.

More men and women came to help, and they were slowly making progress. After about an hour, they were through to what had been a floor.

'Quiet, everybody,' shouted a soldier who had joined them.

They all stood still.

The soldier got down on his knees and shouted, 'Anybody there?'

For a few seconds everybody held their breath.

Then there was a faint reply. 'Four of us.'

'Right, we'll be with you in a while.'

'Thanks,' came the reply.

A cheer went up from the workers and everybody began digging twice as hard. It was then that some WVS ladies made their way across the rubble with cans of tea and some mugs.

'I think you ladies and gentlemen deserve a cuppa,' said one of the ladies as she and her friends began pouring out the tea and handing it round.

'I ain't ever been so pleased to have a cuppa before,' said Ted, wiping the sweat from his face and making clean streaks in his dirty face.

Rene looked around. Dawn was just breaking. The sun began shedding its beautiful light on the workers and the wonderful sound of the all-clear filled the air. Rene wanted to cry; despite the situation it was a wonderful sight and sound.

Rene arrived home tired and dirty. When she pushed open the shelter door, she found her children and mother fast asleep. She stood looking at them, and silently thanked God that they were still here and alive.

Maud stirred in her chair. 'Hello, love,' she whispered. Then sitting up she looked at Rene standing before her. 'My godfathers, what happened to you?'

Rene sat down and in a soft voice told her mother about her night.

'And the family was all right?'

Rene nodded. 'The poor kids were terrified. The fear in their eyes was unbelievable.'

'So would I have been if I'd been buried alive. Has the all-clear gone?'

Rene nodded again.

'Look, why don't you go inside and get tidied up and then have a lay-down? I'll look after the kids.'

'Thanks, Mum.' Rene looked at her children; please don't ever let us be in that situation, she thought.

Rene, who had been fast asleep in bed, woke with a start. What time was it? She jumped up. She could hear talking coming from the kitchen. When she walked in, the children were sitting at the table having their breakfast.

'Mummy, Mummy,' said Hazel as she rushed to her mother and held her close. 'Gran said you was back, but you didn't come in to see us.'

'I did, but you were both fast asleep.'

Hazel sat back at the table.

'Sit yerself down, girl, and I'll pour you out a cuppa,' said Maud. 'You look done in. Why don't you go back to bed?'

'I can't. I must go to work.'

'But you ain't had much sleep.'

'I know, but everybody has to make the effort. If we don't, then Hitler will have won.'

Maud smiled at her daughter and felt very proud. She knew that with people like Rene, they would get through this.

As the month went on, so did the raids. They tried to make the shelter as comfortable as they could; they brought Maud's feather mattress in, so at least Rene and her mother could get some sleep between the falling bombs. Everybody was looking tired and exhausted, and the shortages and queues for food didn't help. Maud was always grateful for James's dairy just across the road. At least they could get the essentials when they had them.

One morning in November, Rene woke and didn't remember being awake half the night. Had the all-clear gone? Had there been a raid? She got up very slowly. She didn't want to disturb anyone as she carefully made her way out to the lav. It was bitterly cold. She looked over at Hilda and Ron's. Ron was walking back to the shelter with a pot of tea.

'Hello, love. All right?' he asked when he saw Rene.

'Yes, thanks. Did we have a raid last night?'

'No. I reckon Jerry's got fed up trying to get us Londoners down.'

'I hope so.'

Just then Maud came out of the shelter and saw Ron with his teapot. 'We got water?'

He grinned. 'And gas.'

Rene smiled too. What was it about the British and their tea?

There was the occasional raid during November, but the Luftwaffe was going to other cities, and Londoners were able to get on with living.

One Saturday afternoon, everybody at 38 Glebe Street had their spirits lifted when Betty walked into the kitchen.

Maud hadn't looked so happy for weeks. 'You certainly look very smart,' she said, full of pride.

The house was filled with chatter and laughter that hadn't been heard for months.

'You look good,' said Rene, giving her sister a big hug.

Even Hazel had a smile on her face. 'I like your uniform,' she said shyly. 'I think the air force uniform is the best.'

'So do I,' said Betty, holding her close. 'And how are you all? The street looks a bit of a mess. Mum told me what happened to the Roberts.'

'We've had our share,' said Rene.

'Katie was such a lovely-looking girl.'

'Yes, she was, but as I told you, we were all right,' said Maud, not wanting to talk about sad things.

Betty picked up on it and said, 'I've got a seventy-two-hour pass, and when I go back, I shall only be at Redhill.'

'Where's that?' asked Maud.

'Surrey somewhere.'

'I'll just put the kettle on,' said Maud, looking at her lovely daughter.

'I've got me ration card, Mum.'

'That's good.'

Rene looked at Betty too. There was something about her; she had changed. Her hair was much shorter and she had a sort of glow about her. 'Have you had much bombing up north?'

'Not where we were, but some places have taken a bit of a hammering. I was very sorry to hear about John.'

'Still, at least we know he's alive, even if he is a prisoner of war.'

'Yes, I suppose that's something. Do you know where?'

'Not yet.'

'And what about you two?' she said to Hazel and Peter, who were just standing staring at their favourite aunt. 'I bet you wish you were back in the country.'

'No we don't,' said Peter. 'It was horrible. You gotta come in the front room and see my shrapnel collection. Me and me mate Billy Walker go round collecting it every morning.'

'Mum's a fire-watcher now,' said Hazel.

'I know, she wrote and told me. Are you frightened when the raids start?'

Hazel nodded. 'I don't like it. And I don't like it when Mum's out.'

Betty cuddled Hazel close to her. She could see the child looked worried and concerned.

'So how's the shelter?' asked Betty.

'It's more like home now with all our bits in it,' said Rene.

'Do you go in it every night?'

'Yes. It's not too bad.'

'Mum said your place upstairs is a bit of a mess.'

'Yes, it is. I was worried about the rain coming in, but now we've got a tarpaulin over the holes, at least that keeps the weather out.'

'But we ain't got no winders,' said Peter. 'And it's ever so dark, 'cos they've put wood over them.'

Betty smiled. Peter had certainly changed, from a frightened little boy to someone who appeared to have a lot of confidence. 'And are you back at school?'

Hazel shook her head. 'They ain't open 'cos there's no teachers.'

'Most of them have been called up or evacuated with their school,' said Rene. 'The government is hoping that a lot of the old ones will come out of retirement. There's talk that the kids might be able to go for half a day; that'll be better than nothing. And they've got shelters in the school now, so at least they should be safe.'

'What do you do, Auntie Betty?' asked Peter.

'I was in the map room. I might be doing the same sort of thing when I get to this new place.'

'That sounds interesting,' said Rene.

'It is. We have to monitor the planes as they come in.'

'Any man in your life yet?'

'No.'

'There must be a few good-looking blokes around.'

'There's a few. Mind you, I don't know what this new camp will be like. I'm hoping to learn how to drive.'

Maud looked at her daughter. She was a lovely girl and she knew it wouldn't be long before somebody snapped her up.

'So how's Maggie?'

'Don't see much of her. She working for some bigwig up West. Something to do with the war effort, she said. It's all very hush-hush.'

'I wrote to her and told her I'd got some leave. I hope she comes to see us.'

'That would be wonderful,' said Maud. All her daughters could be together. She couldn't ask for more.

'Maggie said that Tom was in the army now.'

Everybody's life had been disrupted. But at least they were all still alive, thought Maud as she poured out another cup of tea for her daughters.

Chapter 23

RENE HAD A spring in her step as she walked to work. There hadn't been a raid last night, and she'd had a lovely weekend with her sisters. To see Betty and Maggie again and all laugh together had given her and their mother the lift they needed. Even Hazel looked happy. They were sad to see Betty go, but they hoped to be able to see more of her now she was stationed nearer to London.

On Saturday night the girls had gone to the pub and Rene introduced her sisters to Ted.

'My fire-watching mate,' she said, grinning.

'Come and sit with us, Ted. We want to know what our sister gets up to when she's out with you,' said Maggie.

'Not a lot, but I wish she would wear some decent

shoes,' he said when he sat down with them. 'She tries to scrabble over the debris in silly little things and then complains that she's laddered her stockings.'

'Now when do I get time to go and queue up for shoes?'

'I told her she should join up, then she'd get them issued,' said Betty.

'No thank you,' said Rene. 'Besides, who would make parachutes for your blokes?'

Ted grinned and gave Rene's knee a gentle pat. 'Your sister's not a bad 'un. She'll do her share, bless her.'

Betty and Maggie gave her a knowing look.

'I'm glad I don't have to go scrabbling over rubble,' said Maggie.

'Rene said you was working up West and it's all very hush-hush.'

Maggie looked all about her, then, moving closer, said, 'Shh. Remember, Ted, careless talk costs lives.'

'I can see your mother must have had a handful when all you beautiful young ladies were at home.'

They were all very happy as they walked home laughing and talking. Rene reflected on what a lovely few days they'd had. When would they all be together again? She hoped it wouldn't be too long.

Christmas came and everybody knew that things were going to be very sparse. Maud had done her best, and she and Hazel spent many hours queuing.

'Ain't we gonna have a tree?' said Peter a few days before.

'There ain't any,' said Hazel.

'But we always have a tree.'

'D'you know, you can be a right pain sometimes. If you wanna tree, go out and get one,' said Hazel. She was fed up with her brother always moaning about the things he wanted.

The following day Peter came in with a lot of dead twigs.

'What have you got there?' asked his gran.

'It's gonna be our Christmas tree.'

Hazel laughed.

'Don't laugh,' he said, looking cross. 'We've got some green crepe paper in that box.'

He pointed to the box of Christmas decorations that had been brought down from upstairs. They had already found some paper chains, and Gran had made some flour and water paste so that they could stick them together. The kitchen looked festive, but there was definitely something missing.

'And,' Peter continued, 'we can wind it round the twigs and that'll be our tree.'

Maud was surprised at the lad's inventiveness. 'That sounds like a good idea.'

'Thank you, Gran.'

Hazel grinned. 'Come on, let's get started and surprise Mum when she gets home.'

They spent the afternoon cutting strips of paper and carefully winding them round the branches. When they'd finished, they hung a few baubles on the tree and put it in Gran's aspidistra pot in the middle of the table.

'That looks really grand,' said Maud. 'Let's put the bits we've got hold of round the bottom.'

Hazel went and fetched the few things she'd managed to buy that were off rations. There was a tin of Zubes for her gran when she had one of her tickly coughs, and she had been very lucky, as when she was in the chemist buying her gran's present, they had brought out some hairbrushes. She was nearly trampled on as women pushed their way to the counter, but she knew her mum would like one of those. She had also bought her brother a bar of chocolate. How different this Christmas was going to be.

Gran had put her name down at the butcher's for a piece of beef, and they had gone without meat for a few weekends in order to save their rations.

Hazel looked round the room. It would be wonderful if Auntie Betty and Dad could be here, but she knew that wasn't to be.

There wasn't a raid on Christmas night and everybody felt happy, but what would 1941 bring?

On Sunday the twenty-ninth of December, Rene woke with a start. There was a raid on and she could hear bombs falling and the usual noise from the guns. The wardens and fire-watchers were blowing their whistles. There must be some fires nearby.

She peeped out of the shelter. To her horror, she could see that next door's upstairs curtains were alight. She quickly woke her mother. 'I'm just gonna help next door.' She put her coat on and rushed off.

Maud was disorientated. She looked out and said, 'Bloody hell.' Then she put on her own coat and started to follow her daughter.

'Mum, get inside,' said Rene, who was banging on the Fords' shelter door.

When Ron opened it, Maud could see Rene pointing to the upstairs window.

'Mum. Get inside. I'm gonna see if I can help.' Rene now had her fire-watcher's hat on. She rushed into the house with Ron following on behind.

Maud could hear whistles being blown. She sat back down and waited.

'Maud. Can I come in?' asked Hilda, coming from her shelter.

Maud flung open the door. 'Of course you can. Come in quick.'

'What's wrong, Gran?' asked Hazel.

'Your mum's just had to go next door.'

'Why is Auntie Hilda in here?' asked Peter.

'I didn't want to be in the shelter on me own. Ron's had to go out.'

'Now put your earplugs in and go back to sleep,' said Maud.

'I don't like it when Mum's out in a raid,' said Hazel.

'She'll be all right. Ron's with her,' said Hilda.

Rene went carefully up the stairs carrying the bucket of sand that everybody kept at the bottom ready just in case. They could hear fizzing and crackling from above and could see under the door that it looked as though the back bedroom was well and truly alight.

'Be careful, love,' shouted Ron. 'It might be one of the explosive ones.'

Hitler was now sending over explosive incendiary bombs, which had injured many firefighters.

'Go and see if you can find someone with a stirrup pump,' yelled Rene, taking charge of the situation.

While Ron hurried out, Rene got down on the floor and pushed open the bedroom door with her foot, as she had been taught to do. Hot air rushed out. She could see the bomb; it looked like a giant firework sitting on a chair. She made her way as close as she could safely get and threw the sand over it, causing it to splutter and die. But the chair was still alight, along with the curtains and the lino. Very carefully she backed away; she knew she had to get out of there before the floor gave way. She peered down the stairs, hoping to see someone with a stirrup pump, just as Wally and Ron came bursting through the front door.

215

'All right, Rene?' yelled Wally. 'Come on down, we've got the pump here.'

Rene hurried down the stairs. 'I've put the bomb out, but the room's well alight.'

'Right,' said Wally. 'Give us a hand with this.' He handed Rene the pump and took a bucket of water upstairs. 'Ron, go and get some more water.' With Rene doing the pumping, he gradually ventured into the room and put out the fire.

'Thanks, Rene,' he said, wiping his face. 'That was good thinking.'

'It's only what you taught us. And it was a good job that Ron managed to keep the water coming.'

It was only then that Rene stopped and looked at the sky. It was red. There were fires everywhere, and mingled with the guns and bombs the sound of bells from fire engines and ambulances was all around them.

Ron was full of praise for his neighbour, and Rene was the talk of the dairy the next morning.

'Look at the state of her hands,' said Maud, grabbing her daughter's hands and showing everybody.

'Leave it out, Mum.'

'You need some Germolene on them,' said Mrs James. 'Have you got any?'

'Yes thanks.' Rene was embarrassed at all the fuss.

The papers were full of the night's events; they were

comparing them to the Great Fire of London. The picture of St Paul's Cathedral standing alone and unscathed seemed to be a symbol of the city's defiance.

Rene and many others were helping Ron to clear up the mess. 'Hilda ain't that happy about all the water dripping through the kitchen ceiling. Still, I told her, when this lot's all over I'll do a bit of decorating, but I ain't gonna bother just yet,' he said.

Rene smiled. 'I think you might have a bit of a job getting hold of paint and wallpaper.'

Ron grinned. 'That's another reason.'

'Ain't you going to work today?' asked her mother when she took some cloths next door to help with the cleaning up.

'I'll go in this afternoon. Ernie knows that sometimes we have to stay at home and help our friends.'

'That's all right, then.'

When Rene finally got into work, she was worried because Joan wasn't in. One of the first things everybody did was ask about friends.

'You live near Joan,' she said to Ada. 'Is everything all right in her road?'

'Can't tell yer. I've been away.'

Rene knew that when she finished work that day, she would have to go and call on her friend.

Chapter 24

THAT EVENING WHEN Rene finished work, she went to see Joan. She was happy to find that she and her family were well. It seemed that Sam had a rash and Joan had taken him to the doctor's, but the doctor was out attending some of the wounded and it was a while before she was told it was nothing to worry about.

'I thought about your Peter when he had scarlet fever and that worried me,' she said. 'So I decided to stay at home with him, just for the day.'

'I don't think Ernie will be that annoyed. He's lucky to get us in at all after some of the nights we've had.'

Joan smiled. 'That's true.'

Although the raids continued, people were beginning to get used to them and lived their lives round them. It was only when they heard of someone they knew, no matter how casually, being injured or killed that the reality of how awful this war was hit home.

It was like that the morning Rene went to work and saw that the row of terraced houses where the man and his wife who didn't like rats lived, and with whom she often passed the time of day, was now just a pile of rubble. The policeman said they had both been killed. She was upset about that all morning. What had these people done? Why was it the ordinary folk who were suffering? But as Ernie told her, they were all in this together.

Maud was beginning to look very tired. She blamed it on all the queuing, but Rene knew that the broken nights were beginning to take their toll.

'Thank goodness for Hazel. She's a good kid and stands for ages not knowing what she's waiting for.'

Rene was pleased to get a letter from Betty telling her that she was now learning to drive.

'What she wanna learn to drive for? She can't afford a car.'

'No, but she reckons she might be able to get a driving job when this is all over.'

'I don't know what's wrong with you girls today. Seems you can't wait to do the men's jobs.'

Rene didn't pursue this conversation any further; she knew her mother still wanted her daughters to be her little girls.

A few weeks later, as they were getting ready to go to the shelter, Rene said to her mother, 'Mum, I'm thinking of going down to see Betty. In her last letter she said that she's getting out and about and that Redhill's a smashing place. It might be nice to go and live there.'

'What? I ain't moving from here. Been here all me married life and all you girls were born here.'

'I know, but we'd be safer there.'

'You can go, but you won't get me moving.'

'Now you know I won't be going anywhere without you.'

'Well that's settled, then. I'll fill the flasks.'

At the beginning of February, Rene was having her piece of toast when she heard the postman drop something through the letter box.

'I'll go,' said Hazel. 'It might be a birthday card for me.'

'It's a miracle to me that any post manages to get through. I reckon those posties deserve a medal, looking for an address with half the road missing,' said Maud as she poured out the tea.

'Well Mr Churchill tells us we must keep going,' said Rene.

'Mum, Mum!' yelled Hazel as she burst into the kitchen. 'It's from Dad.'

Rene dropped her cup with a clatter and stared at the card Hazel handed her.

'Well,' said Maud. 'What does he say?'

'It's only a card, and he says he's well and we're not to worry about him.'

'Does he say where he is?' asked Peter, wide-eyed.

'No.'

'Can you write to him?' asked Maud.

'The Red Cross have put a London address on it so I can write there. I've been told they can send letters on.'

Rene sat staring at the card. She couldn't believe that she had at last heard from John. Tears ran down her face. It was very emotional. She walked away from the table and went into the front room and sat on the bed and cried. When would she see him again?

A light tap on the door made her wipe her eyes.

'Can I come in, Mum?' asked Hazel as she poked her head round the door.

'Of course, love. Come and sit with me for a little while.' Rene put her arm round her daughter and held her close.

'Mum. That card you've got. I reckon it's the best card I'll ever have on my birthday.'

Rene couldn't speak. It was as though John had deliberately waited to send this card. 'I think so too.'

On February the twenty-fourth, Hazel turned twelve. Rene held her daughter tight. 'I'm so sorry I couldn't find much for your birthday.'

221

'That's all right, Mum. I love my blouse.' She held up the white blouse her mother had made her out of parachute cut-offs. 'It's really lovely. When this war's over, we can have a party and I'll be able to wear it then and show Dad.'

Rene fought back a tear. Hazel was growing into a lovely girl, and she had the nature to go with her good looks. She helped her gran so much. She would wait in queues for anything the shops had in, and she'd go to the coal yard with Peter for coal. So much had happened in her short life.

Although there were still raids, they were managing to get a full night's sleep now and again. Rene was worried that her children's education could be suffering, and she was pleased when the government announced that some schools could soon be open and the children would have a half-day's classes. At least now they would be occupied for part of the day. And Hazel was right. When this wretched war was over, John would be home and they would have a party that would go on for days.

'So what was school like?' asked Rene when she got home from work.

'Not bad,' said Hazel. 'The teacher's a bit old.'

'Still, it's nice to have something to do in the mornings.'

'Suppose so. Trouble is, we're all in together. I'm

not as clever as some in my class, and then there's others that are a bit dim.'

'I'm sure the teacher will sort it out soon.'

'We had to have air-raid drill this morning. It's dark and smelly in the shelter, and if you wanna go to the lav there's a bucket behind a curtain. I don't wanna go in that.'

Rene grinned. 'It's got to be better than sitting in wet knickers.'

Hazel went to school in the mornings and Peter in the afternoons.

'And how was your first day?' Rene asked Peter.

'All right. I'm glad me mate Billy's in the same class as me.'

'Now don't you two muck about. You're there to learn.'

'Billy said there ain't a lot of use us learning, we might all be blown ter bits next week.'

'Peter, that's a dreadful thing to say,' said his gran.

'It wasn't me, it was Billy.'

Was this how the children were beginning to look at life?

They had the occasional daylight raid, and Maud worried when it happened while the children were at school.

Hazel said it was hard to do writing in the shelter, as it was dingy, with not much light. 'We've only got a

223

couple of hurricane lamps. So most of the time we have to say our tables.'

'Well at least you'll be able to add up quick,' said Maud, trying to make light of it. 'What about you, young man?' she asked Peter.

'We make paper aeroplanes and chuck 'em at each other.'

'Very grown up, I'm sure,' said Hazel.

'Mum, I'm gonna write and ask Betty if me and the kids can go and see her at Easter.'

'What? Will she be able to see you?'

'I don't know. I'm gonna ask her if she's allowed some time off.'

Maud looked unhappy. 'You will come back?'

'Course we will. Would you like to come with us?'

'No. I can't be doing with traipsing round and about on trains.'

'You might like it down there.'

'Is that why you're going there? To see what it's like?'

'No,' said Rene, but she knew that was a lie. She really did want to take the children away from London, and Betty had painted a very nice picture of Redhill. 'Anyway, she might not be able to get time off.'

A few days later, Rene was pleased to get a letter from Betty telling her that she could get that Sunday off, and if Rene would like to come down during the day, she could see what Redhill was like for herself.

Rene said casually, 'Betty said we can go and see her Easter Sunday. Why don't you come with us, Mum?'

'Oh please, Gran,' said Hazel.

Rene had already told the children what she hoped to do.

'Can we go and see that room Auntie Betty was telling us about?' asked Peter. 'You know, the one with all the wooden planes she pushes about on a big map.'

'No, we can't, and you mustn't tell anyone what Auntie Betty told you. She could be had up for being a spy.'

'She ain't a spy,' Peter said.

'We know that, but if you start talking about what she does, someone might overhear you. Anyway I think she is doing more driving now.'

Peter had a big grin on his face. This war was the most exciting thing that had happened in his life, although it was a bit scary at times.

'So what about it, Mum?' Rene said.

'I told you before, I ain't going nowhere,' said Maud.

'But what if there's a big raid that night and we can't get back? I'll be worried sick about you.'

Maud didn't answer.

'Mum, I promise not to move down there.'

'That's what you say now. What if yer sees a nice house with a cheap rent?'

Rene knew she couldn't answer her mother.

'You wanna think about John. How will he feel when he gets home and finds you've upped sticks and left?'

'I'm only going to go and see Betty.'

'Please, Gran,' said Hazel. 'Don't you want to see Auntie Betty?'

'I can wait fer her to get some leave and come here.'

Chapter 25

IT TOOK A while for Rene and the children to get to Redhill. The trains were full of service personnel with kit bags and luggage, and it was very crowded. At one station they had to leave the train and get a bus; someone told the bewildered passengers that the track had been bombed the night before.

They finally arrived at lunchtime. Betty had told them where to go, and when they told the RAF sentry behind the locked gate who they were, he asked them to wait while he contacted her.

After a while, Rene could see her sister running across the tarmac. When she got through the gate, she ran into Rene's arms.

'It's so good to see you all,' she said, bending down

and kissing first Hazel then Peter, who looked a little bit embarrassed when the man at the gate grinned at him.

'I can get out for a while, so we can go and find somewhere to eat. I expect you two are starving.'

Peter nodded.

'We've eaten the fish paste sandwiches I made. Is there anywhere open?' asked Rene.

'I know a couple of places.'

The four of them made their way to a teahouse. On the way, Peter was fascinated to see his aunt salute a man who passed them.

'This is such a pretty place,' said Betty when they were settled and had ordered. 'I was hoping Mum would come with you.'

'She's dead against it. She thinks I'm coming down here just to find somewhere to live.'

'I'll stay with Gran if you move here,' said Peter. 'I don't like the country. We lived there once.'

'Yes, but that was when we were on our own,' said Hazel. 'Do you get many bombs here?'

'Not as many as you. And we sleep in a bed.'

'I'd love to sleep in a bed again,' said Rene.

'Mum said you can drive a car now,' said Peter, desperately wanting to take the subject away from moving.

'Yes. It's great to get out and about.'

'I thought you liked the job you had before,' said Rene.

'I did, but we have to have a break now and again as it can get very stressful, and I was pleased to have the opportunity to learn to drive. You never know, it might come in useful after this is all over.'

'Whose car do you drive?' asked Peter.

'It belongs to the camp. Sometimes I have to collect pilots from different places and bring them here.'

'I'd like to do that,' said Peter.

When they had finished their tea and sandwich, they went for a walk.

'This is certainly a nice place,' said Rene, looking around. 'And look at all those lovely daffs. I could live somewhere like this.'

'I love it,' said Betty. 'It's so clean after London.'

Hazel looked at her brother, who was scowling. She knew he would never move away from his friends.

All too soon it was time for them to go.

'I think we'd better be making a move,' said Rene.

'I wish I could stay here with you, Auntie Betty,' said Hazel.

Betty held her close. 'I wish you could as well.'

Betty walked with them back to the station.

'When are we likely to see you again?' Rene asked her sister.

'I don't know. Soon, I hope.'

As the train chugged and puffed its way into the

station, they hugged and kissed and said their good-byes, then they were off. Betty stood waving till the train was out of sight, then she turned and made her way back to the camp. She was wondering if she would ever see them all again.

Betty was very happy with her new job. Sometimes she drove officers around when they had to go to meetings, and other times she went to various airfields to collect pilots who were being moved about. She also had to collect the young ones who had just got their wings and had never been with a squadron before.

As she walked back to the camp, she thought about the day she had picked up three young lads. To her they had seemed barely out of school. Usually they were full of confidence, but one of the lads was very down. Betty tried to reassure them that this was a good camp to be at and the boys here were great.

'That makes you sound old,' said one of the lads.

'I am compared with you.'

'Not many of us will see old age,' said another of them, who had been staring out of the window.

'Don't talk like that. It don't help morale,' said Betty.

'Take no notice of him,' said the first boy. 'We call him Jonah. He can be a right misery at times.'

'And I thought all you new lads would be full of energy and raring to have a go at the Germans.'

'We are.'

Betty worried about that lad for a while, but after a few sorties and some time in the mess with the other pilots, he soon became one of the boys.

'Is there any entertainment round here?' the third one had asked.

'There's dances at the local church hall.'

'Do you go with anyone in particular?'

'I go with my friend Josie.'

'Is she as good-looking as you? By the way, my name is Dan.'

'Pleased to meet you, Dan. I'm Betty.' She ignored the remark about being good-looking. She was getting used to the flattery and the wolf whistles.

When she arrived back at camp, Betty walked into the billet she shared with Josie. She was good company.

'So, did you see your sister?' Josie asked.

'Yes.'

'How are they?'

'They seem to be all right. Hazel, that's my niece, said she'd like to live here, but me mum won't leave London and Rene won't come without Mum.' Betty sat on her bed. 'I do worry about them being bombed nearly every night.'

'Perhaps Jerry will give up soon. After all, they are losing a lot of planes.'

'I wish that would happen.'

'I heard there's some new pilots coming here soon.'

'We've always got new pilots.'

'Ah, but this lot are Canadians.'

'That could be very interesting.'

'Betty Stevens, you've got a naughty look in your eye.'

Betty laughed. 'Just as long as it's only a naughty look.' She had been hoping to find romance when she joined up, but so far it hadn't happened. She'd had plenty of opportunities to spend the night with some of the boys, but most of them were a lot younger than her and were only living for the moment, and although Betty knew it was hopeless in today's situation, she wanted true love and a long-term commitment.

She thought about her sisters and how they were both happily married. John was her favourite brother-in-law. She always wished he had seen her first. She would have loved to be married to him and have children like Hazel and Peter, but she had always kept her feelings to herself. Her mother would go mad if she knew that she secretly carried a torch for John. She wondered what he would be like when this was all over and he was back here. Would he have changed? What would any of them be like when this was all over? She sighed.

'You all right?' asked Josie.

'Yes thanks, just thinking about what might be in store for us.'

'Now come on, don't get gloomy. Things might get a lot better soon.'

'For us, maybe, but not for my family.'

'Come on. Let's go along to the mess and have a couple of drinks. That'll help cheer you up.'

Betty smiled. 'If you say so.'

'So how was Betty?' asked Maud when they got back.

'She looked fine.' Rene was busy laying the table.

'Has she found you a house?'

'No. Is that why you think I went down there?'

'Well didn't you?'

Rene could see that her mother wasn't very happy. 'I told you I won't go anywhere without you.'

Hazel looked at her gran. Why wouldn't she move away?

Maud could see Hazel looking at her and she asked, 'What about you kids, did you like it down there?'

'I did.'

'Well I didn't. I don't like the country,' said Peter.

Rene just remained quiet. She didn't see the point of causing an argument.

When Rene got to work the next morning, she was telling Joan about her trip to Redhill.

'I've got an aunt who lives in Surrey,' Joan said.

'Do you go and see her?'

'Not that often now. But we still keep in touch. When we was kids, me mum used to take us. She wanted us to move to a new estate they was building, but me dad wouldn't go and leave his mum. But like history repeating itself with Fred's mum not wanting me to go away.'

'What is it about these women?'

'Dunno. I guess they don't like leaving their friends and familiar surroundings.'

'Could be.' Rene thought about the daffodils and wondered if she would ever have a garden. 'Would you like to go and see your aunt again?'

'I wouldn't mind, but with a couple of kids it could get a bit difficult. Besides, Fred's mum would think I was going to leave her.'

Rene continued machining, but her mind was on other things.

Chapter 26

Aᴅᴛᴇʀ ᴀ ʙɪɢ raid in May, the night-time raids were beginning to be very intermittent, and people were taking a chance and sleeping in their proper beds. It was Peter's ninth birthday in June, and when Rene looked at him, she felt so proud and sad. He had witnessed so much in his life. He was beginning to look a lot like John and even had some of his ways. She wished John was here to help her and see how their son was changing. Despite the food shortages, Peter was getting taller, and now that clothes were on ration, that was proving another problem. Maud went to jumble sales to see what she could find, but as most people were in the same situation, there wasn't a lot of decent stuff for sale. Rene did start looking at some of John's clothes and knew that soon she would have to

235

do some alterations. When the children broke up for the summer holiday, Peter was more than happy to be street-raking with his best friend Billy and didn't worry about what he wore.

Rene was still worried about the daylight raids and had tried to drum it into Peter that he had to go home as soon as the air-raid warning sounded. Often when Hazel and her gran were out shopping they would head for the nearest shelter. Maud always complained that the public shelters smelt like a lavatory.

'I dunno how people can spend the night in 'em.'

'If they ain't got anywhere else to go I suppose it's the lesser of two evils: stay at home and hope you don't get killed or injured, or go to a smelly shelter,' said Rene.

'S'pose you're right. Good job we've got our own shelter.'

Rene grinned. She could remember the fuss her mother had made about it when it was being built.

Rene and the rest of the girls at the factory were now working in the basement, so they knew they were safe. So many times since she had been to see Betty, she wished she was away from all this damage and death.

It was a Friday evening when Betty came home on a twenty-four-hour pass. As soon as she walked in, Rene noticed a change in her sister.

'You look happy,' she said as she held Betty close.

'I am.' She smiled.

When they were alone in the scullery doing the washing-up, Rene asked, 'So who is he?'

'Now how did you guess?'

'The grin on your face for one thing. Well?'

'His name's Luke and he comes from Toronto.'

'Toronto in Canada?'

Betty nodded.

'And I suppose he's tall, dark and handsome?'

'Well he's tall and I think he's handsome, but his hair is more of a mousy colour than dark, and he has the loveliest hazel eyes I've ever seen.'

Rene laughed. 'So when are we likely to meet this good-looking hunk who has stolen my sister's heart?'

'When we can both get a pass together.'

'And you do like him?'

'This sounds like an interrogation, but yes, I do.'

'I'm so happy for you,' said Rene as she hugged Betty again.

'Get off. Your hands are all wet.'

'When you telling Mum?'

'Dunno.'

'You know what she's gonna say?'

'Don't remind me. I can remember when I brought that Tom home; she nearly went mad.'

'Yes, but you were only fifteen at the time.'

'I know.'

Later that evening, as the siren went, they made themselves comfortable in the shelter. Rene was on fire-watching duty, so Betty could have her share of the mattress.

'Can't you have a night off?' asked Betty.

'No. Duty calls.'

'Well, be safe.'

'I've still got Ted with me, remember.'

As Rene and Ted walked the streets, she told him about Betty's news.

'She's a pretty little thing. I'm surprised she hasn't found love before,' Ted said.

'I'm worried that if she likes this Luke enough to marry him, she could be off to Canada.'

'I'm afraid you won't be able to stop that,' said Ted.

'Mum won't be very pleased about it.'

'This war's splitting lots of families.'

'I know that.'

'Sorry, love. I forgot about your John.'

'That's all right. Now, about these clothing coupons.' Rene quickly changed the subject; she didn't like to talk about John, as it upset her. His cards were so few and far between. 'If you've got any to spare, think of me.'

'I might be able to sell 'em on the black market.'

'Why, you spiv. I'll report you to the police,' laughed Rene.

They continued walking along and chatting. Rene liked Ted; he was so easy to talk to.

One day near the end of July, Rene got home from work and as usual called out, 'Coo-ee. I'm home.'

'We're in here,' called her mother from the front room.

Rene was puzzled. Why was Maud in their bedroom? Was she feeling unwell? Was it the children? She quickly opened the bedroom door and found Hazel and her mother trying to console Peter, who was clinging to his gran sobbing uncontrollably. His face was deathly white and he was crying like Rene had never seen before.

'What's happened?' she asked her mother, totally bewildered, as she sat next to her son and held him close.

'Hazel, take yer mum in the kitchen,' said Maud, 'and tell her what's happened.'

In the kitchen Hazel wiped her red eyes. She too had been crying.

'What is it? What's wrong?'

'It's Billy Walker. Mum, it's horrible and it could have been our Peter.'

Rene got hold of Hazel and said forcefully, 'Tell me what's happened.'

Hazel sobbed. 'Billy Walker was machine-gunned this afternoon.'

Rene plonked herself in a chair. 'What? Is he badly injured?'

Hazel gave a sob. 'Mum, he's dead.'

Rene put her hand to her mouth. 'Oh my God. And our Peter was with him?'

Hazel nodded. 'They was out playing.'

'What happened?'

'They was playing on a bomb site when this plane just came from out of the sky and—'

'How many times have I told him to get in the shelter when the siren goes?'

'There wasn't a siren. There wasn't an air raid. The warden said it was just a lone plane that got here.'

'Is Peter all right? He's not injured at all?'

'No, it seems he was round behind a pile of bricks having a wee. Mum, it could have been him as well.' Hazel began crying again.

Rene held her close. 'Come on, let's go and sit with Peter.'

As they moved towards the bedroom, Rene couldn't stop thinking that she had to get the children away from all this.

Peter looked up when his mother walked in and she held him close. He wiped his nose on his sleeve. 'Mum, I'm so sorry.' He gave a deep heartfelt sob.

'Shh, don't worry about it.'

'You should have seen the way Billy was spun round when the bullets hit him. It was horrible. There was blood all over him. His pullover was covered.'

Rene let a tear fall. She knew this was going to scar her son for the rest of his life. But it could have been him. She looked up at her mother.

Maud walked away; she knew what her daughter was thinking. She would say it was her fault for not wanting to move away.

July had brought coal rationing, but everybody was happy in the warm sunshine and the extra hour of daylight that double British Summer Time had given them.

One afternoon Maud was sitting outside by her front door when Hilda came back from the shop. Seeing her friend deep in thought, she brought out a chair of her own and sat next to her.

'What's bothering you?' she asked.

'What you talking about?' said Maud.

'You've had a face as long as a fiddle fer days. Come on, out with it.'

'It's young Peter. He's so sad.'

'Well, what d'yer expect? Poor little bugger must 'ave been scared out of his life.'

'All he does is sit indoors and read.'

'Is that such a bad thing?'

'Not in some ways. At least I know where he is. But it's not good for him. He should be out with the other kids.'

'He lost his best mate.'

'I know,' said Maud. 'I sometimes wish they was still evacuated.'

'They wouldn't like that.'

'I know, and I know that Rene wants to move away.'

'But you don't.'

'No. D'you think I'm being selfish?'

'Wouldn't like to say.'

'Why's that? You always say what you think.'

'Well it's up to you.'

'I know. But she won't go without me.'

'You could go and stay with Maggie.'

'Don't see a lot of her. She's been moved to some special place in the country. It's all very hush-hush.'

Hilda sat back and let the sun warm her wrinkled face. 'What you got to stay here for?'

'Dunno. Me friends, I suppose.'

'Well me and Ron ain't gonna be here for ever.'

'Why? Where you going?'

'One day we'll be going to that great place in the sky.'

Maud laughed. 'And what makes you think you're going up there?'

'Wishful thinking, I suppose.'

Maud smiled at her. How could she leave her friends and her home? But what about her family?

Chapter 27

RENE WAS VERY worried about Peter. He seemed to have gone into a shell. Billy's death was having a profound effect on him. The screams and shouting at night were horrible, and despite the cold weather he would wake from his nightmare bathed in sweat. Rene knew he was a sensitive boy, and she would hold him close and whisper to him that he was safe, hoping to calm him down. All the time she wondered when these nightmares would eventually cease.

One Saturday afternoon there had been a raid. Peter was outside with Hazel, and as soon as he heard the siren he rushed into the shelter. Rene could see he was visibly shaking and his face was ashen.

She put her arms round him. 'It's all right. You're safe in here with us.'

'I'm frightened, Mum.'

'Of course you are, but I won't let anything happen to you.'

'Mum, I'm worried sick about him,' said Rene after the raid was over. 'What can I do?'

'I don't know, love. Would you like me to take him to the doctor?'

'What can a doctor do?'

'Give him something to make him sleep.'

Rene was getting agitated. 'Mum, if we could get away from all this . . .'

'Don't start on that again.'

'Why are you so against moving?'

Maud walked away.

'That's it, ignore the problem. If that had been Peter and not Billy, I would have said it was your fault. If John was here—'

'Well he's not, and you've got to make your own decisions and that don't include me.'

'It should.'

'Why?'

''Cos I'm the one who's living here,' shouted Rene.

Maud looked at her daughter with shock. 'Is that what you think? That you've got to look after me?'

'I didn't mean that.'

'Well that's what it sounded like.'

Rene sat at the table. 'I'm sorry, Mum.' She wiped

her eyes. She had never shouted at her mother before. 'I'm so worried about them, and I'm at my wits' end. Hazel and Peter said they wouldn't go away again without me. What can I do?'

Maud didn't answer.

The following week Rene heard from her sister, and that always made her happy. She read that Betty and Luke would be getting a pass for the first weekend in December. She hoped that seeing his aunt's Canadian boyfriend would help Peter. It might be good for him to talk to a man.

Maud wasn't very happy at the thought of another mouth to feed.

'They'll have their ration cards,' said Rene.

'I know that, but it'll still be hard. Things are getting worse, you know. Now they've taken the blinking gate and railings away.'

'I know,' said Rene. She remembered the day she'd come home from work and found the metal gate and the railings that ran all along the top of the walls gone. The government was crying out for scrap metal to help make Spitfires. 'I'm looking forward to meeting this bloke, and we'd better nice to him. He could end up being your son-in-law.'

'Don't say that. She wouldn't, would she?'

Rene shrugged. 'Who knows?'

'I don't want her to go to Canada.'

But Rene was thinking that he was a pilot and that anything could happen to him.

At last the big day came and everybody was ready to greet this newcomer.

'Mum, this is Luke.'

He gave Maud a beaming smile as he shook her hand, and Rene could see that her mother was taken with this tall, clean-cut, good-looking young man, who was just as Betty had described him.

Betty gave Peter a cuddle. 'And this is Peter.'

'Hello, young man. I've heard all about you. We'll have to have a chat sometime.'

Rene knew that Betty had told him about Billy, and she was hoping that as Peter didn't have his dad around, perhaps Luke might be able to help to heal the hurt her son was feeling.

As the day wore on, Rene could see what her sister liked about Luke. He was polite and funny, and Peter sat close to him listening to every word when he was talking about Canada or flying.

'You should see the maple trees in the fall. The leaves go a bright red colour.'

'Do they fall off?' asked Hazel, who was also entranced with this young man.

'Yes, that's why we call it the fall.'

He told them about Niagara Falls and how beautiful his country was. 'But we don't have the history and wonderful buildings that you have.'

'But how many will be left standing when this war's all over?' said Maud.

'A lot, I hope.'

While the sisters were in the kitchen preparing to get ready for the shelter, Rene asked Betty, 'Will he come in with us?'

'No. We did discuss this and he said he would rather sleep in the kitchen, that's if it's all right with Mum. Rene, do you like him?'

Rene held her sister close. 'I think he's wonderful.'

'So do I.'

'And I think Peter's taken with him. He's certainly been a lot more talkative.'

Betty stopped filling the flask. 'That must have been terrible for him, seeing his best friend killed like that.'

'Has he told Luke about it?'

Betty nodded.

'And?'

'Luke told him that he understood, as one of his mates, a navigator, had been killed. Peter asked him if he'd ever machine-gunned kids playing.'

'And?' said Rene again.

'He said he would never do a thing like that even if they were the enemy.'

Just then Peter came into the kitchen. 'Mum, can I sleep in here with Luke?'

Rene looked at her sister. 'I'd rather you didn't.'

'Why?'

'Well I think Luke might want to get a decent night's sleep, and if you keep asking questions all night he won't be able to.'

'He said he don't mind.'

'What about your nightmares?'

Peter looked down. 'I'll try not to think about Billy.'

'I tell you what,' said Betty, grinning. 'What if I sleep in here with you both? That way I can tell you to shut up and give you a poke when you start shouting.'

'Auntie Betty, that'd be great. So can I, Mum?'

Rene raised her eyebrow at her sister. 'I think that'll be all right, that's if you don't mind, Bet.'

When Peter rushed off to tell Luke, Rene said, 'Did you put him up to that?'

'No. But if I'd wanted to stay in here alone with Luke, I don't think Mum would have approved.'

'I'm pretty sure she wouldn't. But with Peter in with you, you'll have to behave yourself.'

'He'll go to sleep at some time.'

'I'm really shocked at my little sister,' Rene said, fanning her face with her hand. 'I would never have thought . . .'

'Come off it, Rene. I can remember before you was married when Mum had gone to Maggie's for the day and John was here and you sent me out to get some shopping.'

'We was engaged.'

'I know, but you tied the string of the front door key round the door handle so you wouldn't be disturbed and I couldn't get in. And when you finally opened the door, you both looked very flushed and ruffled.'

Rene smiled. 'Happy days.'

'I did wonder at what Mum would have said if she'd found your knickers behind the cushion.'

Rene laughed. 'Keep quiet or you could end up sleeping down in the underground. I often wonder how the couples get on down there. You know.'

'Where there's a will there's a way.'

Maud came into the kitchen. 'Is that right, that you and Peter will sleep in the kitchen with Luke?'

'Yes, Mum. Don't worry, we'll behave ourselves.'

'I should hope so.'

After a lovely few days together, it was time for Betty and Luke to leave. Peter threw his arms round Luke's waist. 'You will come and see us again, won't you?'

'If I can get a pass I will.'

Rene held Luke close and said softly, 'Thank you.'

'It was my pleasure, he's a grand kid.'

Hazel looked a bit down at the remark, but Luke added, 'And may I say, young lady, that if your aunt here hadn't stolen my heart, I'm sure you would have.'

Maud looked at her granddaughter. When she smiled, she certainly had a glow about her.

The house seemed very quiet after they left.

'Well, what do you think of him, Mum?' asked Rene.

'He seems a nice polite lad.'

'I think Bet's really taken with him.'

'Time will tell,' Maud said as she made her way into the scullery. 'Time will tell.'

Rene was thinking about the dangerous times they lived in. Would her sister ever have the joy of a loving husband and children?

Later on, Rene and her mother were listening to the wireless when they were told that the Japanese had bombed Pearl Harbor and that America was now in the war.

'Where's Pearl Harbor, Mum?' asked Peter, looking up from his book.

'I don't know. In America somewhere.'

'Is it anywhere near where Luke lives?'

'I don't think so. He lives in Canada. Go and get your atlas.'

'Well that's a turn-up for the book,' said Maud.

'Now the Yanks are in with us, let's hope it'll bring this war to a close soon and our prisoners will be back home.'

Maud patted her daughter's knee. She was proud of Rene. She had been very brave and had tried to keep her feelings to herself. Maud was still upset at Rene's outburst, but she didn't want to leave her home. 'I hope so, love,' she said quietly.

That night Rene was on fire-watching duty, and as they walked the streets, she and Ted talked of the weekend and the latest news from Pearl Harbor.

'Never thought that the Yanks would join in,' said Ted. 'They didn't want ter know till it hit them.'

'I just hope that now they are involved, it'll help to bring this lot to an end.'

'That's all we can do, love, is hope.'

Chapter 28

THIS WAS THE third wartime Christmas they had celebrated, not that there was much to celebrate. With so many shortages things were getting harder, and 1942 didn't hold out many promises.

In February Hazel was thirteen and growing into a lovely-looking girl. How Rene would have loved to have John here to share the joy of seeing their children grow. She couldn't believe that next year Hazel would be going out to work. Although she was a bright girl, her education was suffering, and Rene worried that she might finish up in a factory. When she related her fears to her mother, Maud's reply was: 'Wait and see what happens. A lot can change in a year.'

Peter turned ten in June, and Rene was also worried about her son's lack of education. Since the death of his friend he appeared to be happy to stay at home and not play in the street. He also seemed to enjoy the letters and books Luke sent him about Canada and planes.

Betty's letters were full of Luke and how much he had enjoyed visiting them.

'I'm gonna go to Canada when I grow up,' said Peter, looking up from the book he was reading.

They were sitting listening to the wireless.

Hazel laughed. 'What, you? You didn't like being away from home, remember.'

'I'm talking about when I grow up. You can come with me if you like.'

'Thanks.'

'What about me?' said Rene.

'You'll have Dad and he won't wanna go away.'

'That's probably true,' said Rene wistfully. Would he want to move away?

'Shh,' said Maud. 'I'm trying to listen to the wireless.'

'You know how much your gran likes *It's That Man Again*.'

Hazel and Peter grinned.

It was the end of August. It had been a long, hot summer, and Betty was home again for the weekend.

After the usual hugs and laughter, she sat down at the table and announced that she and Luke were getting married at the end of the following month.

'What?' said her mother. 'That's a bit quick. Do his parents know?'

'Yes, Mum, and I've got a letter from them to you.'

Rene looked at her little sister. 'It's all set then? I'm so very happy for you.' She rushed over to Betty and hugged her.

Betty nodded and smiled.

'And we're the last to know,' said Maud.

'We are both over twenty-one.'

'I know that, don't I. But his parents knew before me.'

'We didn't know how long it would take for the letter to reach them, and I waited till I got a weekend pass as I wanted to tell you in person, not in a letter.'

Maud got up. 'I'll go and make the tea.'

'Oh dear,' said Betty. 'Looks like I've upset Mum.'

'She was like this when both me and Maggie told her we were gonna get married, remember?'

Betty nodded.

'So what date is this big affair?'

'We've got seven days' leave starting September the eighteenth, so we thought we'd get married on the Saturday, the nineteenth. That way you'll all be able to come down to Redhill.'

'What? Mum won't be very pleased about that.'

'I did suggest to Luke that we come here, but he said that with all the bombed buildings, he would rather be married in the country. There's a really pretty church near the camp.'

'I can't blame him for that. But what about all the friends and neighbours?'

'Most of my friends have been called up, and who do we really know who's still around?'

'That's true. Did you want to borrow my wedding dress?'

'No. We've decided to get married in uniform.'

'Oh. Will you regret that in years to come?'

'Rene, we're not stupid. Luke is a bomber pilot, and who knows what might happen. We want to make the most of our lives.'

'That's a bit of a pessimistic view.'

'I know. But it's the way they all think, that we have to live for today.'

Maud came back into the kitchen carrying the tray with the tea things. 'So when's this to be?'

'Like I said, it's next month, September the nineteenth.'

'What's the rush?'

'Luke didn't want to wait.'

'I see.' Maud put the tea strainer on a cup and began pouring.

'Mum, we're gonna get married in Redhill.'

'That'll be nice for you. Don't take too much sugar, we're a bit short at the moment,' she said, pushing the sugar bowl towards her daughters.

'You are going to come, aren't you?'

Rene held her breath. What was her mother about to say?

'I don't know if I can travel all that way.'

'It's not that far.' Betty looked sad. 'Please, Mum, for me.'

'I'll think about it.'

Betty was about to say something when she saw her sister looking at her and shaking her head. She started to drink her tea. Why was her mother being like this?

Rene also started drinking her tea. With her elbows on the table she began wondering about the situation. She was determined to settle it, but how?

'Good. I've always wanted to be a bridesmaid, and to wear a long frock,' said Hazel, smiling when she heard about the wedding plans.

'I'm really sorry, Hazel,' said Betty. 'But we thought we had better get married in uniform.'

'Why?'

'That way we don't have to worry too much about all the trimmings.'

'Will you have a cake?' asked Peter.

'We'll try and have some sort of cake.'

Rene was watching her mother all the while this conversation was going on. What was she thinking? 'If you like, I'll write and tell Maggie,' she offered.

'Thanks. Do you think she'll be able to come?'

'I don't know. Whatever job she's doing, it's very hush-hush.'

When the children had gone to bed Betty said, 'Rene, as I've not got anybody to give me away, will you do it?'

Rene flung her arms round her sister. 'I'd love to. And I shall feel very honoured.'

It wasn't till Betty went back to camp that Maud began to talk to Rene about the forthcoming marriage.

'Why's she marrying him?'

'She loves him.'

'But he's a foreigner.'

'He's Canadian and that's part of the British Empire.'

'And I suppose she'll be going off over there when this is all over. Then I'll never see her again.'

'Mum, let's cross that bridge if and when we come to it. You will come with us, won't you?'

'I suppose I'll have to. Why they couldn't get married here I don't know.'

'It's their choice. D'you think Hilda and Ron use all their clothing coupons?'

'Why?'

'I just thought I'd like to get me and Hazel new frocks.'

'Well I ain't splashing out on anything new.'

'Oh Mum. You can get a new hat, they ain't on coupons.'

* * *

When Maud told Hilda about the forthcoming marriage, her friend was tickled pink. 'And about time too, if you ask me. She's a good-looking girl and should have been snapped up years ago. I must say, her young man is very good-looking. They make a lovely pair. So where's the wedding? Round at St Mary's?'

'No. It's down in bloody Redhill.'

'Oh dear. Sounds like you don't approve.'

'Why she couldn't get married here I don't know. He wants ter get married in the country.'

'Well you can't blame them for that. The scenery ain't all that great here, what with dirty great bomb craters and rubble everywhere. Is she borrowing Rene's frock?'

'No. And that's another thing, she's getting married in uniform.'

'I take it that you're not happy about it.'

'Rene said I've got to go.'

'And I should think so as well. What yer gonna wear?'

'I ain't buying a new frock.'

'Come on, Maud. She's the last one and you've got to make a bit of a show. If you're short of coupons, me and Ron will let you have some.'

'Rene might want them to get her and Hazel new frocks.'

'Tell Rene to pop in when she's finished work and

I'll give her some. You ain't got a lot of time to get yourself something.'

'I know. Don't know why it's got ter be done in such a rush.'

'He's a pilot,' Hilda reminded her.

That evening Rene came back in from Hilda's full of smiles. 'She gave me her book and said I can use as many as I like.'

'That's what I mean about having good neighbours and friends. Wouldn't get that if you moved.'

Rene chose to ignore her mother's remark. 'Right, young lady,' she said to Hazel, 'we can go shopping Saturday afternoon and buy you a new frock, and I'll get Peter some new trousers and a shirt.'

'Can I have long trousers?'

'No. You're too young. Besides, they take too many coupons. What about you, Mum? D'you want to come with us to get a hat?'

'No. I'll pop out one afternoon. I can't be having all that traipsing round the shops.'

Rene was pleased that her mum was at least going to make some sort of an effort.

When they had a letter from Maggie saying that she would be going with them, Rene was overjoyed that they would all be together. If only their husbands were with them it would have been perfect.

* * *

On Saturday the nineteenth of September they made their way to Redhill. Betty was right, it was a pretty church. Rene was so proud as she walked down the aisle with her sister. Betty looked lovely and she carried a very small posy of flowers. When she handed them to her sister, it took all of Rene's self-control not to cry. Her baby sister was getting married. The look of love she gave Luke was something very special. The guard of honour as they left the church was made up of Luke's fellow Canadians and was very touching. Rene was pleased that someone from the camp was taking photos.

'At least we'll have something to look back on,' she said to Betty when they were in a nearby pub having a very simple lunch.

'Thank you for coming, Mrs Stevens,' said Luke to his new mother-in-law. 'I know that it upset you not to have the wedding where you live, but you must agree that this is such a pretty place.'

Maud really didn't want to agree with him.

'When this war's over, me and Betty would like to live here.'

'You wouldn't go back to Canada?'

'No. Of course I shall take Betty over to see my folks, but I love England.'

Rene looked over at her mother, deep in conversation with Luke, and saw her face light up with a smile. She turned to Betty and said, 'I don't know what your husband has just said to Mum, but whatever it was, it's made her happy.'

'He has that effect,' she said lovingly.

Rene looked at her children. Peter was wreathed in smiles as he talked to some of the pilots, and Hazel was looking very coquettish with some of Luke's friends. It suddenly dawned on her that her daughter's wedding could be the next the family would have. Please God, she said to herself. Let it be when this war is over and John is finally safely home.

Chapter 29

IT WAS ON the journey home that Maud told her daughters that Luke had said that he and Betty were going to live in England when the war was over.

'That's wonderful,' said Rene.

Maggie leaned her head back against the seat. 'I wonder where we will all finish up when this lot's over.'

'Is Tom still in North Africa?' asked Rene.

'As far as I know.'

'It's very hot there,' said Peter.

'Someone has been doing his geography,' said Maggie, sitting up. 'Do you like school?' she asked.

'It's all right. I don't like it when we have to go down the shelter. I'm ever so frightened when we have a raid. But Luke said that it's good to be frightened, as it makes you more alert.'

'Luke has certainly captured more than just our sister's heart,' said Maggie.

Rene smiled. Hopefully Luke had helped her son to accept his fear. 'Peter might be able to take some of his exams next year.'

'Does that mean you could go to a secondary?' asked Maggie.

'Dunno,' said Peter. 'I ain't that interested.'

'When I get a chance, I'll send you some of my old school books. That might help you get through your School Certificate.'

'Did you pass?'

'No.'

'But you've got a very important job.'

'Most of which I learnt at work. But things will be different when all the lads come home and want their jobs back.'

'Hazel didn't do her exam; she wasn't at a proper school when she was eleven,' said Rene. 'Besides, I don't know if I could afford to send her to the secondary school if she'd passed.'

'There is talk about making it free,' said Maggie.

'That'll be good.'

'I didn't want to stay at school anyway. I want to go out to work,' said Hazel.

'What do you want to do?' asked Maggie.

'Don't know yet. Might like to work in a shop.'

'There ain't a lot to sell at the moment.'

'I know that, Mum, but this war ain't gonna last for ever.'

Rene was pleased that her children had a positive attitude.

'You're quiet, Mum,' said Maggie. 'What's your opinion of your new son-in-law?'

'He seems a nice enough bloke. Just as long as he looks after Betty, that's all I'm concerned about.'

'And he wants to stay in England,' said Rene, grinning.

'And that'll be a good thing,' said Maud.

The train pulled into the station and once again they were back among the ruins.

Rene looked about her. If only she could persuade Maud to move away from London.

On Monday morning Rene was telling her friend Joan about the wedding. 'I wish she had borrowed my wedding dress, it all looked so stark with them in uniform.'

'At least they got married in a church.'

'I must admit it was a very beautiful old church, and you felt at peace sitting there. It was like being in another world.'

'You old romantic, but it does sound rather nice. If she wanted to get married in uniform, well that was up to her, but I know what you mean. Just as long as in years to come she don't look back on the photos and wish she'd dressed up. Did she like her wedding present?'

Rene grinned. 'I should say so. She'd been having a bit of a moan about not being able to get any nice undies.'

'Good job we can keep some of the offcuts.'

'I should say so.'

'What did your mother think of the country?'

'She didn't say, not that she would anyway.'

'So you couldn't convince her to move down there?'

'No.'

'I was going to suggest you go and visit my Aunt Polly. She said she'd like to see you.'

'You told her about me?'

'Yes. And she said there's plenty of empty houses round her way.'

'Don't tempt me.'

For the rest of the day it was all that Rene could think about. Should she go and see Joan's aunt? Could she persuade her mother to move if she did find them a house?

At the end of the week they had a card from Betty telling them that they'd had a lovely time at the coast. And how nice it was not to be woken by bombers taking off and landing.

'Does she say when she and Luke will be coming to see us again?' asked Peter.

'No. They will have to wait till they get leave,' said Rene.

Life carried on the same, with just the odd daylight raid, and everybody walked about carrying their gas masks. Rene had managed to get a very old skirt from a jumble sale, and she made covers for hers and Hazel's masks. They looked very smart. Women were now making do and mending all they could and trying to make things look less austere. Peter was wearing his father's shirts and Rene had made Hazel a skirt and Peter a pair of trousers out of John's trousers. Every day Maud grumbled about the queues and shortages. To Rene, her mother only seemed to be happy when she was listening to the wireless or, now that the cinemas were open again, going there two afternoons a week. Hazel and Maud would make their way to the Odeon or the Gaumont, and when they got home they would be full of what they'd seen. It was the newsreels that Rene was more interested in, now that the Allies were pushing the Germans back in North Africa and bombing German towns.

'Does that mean that Luke goes over Germany?' asked Peter.

'I don't know,' said Rene.

'But he's a bomber pilot so he must. I can't wait to see him again and ask him all about it.'

Rene didn't answer. She knew what a dangerous job Luke had.

Once again Christmas was fast approaching, and one morning Joan came to work full of smiles.

'Guess what? I had a card from Fred this morning and I think he's on his way home.'

Rene threw her arms round her friend's neck. 'Oh Joan, I'm so happy for you.'

'I can't believe it.'

'You must ask Ernie for a few days off.'

'I will.' She hugged herself. 'I can't wait to see him.'

Rene was happy for Joan; it was nice to have some good news for a change. One of the biggest joys in her life was receiving a card from John. At least that told her he was still alive.

Chapter 30

WHEN JOAN RETURNED to work after her week off to be with her husband, she had a glow about her.

'No need to ask what you've been up to,' said Rene when her friend settled herself at her machine.

'D'you know, I'd almost forgotten how good it was.'

'I know the feeling. So did you do anything exciting, that is anything you can tell me about?'

'As a matter of fact we did. We went for a walk and Fred was really taken aback at all the damage and destruction he saw. He couldn't believe what we'd been through. Anyway, he said that although we seem to be winning this war, he reckoned that Hitler ain't gonna give in that easy and he said that we should move out of London.'

'What did his mother say to that?'

'Not a lot to start with. But after a while he said that we was going to visit my Aunt Polly and see if he could get us a house down where she lives.'

Rene sat back and looked at her friend. 'And did he?'

Joan nodded.

'And?'

'We've got a three-bedroom house and we'll be moving in next month.'

'So quickly? What about Fred's mum?'

'He told her that she's got her own bedroom and there's an indoor lav and bathroom, and he said that her, me and his kids are the most precious things he's got and he doesn't want to lose any of us.' She stopped and wiped a tear.

Rene too choked back tears. Would John feel the same way if he was home and saw what they'd been through?

'So I shall be leaving in a couple of weeks' time, and you must come and see us.'

'I'd like that.'

Rene felt very lonely after Joan left; they had started at the shirt factory together when they left school. But Joan wrote and told her how happy she was, and how even her mother-in-law had made new friends. The children were enjoying their new life and Joan was working part time machining various things including covers for water bottles. Not as nice as parachutes, but just as important.

Hazel was leaving school at Easter and still didn't know what she wanted to do.

'I might go and ask if they want someone in that dress shop in the high street,' she said while they were having dinner one evening.

'They don't seem to do a lot of business,' said her mother.

'Not yet, but wait till this war's over, then everybody will be wanting nice new clothes instead of having to wear this boring old utility stuff.'

'She's got a point there,' said Maud.

Easter was going to be exciting for Rene as well as her daughter. She was waiting for the right moment before she told her mother that on Good Friday she would be going to see Joan. This was something she had been discussing with her friend in their letters. Joan's letters were full of praise about her house and the neighbours, and although they had air raids, most times the planes just passed over. Shirley loved the freedom of their garden and Joan was full of the things she was going to grow. Even her mother-in-law was happy and loved to potter round the garden helping. How Rene wanted this for her and her family.

* * *

It was the week before Easter and Rene told her mother that next Friday she was going to see Joan.

'Is that the one that's moved away?'

Rene nodded. 'Yes. She's got a council house at Morden.'

'Where's that?'

'The last stop on the Northern Line underground.'

'Oh, I see.'

'Can we come?' asked Hazel.

'Of course.'

'Is it in the country?' asked Peter.

'No, not really.'

'Oh, all right. I'll come then.'

'You ain't thinking of moving there, are you?' asked her mother.

'No. She's just asked me to go and see her new house.'

Maud gave her daughter a look that said *I don't believe you*.

'I'll do some sandwiches; I don't want to take any of their rations. Now, young lady, on Saturday shall we go round to Felicity Shaw's shop and see if she'll give you a job after the holiday?'

Hazel's face lit up. 'Can we? Can we really go and ask her?'

'I don't see why not. After all, she can only say no.'

* * *

The following Saturday, Hazel was very shy when they went into the shop. Rene stood back and let her daughter ask about a job. Felicity, the owner, said she didn't have any staff at the moment as her girl had been called up.

'I would love you to come and work for me. I can't afford a lot in wages but it will be an experience. Would you like that?'

Hazel only nodded. As much as she wanted to ask how much she would be earning, she didn't want to just in case Felicity thought she was being pushy.

'You'll have to learn that any new clothes must be sold with coupons. Sometimes the young girls come in here telling me sad stories about their boyfriends coming home and they've nothing to wear, but it's more than I dare do to let them have something without coupons. And you must be the same.'

Hazel didn't say a word.

'Come and see me again when you've left school and we can talk more. That's if you don't change your mind.'

'I won't do that.'

'That's good.'

When they left the shop Rene said, 'Why didn't you speak up?'

'I didn't like to. She talks ever so posh, don't she?'

Rene smiled. 'Not really. And I'm sure you'll be speaking just as nice after a few days.'

'D'you think so?'

'I'm sure of it. I did notice a sewing machine in the corner. I think she must do alterations as well. Now that could be very useful, learning to do that.'

'Mum, I really do want this job.'

'That's good. Now let's go and see if we can find something interesting to have for tea, anything that's off ration.'

'I don't think we'll find anything at this time of day.'

'Perhaps you're right. Come on then, let's get home.'

Rene was pleased her daughter had found something that she would enjoy doing. This war wouldn't last for ever, and Hazel was right, women would want lovely clothes after all the restrictions they'd had to put up with.

Good Friday saw Rene and her children getting off the underground at Morden.

'D'you know where Joan lives?' asked Hazel.

'Yes, but she said she would meet us. Look, there she is.' Rene saw Joan across the road and waved frantically.

Joan was waiting with little Sam by her side, and as soon as she could she hugged Rene.

'You look really well,' said Rene.

'It's all this fresh air and a decent night's sleep. And how are you two?' she said to Hazel and Peter. 'I know we've never met, but I've heard all about you.'

Hazel looked down shyly.

'Hazel starts works after Easter. She's going in a dress shop.'

'That'll be nice. And what about you, Peter?'

'He's working very hard at school.'

'Good. Right, now it's back home. I expect you're dying for a cuppa.'

'I've brought a bit of tea and sugar, as I know how hard it is to feed strangers.'

'Rene, you ain't no stranger.'

'I know, but you know what I mean. Rations are very tight.'

'That's true. It's a wonder we ain't all wasted away. Do you want to hold Sam's hand?' Joan asked Hazel.

'Can I?'

'So how far are you away from here?'

'Just up the road and round the corner.'

As they passed the shops, Rene was taken with the variety. There was a department store and a cinema as well as all the usual little shops.

When they arrived at Joan's house, Rene was more than pleasantly surprised. 'You've got a side gate?'

'Yes, we pay a few shillings more rent for that, but it's worth it. You wait till you see inside.'

Sadie, Joan's mother-in-law, gave them a big smile. 'It's lovely to meet you at last.'

Rene looked at her relaxed, slightly tanned face and she could see that this woman was happy.

As they wandered round the house, Rene was just overwhelmed. It was a dream, and as they went from room to room, she knew this was just what she wanted for her family.

They were upstairs in the back bedroom, looking out of the window. 'Well, what d'you think?' asked Joan.

'I think it's wonderful.'

The children were playing in the garden.

'They seem to be enjoying themselves,' said Joan. 'D'you think you could persuade Maud to move here?'

'I don't know. But I tell you something, I'm gonna have a bloody good try.'

'Good for you. Would you like me to go round to the housing office after the holiday and see if there's any empty houses?'

'Would you?'

'Course.'

'Thanks. That'll be wonderful, that's if I can get Mum to move here.' As Rene looked down on the happy scene, she could almost see herself pottering in a garden.

When they went downstairs Peter and Hazel were talking to Sadie.

'Do you go down that Anderson shelter?' asked Peter.

'Sometimes, when the air-raid warning goes. Can't take any chances,' said Sadie.

275

'And do you sleep in it?' asked Hazel.

'Yes, we have done.'

'Is there spiders?'

'Not since I distempered the walls.'

Rene grinned. This old lady seemed to have a new lease of life. 'You sound as if you like it here.'

'Yes, I do. Mind you, it took a lot of persuading from Fred to convince me and I was very apprehensive at first, but now I'm glad he did.'

'Don't you miss all your old friends?'

'In a way. But I've got some new ones, and there's Joan's Aunt Polly. I go out and about with her sometimes and she introduces me to her friends, and we do a bit of shopping and standing in queues together.'

'D'you know they go to the pictures at least twice a week,' said Joan, smiling.

'Does Aunt Polly live far away?' asked Rene.

'No, not that far, and her or Sadie can always pop on a bus and meet up at the shops,' said Joan.

'Polly took me to her butcher's, and it turned out we went to the same school, though not at the same time, so I got us rationed with him. I managed to scrounge a few sausages from him this week, so how about a bit of sausage and mash, powdered of course?'

Rene noted that her son's eyes lit up. 'That would be very nice, but are you sure you can spare them? I did bring some sandwiches.'

Sadie smiled. 'No, we can have the sausages.'

For the rest of the day Rene, Joan and Sadie sat and talked. The children played in the garden and to Rene this was heaven. When it was time for them to leave, Joan held her tight and said softly, 'I'll go round the housing office on Tuesday and see what they've got.'

'Thanks.'

On the underground platforms, people were getting themselves sorted out and ready for a night's sleep.

'Do they really sleep down here?' asked Peter.

'Those who don't have their own shelter do.'

'I wouldn't like that,' said Hazel.

'It's that or taking a chance with the bombs.'

When they arrived home, Peter was full of the people in the underground, and Joan's garden. 'You should see it, Gran, there was a lovely long bit of grass and I helped Aunt Sadie plant some seeds, then me and Hazel played cricket.'

'They've got one of those Anderson shelters, and Aunt Sadie has painted the inside and it smells all nice,' said Hazel.

'And was your mate all right?' Maud asked Rene.

'Yes, she was.' That was all Rene was going to say for the time being.

Chapter 31

THE NEXT EVENING, Hilda was sweeping her front step when Rene came along.

'It's a bit late for you to be doing that,' said Rene.

'A bloody dog's just shit on me doorstep and Ron's trod in it, so I've had ter wash it down.' She put her broom to one side. 'So how was your day out? Maud said you'd been to the country.'

'It was very nice, but Morden's not really the country.'

'Didn't find yerself a house, then?'

Rene looked at her, surprised. 'What's Maud been saying?'

'Just that she thinks that's what you went down there for.'

'No. I didn't. I just went to see my friend. Mind you, I wouldn't mind living there, and Joan is going to find out all about it for me, but that don't mean we'll be moving.'

'So what does she think about it?' Hilda nodded her head towards next door.

'I haven't said anything and she hasn't asked me. It's only what the children have told her, and they don't know about a house yet. I'll just wait and see if it materialises first.'

'You know what she'll say, don't you?'

'Yes. She'll say she'll miss her mates.'

'Well if you ask me, I think she's being a bit of a silly cow. We ain't gonna live for ever, and she should put you and the kids first.'

'That's up to her. For now I'm going to let her ask me about it herself. I don't want her to think I'm being pushy.'

'Good for you, girl. D'you want me to say something?'

'No. Thanks all the same, but I'll talk about it if and when it happens.'

'Good luck.'

'Thanks.'

As the week went on, Rene knew that Maud wanted to ask about their day out, but she kept skirting round the subject. For the first few days the children were full of their trip to Morden, but Rene never once asked them if they would like to live there. She knew she had to be careful and bide her time; besides, Joan might not be able to get her a house, and even if she did, would she like it? So many things were going round in her mind.

The week after Easter, Hazel started work in Shaw's dress shop. All day while Rene was at the factory, her mind was on her daughter. Was she happy? Was there enough for her to do and not be bored? She couldn't wait to get home to see how she had got on.

'Well?' was her first word when she walked into the kitchen. 'What's it like to be out in the big wide world earning a living?'

'It was all right, but ten shillings a week won't buy me much after I give you half.'

Maud looked at her daughter.

'We all had to pay you when we started work, remember?' said Rene.

'Just wanted you to know the true value of money,' said her mother.

'Can't say I like all the dusting, and we didn't have any customers,' Hazel went on.

'Oh dear,' said Rene.

'Mrs Shaw said that Monday is always the worst day of the week, and that's why it's best to get on with the dusting and clearing up. She was busy doing a lot of alterations and I had to pick up the pins. But I didn't sell anything.'

Rene looked at her mother and smiled.

When they were in the scullery washing up, Maud said, 'D'you think she'll stick at it?'

'Don't know. Give it time. If she's not that happy, we can always look for something else. It's not as if jobs are hard to get.'

'Not yet they ain't, but wait till the boys come back, then things will be a lot different.'

As the weeks went on, Hazel appeared to be settling down, but she still seemed bored and frustrated at not having much to do.

'I wish we had more customers,' she said to her mother one evening when they were sitting in the kitchen listening to the wireless, with Maud as usual doing her knitting.

'Would you like to try something else?' Rene asked her.

'Don't know.'

'Well give it some thought. You never know. With the summer coming, some people might want a new frock.'

'I hope so.'

At the end of that week, Rene received a letter from Joan full of apologies for not writing earlier. Rene had been concerned at not hearing from her friend and thought that she might have changed her mind about finding Rene a house. Joan said she had been to the housing office and they had sent her to look at a couple of places, but she wasn't impressed with the location and one of them only had two bedrooms. But she said not to give up hope; as soon as a house came up, she'd let Rene know. That pleased Rene, and she wondered if she should tell her mother.

'Was that a letter from your friend?'

'Yes.'

'So when you off down there again?'

'Dunno. We ain't made any arrangements.' Did her mother suspect?

'I was talking to Hilda today.'

'You talk to Hilda every day.'

'I know, but she was saying that you'd told her about your friend's house.'

'Yes, I did tell her about Joan's house.'

'And by all accounts it was very nice.'

'Yes, it was.' Rene waited for this conversation to continue, but it didn't.

It was after Peter's birthday that Rene got the letter from Joan telling her that she had seen a house she liked and thought would suit Rene. Although she felt guilty, she knew that for the time being she had to keep this piece of information to herself, as it might cause more distress. 'How d'you fancy going down to see Joan again next Sunday?' she asked the children.

'I don't mind,' said Hazel.

'Fancy coming with us, Mum?' Rene casually asked her mother.

'Don't think so.'

'Oh come on, Gran, it'll be fun. Joan's got a lovely garden and little Sam's ever so sweet.' Hazel was very enthusiastic.

'I wish we had a garden like it,' said Peter. 'Aunt Sadie was telling me all about the things she's gonna grow.'

Rene didn't say a word; she just sat back and let the children tell her mother all about it.

After the children had gone to bed, Rene thought it was a good time to bring up the subject. 'Mum, why don't you come with us on Sunday? It'll do you good to have a day out.'

'You only want me to look at this house your mate's got.'

Rene crossed her fingers. 'Yes.' She wasn't about to tell her mother that she was going to look at a house for them.

As far as Maud was concerned, that was the end of the conversation, and she picked up her knitting and studied the pattern.

Rene knew that although the raids on London weren't so frequent these days, she couldn't just up sticks and move away without her mother. What should she do? If the raids started again, how would she feel about that? Looking at her mother, she knew she would never leave her, not while this war was still on.

Chapter 32

WHEN RENE WOKE on Sunday morning, although the windows were still boarded up, she could see that it was bright outside and she hoped that the sun was shining. She carefully got up, trying not to disturb Hazel, who shared her bed, and moved quietly past Peter, who was now sleeping on a camp bed. She gathered up the clothes that she had set out last night and went and dressed herself in the kitchen.

She had just made a pot of tea when her mother walked in.

'You're up early,' said Maud. 'I thought I heard someone moving about.'

'I want to get an early start.'

'Why's that?'

'No reason. It's just that I want to make the most of

the day. I'll take a bit of tea and sugar with me. Is that all right?'

'Course. I'll do the kids some dried egg on fried bread before you go.'

'Thanks, Mum. I still can't persuade you to come with us, then?'

'No.'

Rene knew it was useless trying to get round her mother. 'I'll do some sandwiches, and don't worry about getting us anything. I expect we'll find a British Restaurant open somewhere.'

When they arrived at the underground, Peter was fascinated by all the people still fast asleep.

'Be careful not to tread on anyone,' said Rene as they moved down the platform.

When the train pulled into the station and the people were getting off, Peter was still looking around. 'How can they sleep with all this racket going on?' he asked.

'Come on, this is our train,' said Rene.

When they got to Morden, Hazel asked, 'Is Joan going to meet us?'

'No. I told her we can find our own way.'

As they walked, Peter shouted, 'Look at those boys in that field playing football.'

'Would you like to do that?' asked Rene as they stood looking.

'Yer. Billy always said he wanted to be a footballer when he grew up.' He stopped and took hold of his mother's hand.

Rene held his hand and they moved on. Would that horror be with him for the rest of his life?

There were hugs and smiles when Joan opened the door. 'Come on in.'

'Hello,' said Sadie. 'It's lovely to see you all again.'

Shirley grabbed Hazel's hand. 'Come and see the new cover I've got on my doll's pram. Mummy made it for me.' She almost dragged Hazel into the garden.

'And I'll take you, young man, to show you the seeds that you helped me plant when you were last here.' Sadie gently eased Peter outside.

'That was all well rehearsed,' said Rene.

'Well, Mum knew that I wanted to talk to you on your own. Kettle's boiled, and we'll sit and have a nice cup of tea and a chat.'

'I'm really looking forward to going to see this house. Is it near here?'

'It's closer to Aunt Polly, but that's not all that far away. It's got three good-size bedrooms and a bathroom indoors.'

'That's got to be a blessing.'

'I looked at some right old places, I can tell you. I can never understand how some people can make so much mess. The house you're going to see is what they call a parlour type. The council will do a few things, but it's nice. It's in a cul-de-sac and you look out over a green, and it's got a side gate.'

'I can't wait. I am a bit worried about the rent, though. You don't get a lot on an army allowance.'

'You can always come and work where I work. They're crying out for machinists now all the twenty-year-olds are being called up.'

Suddenly the back door burst open and the others all trooped in. Rene could see that Sadie enjoyed her children's company.

'They all want a drink,' said Sadie, 'and I'll have a cuppa.' She sat next to Rene in the bright kitchen. It was only small, but very compact.

'Has Joan had a chance to tell you about the house yet?'

'Yes, and it sounds lovely.'

'We can go and have a look if you like,' said Joan.

'You can leave the kids here,' said Sadie.

'Are you sure?' asked Rene.

'What house you gonna look at?' asked Peter.

'And why can't we come with you?' said Hazel.

'Joan's going to show me a house she likes, that's all.'

Hazel and Peter looked at her suspiciously.

'You gonna move away from here?' Peter asked Sadie.

Sadie looked at Joan.

Rene said suddenly, 'It might be for us.'

'Well in that case we'd better come as well,' said Hazel.

Rene looked at her daughter in surprise. 'Well I think you should wait and see what I think about it first, and remember, if your gran won't come here to live, then neither will we. I don't want you to get your hopes up.'

There was silence for a moment or two, then Hazel said, 'All right. We'll stay here then.'

'Good. If I think it's suitable, we'll have another look and get your approval.'

'I'm sorry, Rene, I forgot they weren't to know yet.'

'Don't worry, Sadie, they might have to know, if it's all right.'

Joan took Sam with them, and as they made for the road the house was in, Rene looked all about her. 'Is it very far?' she asked.

'Not that much further.'

'How did you manage to get the key?'

'I asked for it for Saturday, and that way I can hang on to it till Monday. Polly lives in the next road,' said Joan as they turned into a cul-de-sac. 'This is Almond Close.'

Rene was full of apprehension. She could see the green surrounded by houses; she could even imagine her children playing ball there.

'This is it.' Joan walked into a small front garden and opened the front door.

Tentatively Rene stepped inside. A door opened off the passage into the front room. Next there was a dining room, and at the end a small kitchen. Upstairs were three bedrooms and a very small bathroom.

'This is wonderful,' said Rene, wandering from room to room. She stood looking out of the back bedroom at the small garden. Would John be happy here? Would he like to do gardening? She could see him growing flowers and cutting the grass. Tears filled her eyes. 'How much is the rent?'

'It's nine and six a week. Could you afford that?'

'If I can work I can.'

'So what shall I tell the housing office?'

Rene crossed her fingers behind her back. 'Tell them yes.'

Joan threw her arms round her friend's neck. 'I'm so pleased. I know you'll be happy here.'

'But what if I can't get Mum to move?'

'You'll have to get the kids to work on her. Do you want to go and fetch them? If they like it, you're halfway there.'

'Thanks, Joan.'

As they walked back to Joan's house, Rene wondered if she was doing the right thing. She had seen some bomb damage, so they had had some bombs here, but nothing like they had been through in Rotherhithe. If only she could make her mother come, then she would be more than happy.

When the children saw the house, they were both very excited and ran from room to room.

'This is my bedroom,' yelled Peter from the box room.

'And this one's mine,' said Hazel next door. 'You can have the big one, Mum.'

'Oh, thanks. And what about Gran?'

Hazel came out of the bedroom. 'Will she come here?'

'I don't know. Would you like to live here?'

'Yes, I would. And perhaps I could get a job in that big shop we saw near the station.'

Rene was surprised that her daughter had been thinking things through. 'What made you think of that?'

'Dunno. It's just that it looked nice.'

'Joan said the school is just up the road, so you wouldn't have far to go,' said Rene when Peter came out of his bedroom.

'But what if Gran don't wanna come?'

'I don't know.'

'Where would she sleep?' asked Hazel.

'Perhaps she could go in the front room downstairs,' said Rene.

Rene knew she was going to have an uphill fight on

her hands, but she was convinced that this was the best thing she could do for her family. When the war was over and people started to come back to their roots, all the houses would soon be snapped up.

Chapter 33

A s they were leaving for home, Joan held Rene close. 'Good luck.'

'Thanks. I'll let you know what the outcome is.'

At Morden, Hazel said, 'Let's go and look at that department store.'

'It's closed, silly,' said Peter.

'I know that, but we can look through the window.'

Rene was still taken aback by the children's attitude to moving. Hazel seemed very happy, and though Peter was a bit concerned about starting a new school, the grass and the football seemed to appeal to him, and he had been asking Sadie about the garden at Joan's.

As they looked through the many windows of the

store, Hazel said, 'They certainly seem to sell some nice things. I wouldn't mind working here. At least there'd be other girls to talk to.'

Rene didn't say anything. She was thinking about how she would bring the subject of moving up with her mother.

As they walked home from the train, Hazel was full of the house, having her own room and the fact that she could be starting a new job. 'All we've got to do is convince Gran that this is the best thing.'

'I think we might have a job there,' said Rene.

'What we gonna do if she says no?' asked Peter, who also seemed keen on the idea.

'I don't know. After all, someone has to look after her, and if we move away and . . .' Rene stopped. She couldn't even begin to think about that.

'Hello, Gran,' said Hazel as they burst into the kitchen.

'Have you had a nice day?'

'I should say so,' said Peter, throwing his coat on the chair.

'Peter, go and hang your coat up,' said Rene.

'Not till I've told Gran what a smashing time we've had.'

There was no way Rene was going to stop them now they were in full flow.

'We went and saw this house,' said Hazel, looking

at her mother. 'And it's ever so nice.'

Rene saw Maud visibly purse her lips.

'And,' said Peter, 'it's got a smashing garden. And Aunt Sadie said she'll tell me what seeds to plant.'

'So it's Aunt Sadie now, is it?'

'That's what she said to call her.'

'I see.'

'I'll put the kettle on,' said Rene, going into the scullery.

It wasn't long before Maud followed her. 'So you've been to look at a house?'

'Yes.'

'And?'

'I want you to come and see it.'

'Seems like the kids have already made up their minds. And you know my feelings about moving.'

'Yes. But if you could see how nice it is and how happy Sadie is, I'm sure you'd change your mind.'

'It seems you've already decided.'

'But Mum, we can't leave you on your own.'

'I can assure you that I am quite capable of looking after myself.'

'I know you are, and you look after us too. But you're my mum and these are your only grandchildren; don't you want to see them grow up and be healthy? If Betty was to go to Canada you wouldn't see her children.'

Maud didn't answer.

Rene picked up the tray and took the tea things into the kitchen. She wasn't going to tell Maud that she had paid two weeks' rent; she knew that at the moment it was pointless getting into an argument.

The next day when Rene came home from work, Hazel was telling Maud about the department store.

'Hello, Mum. I was just telling Gran about that shop. I said I'd love to work in a big shop like that. To work with other girls. I bet they can get stuff to sell.'

Maud just sat there knitting.

'Is Peter home?' asked Rene.

'He's out somewhere,' came the curt reply.

Hazel followed her mother into the bedroom. 'Mum, if Gran don't want to move and you have to stay here, could I go and live with Joan?'

'What?'

'It'll be a bit like being evacuated, only much better.'

'I don't know. We've got to wait and see if we can get Gran to come with us.'

When Hazel left, Rene sat on the bed. What should she do? Perhaps Betty could persuade their mother?

Rene wrote to both Betty and Joan explaining the situation; she also sent Joan a postal order for another month's rent. She didn't want to lose that house.

Betty wrote back and said that as soon as she could she would get a forty-eight-hour pass and come and see them. Rene sat looking at her sister's letter. Would they be able to make their mother understand?

For the next few weeks everything carried on as normal, despite the cool feeling that Maud had adopted towards her daughter. Rene hadn't told the children that she had paid the rent, so the subject had been dropped and they just carried on as usual, although Hazel was disappointed at not going to live in Morden.

Rene had decided to go to Morden the following Sunday when she had a letter from Betty. She had got a weekend pass and was coming to see them the weekend before.

There were the usual hugs and kisses when Betty walked in.

'You look ever so nice,' said Hazel.

'And look at you, all grown up and going out to work.'

After giving her daughter a hug, Maud said, 'I'll go and make a cup of tea. I expect you could do with one after that journey.'

'It ain't that far away, Mum.'

Maud didn't answer as she left the room.

'Is Luke with you?' asked Peter.

'No, he's been night flying and has to get a bit of sleep. I might be moved from the camp.'

'Why's that?' asked Rene.

'They don't like husbands and wives together.'

'That's a shame. You'll miss him.'

'Yes, I will. But it's such a worry when he goes off, especially now they're doing such a lot of night flying.'

'I can imagine that. D'you know where you'll be sent?'

'No.'

'Let's hope it's not too far away.'

'At least the war seems to be going in our favour,' said Betty.

Maud came back in with the tea tray. 'I suppose Rene's been telling you about this place out in the country?'

'No. She did write and tell me she'd been to see her friend Joan who lives at Morden. That ain't in the country.'

'It's ever so nice,' said Hazel. 'I'd like to live there, and there's a smashing shop that I'd like to work in. I did ask Mum if I could go and stay with Auntie Joan, but she said no.'

Maud looked shocked at that. 'You didn't tell me that. I thought you didn't want to be evacuated again.'

'It's not like being evacuated.'

'So why don't you go and look at it, Mum?' asked Betty.

'What's she been telling you?'

'Not much. But it does sound rather nice.'

Maud continued pouring out the tea.

'It's no good keeping on, Bet.'

'Well I would rather live somewhere that had windows and a garden.'

Hazel grinned. 'So would I.'

Later, Rene was getting ready to do her fire-watching.

'You still doing that?' Betty said.

'Yes, but it's much better now we don't have so many raids. And that's all down to blokes like your Luke.'

'And how's your fire-watching friend?'

'He's fine.'

'What does he say about this business with Mum and the house?'

'The same as everyone else. Bet, I think we should drop the subject. It's not going to do any good.'

'What does Maggie think about it?'

'The same as you.'

After Betty left, Rene told her mother that they were going to see Joan again. She didn't even invite Maud; she knew that was hopeless.

It was Saturday night and they were quietly listening to the wireless when Maud suddenly said, 'I think I'll come with you tomorrow.'

'What?' Rene was stunned. 'What's brought this on?'

'Her next door. She's been on and on at me and it's anything for a quiet life.'

Rene said a silent thank you to Hilda.

So Sunday morning saw them all off to Morden. Rene could hardly believe it. She hoped that Sadie and the house would make a good impression. With a bit of luck they could be moving in a few weeks' time.

Chapter 34

RENE WAS SO pleased that the sun was shining. When they got out of the underground at Morden, Hazel quickly took her gran across the road to show her where she would like to work.

On the way to Joan's, they stopped and looked at the boys playing Sunday morning football again.

'Can I stay and watch 'em?' asked Peter.

'Of course. You know your way to Joan's.' Rene was pleased that Maud could see how much the children wanted to be here. It was a world away from Rotherhithe.

There was the usual greeting from Joan and Sadie when the door was opened, and Shirley giggled as she took hold of Hazel's hand and led her into the garden.

'Lovely to see you, Maud. I've heard so much about you,' said Sadie.

'I bet you have.'

Sadie pulled out a chair from under the kitchen table. 'Sit yourself down while I just put the kettle on. I expect you'd like a cuppa.'

'Yes please. We've brought some tea and sugar.'

'Was it very crowded on the tube?' asked Sadie.

'Not too bad. But I couldn't get over all those poor devils sleeping on the platform, with people stepping over 'em and trains stopping and starting.'

'Even though things are getting better, I expect they feel safer down there just in case anything happens.'

'S'pose so.'

Rene looked at her mother, who seemed to relax.

'I got your letter and managed to get the key again.' Joan wasn't going to let on that Rene had paid the rent for six weeks.

'Thanks. Would you like to go and look at this house then, Mum?'

'It's very nice,' said Sadie.

'I don't know why she's bothered to drag me down here. She knows I don't want to move.'

'D'you know, I felt exactly the same. But it was the best thing we did. Young Shirley looks a picture of health and I feel a different person.'

'I know this is why she wanted me to come here.'

'Well just go and have a look when Peter gets here.'

Rene could have thrown her arms round Sadie. She was saying all the right things, but would it change her mother's mind?

Later, as they made their way to Almond Close, Peter ran on ahead.

'This is the house, Gran,' he called out.

Rene had warned them not to say too much, but she could see that her children were having a job keeping their feelings in.

Inside, Rene showed her mother around. She was having trouble not to tell Maud where she was going to put things and how much she wanted to move here.

After a while she said, 'Well, what d'you think?'

'It's very nice, but a bit out of the way. You ain't got a local shop just across the way.'

'I know. Joan's Aunt Polly lives in the next road and Joan said she gets a lot of her stuff from the blokes who come round with vans.'

They were at the window in the back bedroom that overlooked the garden. The children were sitting outside talking, and every now and again they looked up and gave their mother and grandmother a wave. How could Maud not want to live here?

'Well, what did you think?' asked Sadie to Maud when they got back to Joan's house.

'Very nice,' was the short answer.

For the rest of the day nothing more was said about the house. Rene thought it was best to let her mother make the first move on that subject.

They had just arrived home and were pulling the key through the letter box when Hilda, followed by Ron, came out of their door.

'I've been waiting for you, been watching for you out the window,' said Hilda.

'Maud. Rene. You'd better come in here,' said Ron.

The two women looked at them. They could see that their neighbours were in a state of shock.

'What is it?' asked Maud.

'Come on,' said Ron, taking Maud's arm.

'Can we come?' asked Hazel.

Hilda nodded.

Once they were in Hilda's kitchen, Maud said slowly, 'Is it Luke?'

Ron shook his head. 'I'm sorry, Maud. It's Betty.'

Maud went deathly white. 'Betty? My Betty? What's happened to her?'

'I am so sorry, Maud,' said Ron again.

Maud looked at him in disbelief as she said softly, 'Is she . . . ?' She couldn't finish the sentence.

Hilda took hold of Maud's hand. 'I'm so sorry.'

Rene just sat staring at them. She couldn't believe what she was hearing. Suddenly she said, 'How do you know?'

'Her husband came this afternoon. We told him you'd gone out and he told us what had happened. Poor lad, he was in such a state.'

'Where is he now?' asked Rene.

'He said he'd come back later, I told him to stay here, but he said he needed to be on his own.' Hilda dabbed at her eyes.

'Mum. Is Auntie Betty dead?' asked Hazel.

Rene could only nod.

Hazel began to cry. 'She can't be, there ain't been any air raids.'

'How did it happen?' asked Rene.

'It seems she was in a car and she hit a lorry, that's all the lad said.' Ron was having a job to keep his emotions under control. 'Maud, I'm so sorry.'

Dry-eyed, Maud said, 'We'd better go next door just in case he comes back.' She gathered up her handbag and stood up. 'I'll see you tomorrow.' With that she left the room.

'She's in shock,' said Rene as she followed her mother.

Back indoors, Maud went into the scullery without even taking her hat off and busied herself.

Rene sat at the kitchen table and listened to her mother banging the crocks and tea things. Hazel had gone to the bedroom. Peter sat next to his mother and took her hand, and Rene tried to smile although her heart was breaking.

'I know how sad you are,' Peter said.

Those few words brought forth floods of tears, and Peter held his mother close and gently patted her back.

After a while, when Maud brought in the tray, Peter went and joined his sister.

'Why did he have ter come and tell us? We're her family, we should have been told first,' said Maud.

'Mum, Luke's her next of kin.'

'But they ain't been married that long.'

'I know, but he was her husband.' Rene gave a sob. Suddenly it began to hit home. She'd never see her lovely sister again.

Maud put the tea strainer on the cup and poured the tea. 'Will you write and tell Maggie?'

Rene could only nod, as she clutched the cup that Maud passed her. Her mind was in turmoil. If only John was here. Life was so unfair.

'I wonder what time he'll be here? Will he want a bit of dinner?'

Rene wanted to scream at her. She didn't seem to be taking it in that her youngest daughter was dead.

She got up and went into the bedroom. Hazel and Peter were sitting on the bed. Hazel had been crying; her face was red and blotchy.

'Mum, what we gonna do?' asked Peter.

'What do you mean?'

'Will we still be able to move?'

'I don't know, love.'

'I don't want to stay here,' said Hazel. 'I loved Auntie Betty, we had such good times together.'

'I know you did. We all did.'

'Will she have a funeral like Billy's?' asked Peter.

'I expect so.'

They sat in silence for a while, and Rene felt guilty at leaving her mother alone. But why hadn't she cried?

When she got back into the kitchen, Maud was looking at the photos of Betty's wedding and the tears were rolling down her cheeks. She looked up when Rene walked in. 'She was so lovely.'

'Yes, she was.'

The knock on the front door sent Peter scurrying to open it.

Rene opened the kitchen door. 'Hello, Luke,' she said and held him close.

He kissed her cheek and went to Maud and held her.

Rene wiped her eyes. 'Can I get you a cup of tea?'

He nodded.

In the scullery, Rene couldn't get over how different Luke seemed. He was gaunt and sad-looking. What trauma had this lad been through?

When she took the tea in, Luke was sitting at the table with Maud. He was holding her hand.

'What happened, Luke?' Rene asked.

'She was an excellent driver and it wasn't her fault. She was going somewhere to pick up some new boys. The lights on the cars are very dim because of the blackout, and it appears she went round a corner and there was a broken-down lorry and she just went into it.'

'Did she suffer?' asked Rene.

He shook his head. 'The police said it was instantaneous.'

'When did it happen?' asked Rene.

'Friday.'

'Friday?' repeated Maud. 'Why has it taken so bloody long for us to hear?'

'The accident wasn't discovered till very late Friday night. It took almost all day Saturday for the police to find out where she was stationed. Because of security, she couldn't carry any information on her about where she was stationed; just where she was going. I was flying over Berlin and I didn't know about it till late Saturday night when I got back to camp.' He stopped, then added softly, 'I had to go and identify her.'

Rene let the tears run unchecked down her face.

'I am so sorry,' Luke said.

She sniffed back her tears. She knew she had to be practical. 'I'll write and tell Maggie; I should think she'll get time off for the funeral. When's that likely to be?'

'Next Friday, if that's all right with you?'

'I can get time off.'

'It will be at the church where we were married.'

'What?' said Maud. 'Why can't she be buried here in her local churchyard? Where her dad is?'

'This is what she wanted. It was something we'd discussed.'

'You discussed this?' said Maud.

'Yes. But not for her, for me. You see, in this game we have to be prepared, and I said that if it happened I wanted to be in that beautiful churchyard, and so did my Betty.'

'Will you go back home when this is all over?' asked Rene.

'Not till the job is done.'

'When are you flying again?' asked Rene.

'I'm on compassionate leave at the moment.'

'Where are you going to stay?'

'I thought after Friday I might go down to the hotel where we spent our honeymoon.'

'Won't that have too many memories?'

'Yes, but very happy ones.' He let a slight smile lift his sad, handsome face.

As much as Rene tried to persuade Luke to stay, he insisted on going back to camp.

They stood at the door saying their goodbyes.

'As soon as all the arrangements have been made, I will come and let you know.'

'Thanks, Luke.'

Hazel hugged him. 'I loved my Auntie Betty,' she said.

'I know, and she loved you, very much.'

Peter was next in line. 'You will come and see us, won't you?'

Luke ruffled his hair. 'Of course.'

He kissed Maud's cheek and left. He never turned round at the bottom of the road, and the sad party went back indoors.

Chapter 35

THAT EVENING RENE sat and tried to write the letters to Maggie and Joan. It was very hard. How could you put such a tragedy on paper and not make it sound so cold and unemotional?

'I won't be able to go and put flowers on her grave,' said Maud, who had cast her knitting aside.

'I can always take you.'

'Not if you're not living here.'

'Mum, please don't start on that again.' Rene went into the scullery and then out to the lav. As she passed the air-raid shelter, she almost felt like going in there to get away from this nightmare. If it wasn't for the war, her sister would still be here. Her thoughts went to John. And so would he. How different all their lives would have been. How would John feel when he learnt about Betty? He had loved her.

Back in the house, her mother said she was going to bed, so Rene got on and wrote the letters. She began: *I can't believe that this time last year we were celebrating Betty and Luke's wedding. Now I have to write and tell you of the terrible tragedy.*

She went on to explain what had happened and where and when the funeral would take place.

When the letters were finished, she propped the envelopes against the clock on the mantelpiece and went to bed.

Although Rene was tossing and turning, and trying to avoid waking Hazel, she must have fallen asleep, as it was light beyond the wooden shutter. The sun would be shining through those lovely windows at the house in Morden. Would she be able to move away from here now? She lay thinking about yesterday. Was it all a bad dream? But she knew the answer to that. She could hear her mother moving about. She knew she had to get up for work; everybody did, no matter what horrors had happened the day before. As she got out of the bed, Hazel sat up.

'I'm not going to work today.'

'I think you should.'

'I don't like boring Mondays. Besides, I shall keep thinking about Auntie Betty and crying.'

'I know, love. We all will. But working will take your mind off it. Besides, you'll have to tell Mrs Shaw that you want Friday off; that's if you want to go to Betty's funeral?'

'Of course I want to go.'

Peter sat up. 'I didn't want to go to Billy's. His mum said I could as I was his best mate, but I didn't want to.'

'You don't have to come,' said Rene. 'You can stay with Ron and Hilda.'

'No. I must be brave like Luke. He will be there, won't he?'

'Yes, he will.'

Peter settled himself down again. This week it was school in the afternoon for him.

Friday saw the family leave for Redhill wearing the black armbands that Rene had made for them. Unless you already had a black coat, it was very hard to give up your coupons for something you might not want to wear again.

Luke had written and told them that the service would be at two o'clock and they were welcome to come whenever they wanted, as the local pub where they had had their wedding reception was going to look after them.

They collected their wreath from the florist and made their way to the train. It was a very sad party that arrived at the pub.

Luke came out to meet them and hugged them all. 'I've got a car to take us to the church; Betty is there already.'

Maud sat stony-faced. She had been quiet all the way. In the church there were quite a few service personnel. Luke had told them that Betty was very popular.

Rene didn't really listen to the service; her thoughts were on the last time she'd been here. She shivered although it was a warm September day. Instead of seeing a coffin in front of her, she remembered Betty as a happy, lovely bride, smiling and looking up at Luke with love in her eyes. She glanced at Luke. He looked a different man.

As they stood round the grave, Hazel was inconsolable and was being comforted by one of Betty's friends. Peter just stood clutching Luke's hand and Maud cried gently as Maggie held on to her. Rene wanted to run away. She didn't want to be here. She didn't want to see her sister put in this dark hole. She walked away.

She watched from a gravestone she was sitting on. She was angry. Why had her lovely sister been taken like this?

When it was over, she made her way back to the others and on to the wake. All she wanted to do was go home.

On the journey home, Peter was full of the pilots he'd been talking to. 'Luke is going to write to me.'

'That's nice,' said Maggie. 'And how about you, Hazel? D'you like your job?'

'Not really, there's not a lot to do. I want to go and work in the store at Morden, but Mum won't let me go and stay with her friend Joan.'

'Oh dear,' said Maggie.

'We can talk about that another day,' said Rene.

Hazel looked at her mother. Was she going to give in?

When they arrived home, Maggie and Rene were alone in the scullery making a cup of cocoa before going to bed.

'Rene, would it help for me to have a word with Mum tonight?'

Maggie was staying for the night and would be in Betty's bed in their mother's room. Rene had told her all about the house and wanting to move.

'I honestly don't know. Hazel really does want to move and I think Peter feels the same way, but you know what Mum's like.'

'I know. What happens to the house if you don't move in? Will the council take it back?'

Rene shrugged. 'I don't know. I suppose all the time I can pay the rent it'll be all right, but I don't really know how long I can do that for.' She wiped away a tear.

Maggie held her sister close. 'It's been a bad day for all of us. Go on off to bed.'

She kissed Rene's cheek.

* * *

On Sunday Rene was changing her bed when her mother walked in.

'So what do you think about Hazel going to stay with Joan?'

'Well, I had said no to her.' Rene stood up from tucking the sheet in. 'But I've been thinking about it. Hazel's not happy where she is and I know she wants to get away from here. I was going to write to Joan and ask her.'

'Would she have the room?'

'Dunno.'

Maud turned and was going out when Rene asked, 'Why did you ask?'

'Nothing. You don't want to build her hopes up too high, you know.'

'I know. But I want her to be happy.'

Maud closed the door and Rene sat on the bed. Was her mother backing down? What had Maggie said? Was there some light at the end of this very dark tunnel they were in?

Joan had written and sent her and Sadie's condolences. She also said that they had been to the house and put some of their old curtains up at the front windows to give it a lived-in look. She had spoken to the neighbours too and explained the situation to them. 'They seem very nice,' she had added.

Rene finished making the bed. She knew then that

she was going to tell her mother that they would be moving in a few weeks' time. With or without her.

Rene went into the kitchen and sat at the table. 'Mum. You know that letter I had from Joan?'

Maud looked up from the paper she was reading. 'Do you know, they are talking about opening a second front. That means that this war could be over very soon.'

'I hope so. Mum, I've been paying the rent on that house we looked at and we shall be moving soon.'

Maud put the newspaper down. 'When you say we, I hope that doesn't include me?'

'Well yes, it does.'

'You know my feelings.'

'All too well. You have made it very clear. I'm sorry, but my children need to get away. To be in a house where they can see out of the windows. To be in a house that has a garden for them to enjoy. And I need to get away too.' Rene sat back. She felt exhausted.

'That was quite an outburst.'

Rene had tears running down her cheeks. 'Please, Mum.'

Maud stood up. 'I'm going to talk to Hilda.' She left the room.

Rene picked up a cup and threw it at the door.

* * *

The following week saw Hazel, Peter and Rene going to Morden. Maud was noticeably absent. They were carrying some of their possessions and Hazel was so excited. Rene had told them they were going to move as soon as she gave in her notice, and she had told Hazel to do the same. She also told Peter to get some kind of reference from his teacher. He said he would write to Luke and give him their new address. Rene had been busy trying to find a firm that would move them.

Hilda was very upset when she heard they were going. 'I'll miss you lot,' she'd said.

'And we shall miss you. We'll be back to see Mum.' Rene had been very upset over the row she and her mother had had last Sunday, and later that afternoon, when her mother came back, she had gone and sat in Hilda's kitchen. She needed someone to talk to. 'I feel rotten about this,' she said. 'But I'd hoped Mum would see it my way.'

'She can be very cantankerous.'

'I know.'

'So when are you going?'

'We're going down next Sunday, and it should only be a week or two after that. It all depends if I can find someone to move us.'

'I'll get Ron to ask around. Have you had a word with Wally at the warden's post?'

'No. I never thought of him.'

'Well he seems to know everyone.'

'That's true. Thanks, Hilda, I'll go along and see him.'

As they sat on the train, all these thoughts were going through Rene's mind. She was waiting for the date to be arranged with a friend of Wally's.

Chapter 36

Rene, Joan and the children spent the morning cleaning and putting their few belongings in cupboards. It was a happy scene with plenty of laughter.

'I'll have to go and get dockets for bedding and curtains and everything we need,' said Rene.

'As you've been blasted out of your home, you get extra,' said Joan.

'But will I, as Mum will still be living there?'

'Don't know about that,' said Joan, tucking back the stray strands of hair that had escaped from under her turban.

There was a knock on the front door.

Rene and Joan looked at each other.

'Who knows we're here?'

Joan shrugged.

Rene ran her hands down the front of her pinny. When she opened the door, she was surprised to see a slim, smart grey-haired woman standing there.

'Hello,' said the woman, smiling. 'I'm Doris Barker and me and Stan, that's me husband, live next door. As it's a bit warm today and we can see that you're all busy, we thought you might like a glass of lemonade.'

Her husband, a well-built man, was standing behind her with a tray. He gave Rene a nod.

Now Joan, Hazel and Peter had joined Rene at the door.

Rene smiled. 'Thank you so much, that's very kind of you.'

'I looked over the fence and saw there was four of you,' said Stan.

'We met the other day,' said Joan, going forward and shaking Doris's hand. 'I'm Joan, Rene's friend.'

'Come on in,' said Rene.

'When are you moving in?' asked Stan.

'As soon as I can give in my notice on my job,' said Rene.

'Is it just the three of you?' asked Doris.

Rene nodded. 'At the moment, my husband is a prisoner of war.'

'Sorry to hear that.'

'I was hoping my mother would come and live with us, but she don't want to leave her friends and neighbours.'

'I can understand that,' said Doris. 'We felt the same till we was bombed out.'

'This war has certainly caused a few upheavals,' said Stan.

'And what's your name, young lady?' asked Doris.

'I'm Hazel, and this is me brother Peter.'

'And will you both be going to school round here?'

'Peter will. But I want to work in the big shop at Morden.'

'That's a lovely store. Nice girls work there.'

'Come on, love, let these good people get on with their work,' said Stan.

'Yes. I'm sorry.'

'No, that's all right. We deserve a break,' said Rene. 'Thank you for the lemonade.'

'Leave the glasses on our doorstep when you go,' said Doris as they made their way out. 'And we look forward to seeing you again.'

Rene closed the door behind them. 'They seem a nice enough couple.'

'I think so,' said Joan.

On the way home, Hazel and Peter were full of the house and where they were going to put their things.

'Hello, Gran,' said Peter when they walked in. 'You wait till you see my bedroom. I'm gonna put all my shrapnel collection on the windowsill.'

'That's nice.'

'Mum said she'll try and get me a small dressing table,' said Hazel. 'Only a second-hand one, but I don't care as it will be in my own bedroom.'

Rene asked her mother if she wanted a cup of tea.

When the children had gone to bed, she told Maud about her neighbours. She tried not to sound too enthusiastic. But she could see that her mother wasn't that interested.

'Wally came round this morning. He said for you to go and see him.'

'Did he say anything else?'

'No.'

'Mum, I know you're angry with me, but please don't let me go away with bad feelings.'

'I'm going to bed.'

She left Rene sitting alone. What should she do?

Wally had arranged with his mate to move them the following Saturday. Although Rene was pleased about it, she was also very apprehensive. She told Hilda, who promised that they would keep an eye on Maud and get in touch if necessary. 'If it's anything bad, I'll send you a telegram.'

That didn't help to dispel Rene's fears and guilt.

Over the next few days, boxes were filled with crocks and clothes, labelled and sealed up. The atmosphere between Rene and her mother was almost unbearable.

One night Rene was gently crying when Peter came and sat on the bed.

'What's wrong, Mum?'

'Nothing.'

'Is it 'cos Gran won't come with us?'

Rene nodded.

'I told her what a smashing house it was and that she would like it. Why won't she come with us?'

'I think deep down she wants to, but it has gone on for so long now that she won't give in.'

'Well I think she's silly.'

Rene kissed her son. 'Go back to bed. And remember that after Saturday you'll be in your own room and your own bed.'

He gave her a hug and crept back on to his camp bed.

Rene had a letter from Maggie. In it she said that she'd told their mother not to be so damn difficult. Rene smiled. Her sister was very direct. But Maggie didn't say if Maud had said anything about changing her mind.

Both Rene and Hazel left work with glowing references, and Peter's teacher had given him a wonderful report.

'I didn't know you was so clever,' said Rene as she read it. 'Have you seen this, Mum?'

'Yes. He's a very clever boy.'

Rene smiled at him proudly. 'So what have you two been up to this afternoon?' She was trying to keep the atmosphere light-hearted.

'Well me and Gran had a very long talk.' Peter looked at his grandmother. 'And I told her that she was being very silly.'

'Peter, you shouldn't.'

Maud held up her hand. 'Let him finish.'

'Well,' said Peter, full of pride, 'I told her that when I was in hospital I was all alone and I was scared and didn't like it, and that she has to come with us as winter is coming and I won't be here to get her coal and wood and she'll be all alone and cold and scared if the bombs start again.'

For a few minutes Rene was speechless. 'And?'

'She said I was right and she wants to come with us.'

'What with him, Hilda and Maggie, I thought I'd better go with you, otherwise I'd never hear the last of it.'

Rene didn't know who to hug first, her son or her mother.

When Hazel walked in, all she could see were happy faces.

They all went in to Hilda's, and Rene took in the bottle of whisky that she had been given by Ted and Wally as a goodbye present. This was a very happy day for her.

* * *

Saturday the thirtieth of October 1943 saw the family moving away from Glebe Street, Rotherhithe, to start their new life in Surrey. They watched the van move away, and as they made their way down the road, there were many hugs and kisses and promises to write. A few tears were shed as well. Rene had very mixed feelings as she watched her mother with tears in her eyes say goodbye to the street and the neighbours she had known all her married life. She had so many memories, though not all of them good. Rene also felt sad; this had always been her home. Where she had grown up and where she was married from and where she'd lived with John. They would never come back here. She had written to the Red Cross and given them her new address. She only hoped that John would be happy in their new home.

They sat back quietly on the tube, all with their own thoughts.

They called in first at Joan and Sadie's, then they all went on to the house. Doris and Stan were waiting for them, and after Maud was introduced to their neighbours, tea was swiftly brought out.

'You shouldn't have done that,' said Rene. 'We can't take your rations.'

'When all your goods arrive, the next cuppa is on you,' said Stan.

It wasn't long after that that the van arrived and everybody set to and helped.

Stan was a retired builder, so he had plenty of muscle and was helping to bring in the furniture. Boxes were being opened and crocks put in cupboards and clothes hung in the fitted wardrobes. Rene was upstairs telling the men where to put beds and the like. The piano went into the front room along with Maud's bed. Everybody worked hard, and when the kettle was found, Sadie made some tea.

'I'll have to get us registered at the shops. Are they very far away?' Maud asked Sadie when they were busy in the kitchen.

'No. I'll take you Monday morning and you can be with ours.'

'You with Jock the butcher?' asked Doris.

'Yes,' replied Sadie. 'D'you know him?'

'Used to go to the same school. Nice bloke.'

Sadie and Doris talked about their school, and there was plenty of laughter coming from the kitchen. Rene looked at her mother in amongst it all. Maud seemed to have shed years in such a short time.

By the time everybody had gone, the house was looking like a home. The children were in bed and Rene and Maud were sitting in the dining room listening to the wireless.

'We've all done a good job today,' said Rene.

'We certainly have. What nice people next door.'

'Yes, they said that those on the other side are at their son's for the weekend, so we'll meet them on Monday. In the morning I'm going with Hazel to the store to see about a job for her, and then on to the school with Peter. Then I'll go along to where Joan works and see about working there. So you can introduce yourself to next door.'

'I'm going to the shops with Sadie and Doris. They're gonna show me the best places to get registered with, then we might go to the pictures. It seems both of them trot to the cinema a couple of times a week. Stan said he's looking forward to taking a trio of ladies out. He's such a charmer,' said Maud with a grin.

Rene smiled. Suddenly her mother was a different woman. 'Any regrets, Mum?'

'Yes.'

Rene sat up. 'What?' she asked.

'That I didn't do this earlier.'

Rene went to her mother and held her tight. This was one of the best days of her life, and she knew that even better was yet to come. That day would be when the war was over and she was in John's arms again.

Chapter 37

IT DIDN'T TAKE the family long to settle down in their new life, and they were all very happy. Hazel loved her job in Jones' department store, selling clothes on the baby counter. Peter had joined the school's football team, and Rene was working with Joan again; this time they were making uniforms for the forces. It was heavy, hard work but she loved it. They had an Anderson shelter in the garden but they didn't sleep in it. They only had the occasional air raid; mostly the planes went over them. Luke was writing to Peter, and Maud was more than happy with her new life. The Hoopers, who lived the other side of them, were just as welcoming as Doris and Stan.

Christmas was fast approaching and everybody was making plans. Stan and Doris were going to stay with their daughter in Somerset, and Joan and Sadie and the children were coming to Rene's for the day. Everybody was combining rations and looking forward to a feast, and trying to find things to give or make for presents. Peter was so happy when Luke said that he would like to spend the holiday with them.

When he arrived with tinned food, the like of which they hadn't seen for years, they all knew this was going to be a good Christmas.

On Christmas morning Rene stood and looked at her table, which had been laid last night. All the best china had been brought out and Luke and Peter had been to the woods and cut down a tree. The trimmings were once again brought out and there were a few presents underneath and it all looked lovely. She couldn't help herself as a tear slowly ran down her cheek. Betty and John wouldn't be here to share it with them, but one day John would be; then they would have the best time ever.

'Good morning.' Luke's voice startled her. 'Rene, are you all right?'

She quickly ran her hand over her cheek. 'Just wishful thinking.'

'I know what you mean. I went to Betty's grave and placed a holly wreath on it before I came here.'

'Luke, you should have said. We would have got you to—'

He raised his hand. 'I put one there from all of you as well.'

Rene began to cry again.

Luke held her close, and Maud walked in. She looked at them. 'Are you all right?' she asked.

Rene nodded.

'I was just telling Rene that I placed two wreaths on Betty's grave and she got a little overcome.'

'Thank you, son. I'll go and see to the dinner.' Maud quickly walked away.

All too soon Christmas was over, but people were full of hope for 1944, with the talk of a second front filling the newspapers. Everybody was waiting and talking about the end being in sight; they were weary of shortages and longed for the days of plenty again.

In February Hazel turned fifteen. She was growing up to be a lovely girl.

'You'll soon have all the boys after you,' said Sadie when her family were round at Almond Close for a birthday tea.

With that Hazel blushed.

'That boy at the garage likes you,' said Peter.

'Shut up.'

Rene smiled. 'Are you going out with someone?'

'No. Me and me mate Ros see Ben at the jive shack sometimes.'

'Jive shack?' asked Sadie.

'It's the name they give the Scout's hut when they have dances there,' said Rene.

'And he gives her a wolf whistle every time she goes past,' said Peter.

'You should mind your own business,' Hazel said angrily.

'You know you can always bring him home any time,' said Rene.

Hazel looked horrified. 'What? I told you, he's only a friend.'

'So, you bring friends home,' said Peter.

'I know, but not boy friends.'

'Ah. See. I told you he was a boyfriend.'

Hazel ran from the room. 'Shut up. I hate you,' she shouted out.

Peter laughed.

'That wasn't very kind,' said Maud.

'Sorry, Gran.'

'It isn't me you should be apologising to.'

'Go on, Peter, go and say you're sorry,' said Rene.

Peter left the room. He didn't want to upset his sister. He thought the world of her. She was always there when he needed her.

He knocked gently on her door.

'Go away.'

'Please, Haz, let me come in.'

She opened the door.

'I didn't mean to upset you, especially on your

birthday.' He sat on the bed. 'You know what they say? You mustn't cry on your birthday as you'll cry all the year round.'

Hazel smiled at him. She couldn't be angry with him for long.

'Do you like Ben?'

Hazel nodded.

'So what's the problem?'

'I'm only fifteen.'

'Have you been out with him?'

Again Hazel nodded. 'I always see him at the jive shack, he's a good dancer, and we did go to the pictures once.'

Peter took her hand but she pulled it away.

'Hazel, this might sound silly from me. But if you like him, then give him a chance. Remember Billy and Auntie Betty?'

Hazel looked at him, shocked.

'I always think of them whenever I'm not sure whether to do something or not. Luke said that we should make the most of every moment.'

'Is that why you're studying hard at school?'

He nodded. 'Luke told me I should grow up to be someone they would be proud of.'

Hazel put her arms round him and gave him a hug. 'You're not doing too bad. Come on, let's go downstairs.'

* * *

Every day brought news of more victories and hope for Britain and her allies. Then on June the sixth the big invasion began.

Although they had heard it on the wireless, to see it on the newsreels at the pictures was wonderful. Hazel and Ben had been out together a few times, and when a big cheer went up among the audience, Ben turned to Hazel and hugged her.

'It'll soon be over now,' he said.

'I hope so, then my dad will be back.'

In the days that followed, it seemed that the sun was always shining and everybody was happy. Stan kept them all up to date with a wall chart he had been keeping since the second front opened.

June the eighteenth was Peter's birthday. Despite his protests, they were having family and a few friends to tea.

One of Peter's football friends was in the kitchen telling Rene what a good player Peter was. 'I reckon when he leaves school one of the clubs will sign him up.'

Rene looked at him, surprised. 'You don't really think that, do you?'

He nodded.

'What does the coach have to say about it?'

'He thinks the same.'

Rene took the sandwiches into the dining room. She smiled at her son. This was something he'd kept very much to himself.

Peter was disappointed that he hadn't heard from Luke for a while and was beginning to get upset about it. 'I thought he would have sent me a letter for me birthday,' he said to his mother the next day.

'Perhaps he's busy.' Everybody knew what a risky job Luke did, and Rene crossed her fingers. Please don't let there be another death in her son's short life.

It was a week later that a letter arrived for Peter from Canada. He had already left for school. Rene looked at it with horror.

'What shall I do, Mum?' she asked Maud.

'What d'you mean?'

'Should I open it?'

'I don't think so.'

'But what if it's from Luke's parents telling Peter . . .' She couldn't finish the sentence.

'I don't know, love.'

'Don't give it to him till I get home.'

'Well all right, but it might not be bad news.'

'I'm not taking that chance.'

Rene left for work. All day her mind was on that letter and the effect it would have on her son if it was bad news. After all, Luke's parents were his next of kin.

When Rene arrived home, she took the letter to Peter in his bedroom.

He looked at the envelope. 'When did this arrive?'

'This morning.'

'Where's it been? Why didn't Gran give it to me when I came in?'

'I wanted to be here with you.'

Slowly Peter opened the letter and Rene waited for his reaction. Suddenly his face broke into a big smile. 'He's home. He says he's sorry he wasn't here for my birthday but he was on his way home. He'd been shot down and injured and now he's back in Canada.' He passed the letter to his mother.

Rene read it, then hugged her son. Both stood with tears running down their cheeks.

When they told Maud, she too let a few tears fall. 'He's a lovely lad. I hope we see him again one day.'

Hazel too was pleased. She also loved Luke; after all, he was one of the family.

A few days later, Hazel and Ben were walking home from the pictures when a funny noise filled the air. They looked up and saw a small plane going along in the middle distance. It was on fire. Suddenly the engine stopped and the plane fell to earth with a loud explosion. They looked at each other.

'I don't reckon that pilot stood a chance,' said Ben.

'I wonder if it was British or German?'

'Must have been British. We ain't had any warning go off.'

That was the first time V-1 rockets were seen or heard of. They quickly became known as doodlebugs.

Chapter 38

A
LTHOUGH BRITAIN AND her allies were gaining ground every day, Hitler wasn't going to give up that easily, and another new menace began to fall from the sky. The V-2 was even worse than the doodlebugs; these rockets just fell to earth with no warning at all.

The war was still dragging on and everyone was tired. Gradually even the V-2s began to cease and people had hope again.

Christmas came and went, and they knew that the end was near. By the spring of 1945, people had started to think of the future. Street parties were being planned, and Joan and Rene had the job of making the bunting that was going to be draped from window to window all round the close. Everybody was bringing them scraps of material of all colours; they were cut into triangles and sewn on to yards of tape. Shirley and Sam thought it was a new game as they threw themselves into the heap. The food was going to be laid out on tables from the Scout's hall. It was amazing that suddenly tins of salmon, fruit and other goodies were found in cupboards and put in the store cupboard in Doris's spare bedroom. People were going to celebrate this victory in style; they had waited six long, weary years for it to happen.

Hazel was upset when Ben told her that he'd passed his medical and would soon be called up. He was going into the air force. But at least she knew that he wouldn't be in as much danger now the war was over.

Today it was official: May the eighth was going to be called VE Day. There were so many tears and hugs of joy, even with complete strangers. Mr Churchill had told the nation that the day was going to be a holiday.

Hazel brushed the tears from her eyes as she looked around at the happy faces. At last the war was over. The street party was in full swing and today would go down in history.

'You all right, love?' asked Ben as he put his arm round her slim shoulders.

'Yes thanks. Just happy, that's all.' She reflected on the past six years and all that had happened to her family. Her beloved Auntie Betty was no longer here, but hopefully her dad would be home soon. Her dear dad. How much had he changed? Would he be happy living here in Surrey?

Everybody was singing and dancing, and her mum, who was dancing with Peter, whisked Hazel and Ben along with them in the conga round the green.

Peter would soon be thirteen and had surprised everybody by playing football for the local semi-pro team. He was a very bright boy and he loved looking after the garden with Sadie and Stan's help. Their dad would be so proud of him.

The music stopped and everybody sat down to get their breath back.

Hazel began thinking about Betty. She had been very fond of her aunt and wanted to be like her. Why did she have to get killed? She wasn't even in London. If she had still been alive, she would be talking about going to Canada to be with her husband Luke now. He was a smashing bloke and they all loved him, and he'd promised to come back and see them one day.

'You sure you're all right?' asked Ben as tears began trickling down her cheeks.

She nodded.

'Look, how about you and me going up West tomorrow? The celebrations will still be going on.'

'I'd like that.'

'Good.' He leaned over and kissed her on the lips.

Hazel knew that in the past six years she had grown

up, and she also knew that Ben could become a very important part of her life.

She sat remembering when they had first moved here to Morden. Her gran had been against the move but now she was more than happy to be with their neighbours Doris and Stan and Joan's mother-in-law Sadie. Hazel looked across the green at them sitting laughing and drinking. Her mother was smiling at her, but Hazel knew that her mother's happiness wouldn't be complete until John was home. Every day they waited for a letter telling them that her dad was back in England. Hopefully that letter would arrive very soon. Then they really would be celebrating.

Joan's daughter Shirley ran up to Hazel and climbed on her lap. She was such a happy child and Hazel adored her. It wasn't long before little Sam came waddling over as well.

'These two really like you,' said Ben.

'I hope so.' As she sat looking at them, she thought of everything that she and Peter had been through. Being evacuated and sent away from home when they were just children had been very traumatic. Being in the Blitz. Losing Auntie Betty had been so very sad, and Peter had had the added pain of seeing his best mate Billy gunned down. Such things must never happen to these children. Hazel gave a sigh.

Ben took her hand. 'Don't be sad.'

'I'm not really. I was just thinking of all that's happened.'

'Haz, you will write to me, won't you?'

'Of course I will.'

Shirley and Sam slipped off her lap and ran across to their mother, who was passing out some lemonade.

'At least I'm going in the air force when the war's over.'

'Yes, my only worry is that you'll meet some nice girl.'

'And why should I do that when I've got the best there is right here?'

He kissed her again, and Hazel knew that from now on things could only get better.

A Moment to Remember

Dee Williams

High hopes and shattered dreams . . .

Milly Ash is born into terrible poverty in the back-streets of London's East End. One of a huge family in which there is never enough food to go round, Milly has always dreamed of escape.

Her chance comes when she lands a position as a lady's companion to Jane Green, the disabled daughter of a well-to-do family. The Greens take Milly into their home and their hearts, and she even starts to develop feelings for Jane's older brother, Richard.

But then a tragic accident means Milly must suddenly leave the Green household and the life she so loved. As Milly tries to piece her world back together, will she ever find happiness, and love, again?

Warm acclaim for *Sunday Times* bestseller Dee Williams's novels:

'An inspiring tale' *Woman's Weekly*

'Harsh times, brave hearts and always a hint of hope' *Northern Echo*

978 0 7553 5889 2

headline

This Time for Keeps

Dee Williams

Love and war. Passion and heartache . . .

When Babs Scott loses her beloved parents in an air raid, she finds herself homeless and alone in Rotherhithe. The Land Army offers her an escape and, despite the backbreaking toil, Babs loves the peaceful green fields and the fresh, clean air of Sussex.

With the support of fellow Land Girl Lydi Wells, Babs forges a new life for herself. But, still haunted by her parents' death, her resolve gives way to resentment when two Italian prisoners of war are sent to the farm. And when her new RAF sweetheart Pete dies on his return to the skies, Babs is grief-stricken once more.

After the war and back in her home town, a foolish mistake changes Babs' life for ever. She fears she has lost her one chance for happiness, but then a letter from abroad arrives, offering an unexpected ray of hope . . .

Sunday Times bestseller Dee Williams' novels have been warmly acclaimed:

'An inspiring tale' *Woman's Weekly*

'Harsh times, brave hearts and always a hint of hope' *Northern Echo*

978 0 7553 3958 7

headline

All That Jazz

Dee Williams

Step into the colourful world of the Jazz Age . . .

1921. When the influenza epidemic sweeping the nation claims the life of their mother, Daisy Cooper and her sister are left all alone in their squalid rooms in Rotherhithe. Working long hours to keep a roof over their heads, Daisy hates leaving little Mary alone so often, but what else can she do?

The arrival of moving pictures offers the sisters a glimpse of a magical world, and Daisy dreams of joining the beautiful dancing girls on the stage. When a chance meeting leads to an audition for the chorus line, Daisy wonders if this will be the door to a brighter future for her and Mary. But just as Daisy embarks on the glamorous path to fame, tragedy strikes . . .

Sunday Times bestseller Dee Williams' novels have been warmly acclaimed:

'An inspiring tale' *Woman's Weekly*

'Harsh times, brave hearts and always a hint of hope' *Northern Echo*

'Another wonderfully warm-hearted winner from Dee Williams . . . Her readers will be queuing up for this one' Gilda O'Neill

978 0 7553 3956 3

headline